"What happened that n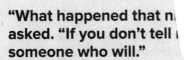**asked. "If you don't tell someone who will."**

"You ask so many questions," Rory murmured. "Occupational hazard?"

"I just have so many questions," Brittney said. "I always have."

"So that's why you became a reporter?"

"You ask a lot of questions, too, Mr. VanDam," she pointed out.

Rory shrugged. "I usually don't. But I'm interest—no, I'm curious."

She was amused that Rory had stopped himself from saying *interested*. So to tease him, she batted her eyelashes and stepped closer to him. "About me?"

"About why someone would threaten you and force you off the road," he said.

"I'm curious about that, too," Brittney said. "It has to be related to the plane crash."

"You ran that story months ago," Rory said. "And you already covered it. So why would anyone be trying to back you off from what you've already done?"

"Because they know what I know, that there's more to that story."

Dear Reader,

Welcome back to Northern Lakes, Michigan, for another installment in my Hotshot Heroes series with Harlequin Romantic Suspense. I hope you've all been looking forward to finding out more about Rory VanDam and that mysterious plane crash he and Ethan Sommerly survived five years ago. And if anyone can find out the truth, it will be determined reporter Brittney Townsend. But Brittney's quest for knowledge just might get both her and Rory killed as there are numerous attempts on their lives. Being a hotshot has never been more dangerous for Rory.

With so many recent wildfires in areas in Canada and in the US, including the town on which I've based Northern Lakes, hotshot firefighters are being hailed as the heroes that they are when they selflessly put their lives on the line to battle these unpredictable blazes.

I have so much respect for the dangerous job that hotshot firefighters do. They are definitely the perfect heroes. And I love writing about the perils of their careers and their private lives in my Hotshot Heroes series. I hope you've been enjoying the series as well. Or if you've just discovered it, I think you'll be able to jump right in and know what's been going on in Northern Lakes—a lot of danger, betrayal and romance.

Happy reading!

Lisa Childs

HUNTED
HOTSHOT HERO

LISA CHILDS

Recycling programs for this product may not exist in your area.

ISBN-13: 978-1-335-59400-6

Hunted Hotshot Hero

Copyright © 2024 by Lisa Childs

For questions and comments about the quality of this book, please contact us at CustomerService@Harlequin.com.

TM and ® are trademarks of Harlequin Enterprises ULC.

Harlequin Enterprises ULC
22 Adelaide St. West, 41st Floor
Toronto, Ontario M5H 4E3, Canada
www.Harlequin.com

Printed in Lithuania

MIX
Paper | Supporting responsible forestry
FSC® C021394

New York Times and *USA TODAY* bestselling, award-winning author **Lisa Childs** has written more than eighty-five novels. Published in twenty countries, she's also appeared on the *Publishers Weekly*, Barnes & Noble and Nielsen Top 100 bestseller lists. Lisa writes contemporary romance, romantic suspense, paranormal and women's fiction. She's a wife, mom, bonus mom, avid reader and less avid runner. Readers can reach her through Facebook or her website, lisachilds.com.

Books by Lisa Childs

Harlequin Romantic Suspense

Hotshot Heroes

Hotshot Hero Under Fire
Hotshot Hero on the Edge
Hotshot Heroes Under Threat
Hotshot Hero in Disguise
Hotshot Hero for the Holiday
Hunted Hotshot Hero

The Coltons of Owl Creek

Colton's Dangerous Cover

The Coltons of New York

Protecting Colton's Secret Daughters

Visit the Author Profile page at
Harlequin.com for more titles.

With great appreciation and respect
for all the hotshot firefighters—the real heroes!

Prologue

The hotshot holiday party ended without the bang everyone had been expecting and dreading, no one more so than Rory VanDam. Ever since that reporter dredged up the plane crash that had happened five years ago.

No. Ever since the plane crash.

No. Even before that.

Rory had been waiting for the big bang or the next crash. While he'd been waiting the longest, the other hotshots had begun to expect bad things to happen, too, and not just because of their jobs. Being a hotshot firefighter was more dangerous than being a regular firefighter because they battled the worst blazes—the wildfires that consumed acres and acres of land and everything in their paths. But it wasn't the job that put them in danger lately, it was all the bad things that had been happening to the hotshots. Explosions. Murder attempts. Sabotage.

But tonight, the holiday party ended with an arrest but no gunshots, no fight, not even a fire. The party was over now and the hotshots, who had traveled to their headquarters in Northern Lakes, Michigan, to attend it, were tucked up in the bunks at the firehouse unless they had other places to stay. And, since falling in love and getting into relationships, many of them had other places now. So maybe it wasn't just bad things that happened to hotshots. But for

Rory, to fall in love or have someone fall in love with him would be a very bad thing. He couldn't risk a relationship with anyone ever again.

So, with nowhere else to stay, he was lying on his back on one of the bunks, staring up at the ceiling. Despite that arrest tonight, Rory was still uneasy, waiting for the next bad thing to happen.

The immediate danger was only over for Trent Miles tonight. The person who had been threatening Trent in Detroit, where Trent worked out of a local firehouse when not on assignment with the hotshots, followed him up to Northern Lakes. While the young man had run Trent and his girlfriend off the road the day before, he hadn't harmed anyone tonight. Trent's girlfriend, a Detroit detective, quietly arrested her and Trent's would-be killer. Except for that whole running them off the road thing, Rory was relieved that the killer was the only one who'd followed Trent up to Northern Lakes and not the man's sister again.

Trent's sister, Brittney, was beautiful, with her long curly dark hair and big topaz-colored eyes. But Brittney Townsend was also an ambitious young reporter who would sell out her own soul for a story. Or at least her own brother.

Not that Rory could judge anyone for selling out their soul, not when he'd already done it himself. But it still affected him, leaving him feeling hollow and empty inside and alone even in a bar full of other people like he'd been earlier tonight for the party. His coworkers. His friends. At least he hoped they considered him a friend and not the saboteur.

Who the hell was behind all the damn dangerous "accidents" the hotshots had been having? Broken equipment. Like the lift bucket coming loose with Trick McRooney in it and all of the cut brake lines on trucks that had sent or nearly sent hotshots to the hospital. And the loose gas line on the stove in the firehouse kitchen that had caused the explosion that had taken out Ethan's beard and revealed his real identity as the Canterbury heir.

Rory touched his jaw where stubble was starting to come in again. And his uneasiness grew. His disguise was being clean-shaven and short-haired; something he hadn't been for a while until his hotshot training and his new identity.

His new life. But this new life was proving to be every bit as dangerous as his last one. And he couldn't help but think that this life was going to end, too.

As he lay there, he heard the rumble of an engine and then another and another. The firehouse was on Main Street, but there was never much traffic in Northern Lakes at this hour and especially during the winter. And these engines weren't just passing by, they were running inside the building.

The fire trucks.

Who started up the truck engines?

They hadn't been called out to a fire because the alarm hadn't gone off. It would have woken up everyone in the bunk room if it had. And as far as he knew, he was the only one awake because all around him, other hotshots snored.

Trent Miles stayed behind in Northern Lakes after his girlfriend left. A couple of the younger guys, Bruce Abbott and Howie Lane, stayed because they'd been drinking at the party. And a couple of the older guys, Donovan Cunningham and Carl Kozak, stayed, probably for the same reason.

Michaela was here, too. The female hotshot worked as a firefighter in St. Paul, which wasn't far away, but while she hadn't been drinking, the party ended too late for her to want to make the drive home.

Not everybody staying was a hotshot. Stanley, the kid who

kept the firehouse clean, was sleeping here tonight with the firehouse dog, Annie. Stanley's foster brother, Cody Mallehan, and his fiancée, Serena Beaumont, had recently gotten licensed as a foster home and had taken in a kid who was allergic to Annie. And Stanley didn't like to be separated from the big sheepdog/mastiff mix that had saved his life.

His life wasn't the only one she'd saved, though. She'd rescued many other hotshots and their significant others over the past year since Stanley had adopted her to be the firehouse dog. Maybe she was about to make another rescue because she whined and crawled off the bunk below Rory where she'd been sleeping with Stanley. Then she jumped up, put her paws on the side of Rory's bed, and she whined again, obviously as confused and concerned as he was about those running trucks.

"You hear 'em, too," Rory said, and he jumped down from his bunk. While the diesel trucks didn't emit as much carbon monoxide as gas engines, if all of them were running, like he suspected they were from the sound, the level could get high enough to kill.

The air was already getting thick. He coughed and sputtered, trying to find his voice to wake the others. "Hey…" he rasped out the words. "Hey…"

Annie barked, but it wasn't as loudly as she usually barked. Rory needed her to bark as loud as she had the first time she'd seen Ethan without his beard. He needed her to wake the others, or they might not be able to wake up ever again if the carbon monoxide level rose any more.

And he needed to get the hell downstairs and shut off those trucks. He would pull the alarm in the hall, too, before going downstairs. That would certainly wake up everyone easier than he and Annie could.

But once he stepped through the door to the hall, something struck him hard across the back of the head and neck, knocking him down to his knees before he fell flat on his face. His last thought as consciousness slipped away was: Would he be able to wake up again or was his most recent life ending right now?

Chapter 1

He was having that dream. The one where he was falling through the air, his arms flailing as he kept reaching and reaching, but just nothingness slipped through his fingers. Nothing.

That was all he had now, all that he was now. He had a new name to replace the one he never wanted to hear again. But he'd lost much more than his old name.

And he was about to lose even more.

Before jumping out of the sputtering plane, he'd strapped on a chute, and the weight of it was pulling at his shoulders. It was supposed to open. He had been trained as a smoke jumper. He knew how to do this. But whoever had sabotaged the plane might have rigged the chute, as well. He wasn't the only one who'd jumped out, though.

At least one other chute had opened. He could see it in the distance. Just as he could see the plane, continuing on its doomed flight, spiraling toward the ground as the engine cut out entirely. He was spiraling, too.

Free-falling…

For a second, despite all of his training, he forgot what he was supposed to do. And he'd been trained by the best in the elite firefighting business: Mack McRooney.

But he forgot more than his training. He forgot who he

was now: a hotshot. Mack's voice echoed inside his head. "Breathe. In and out. Relax. And pull the cord."

Mack, with his bald head and booming voice, demanded total obedience. And this student obeyed. He reached for the rip cord, pulling it, and he waited for the jerk on his shoulders, for his body to go up instead of down.

But there was no jerk; it didn't come. The chute hadn't opened, hadn't rescued him. He kept hurtling toward the mountains, to all the pine trees and jagged ridges. And he braced himself for the impact.

For death.

Jolting awake, he jumped and gasped, trying to breathe. But something had been shoved in his mouth and down his throat. Panic gripped him.

They had found him again.

And this time they would, no doubt, make certain that he died.

You are being watched, and if you don't drop this story, you will die.

Brittney Townsend's fingers shook slightly as she held the note she'd just pulled from beneath the windshield wiper of her van. When she'd seen the slip of paper, she figured it was a ticket or a flyer for a restaurant or a food truck. She had not even considered that it would be this: a threat.

After weeks of alternating between feeling paranoid and flattered, she should be relieved that her suspicions were confirmed. She'd had this strange feeling someone was watching her.

It had been easy enough to spot the ones who openly stared at her, some of them because they must have recognized her as the reporter who'd broken the big story, who had discovered that Jonathan Michael Canterbury IV was still alive. Or maybe they'd been staring because they had recognized her from the other stories she did. For the fluff pieces her local Detroit station had hired her to do, like report on gallery openings and concerts and new shops and restaurants.

She hated doing stories like that and figured she got saddled with them because she was young and, as her producer told her, cute. And the way he said it...

She had considered reporting him to HR, but everyone else loved him. So she let the comments go. For now. He was probably harmless enough, and she doubted that he was the one watching her. She also doubted that it was any of the people who'd spoken to her after recognizing her. None of them had given her that uneasy feeling that she kept having.

That creepy sense of foreboding, like whoever was watching her wasn't doing so out of admiration but something else...

Obsession. Anger. Revenge?

Her brother had recently had someone go after him for revenge, because Trent hadn't been able to save that person's loved one from an apartment fire. But Trent was a firefighter. His job was definitely a lot higher stakes than hers.

Except for the one big story she'd done about the hotshots. And that plane crash.

She glanced around now, peering into the shadows of the parking garage. It was late, so the only light was the soft glow from the small overheard fixtures scattered throughout the concrete structure. Was whoever had stuck the note under the windshield wiper out there? Watching her from the cover of the shadows?

Goose bumps lifted on her arms despite the heavy wool coat she wore. She reached for the door handle she'd already unlocked and jumped up onto the driver's seat of the van. She suspected that someone had been watching her when she left the station a short while ago. Because it was late, she was the last one leaving the building for the parking garage. But she'd heard shoes scraping behind her on the sidewalk.

She glanced over her shoulder, but in the darkness, she wasn't able to see anyone. But she knew they were there, just as she'd known all those other times she had that uneasy feeling.

Someone was definitely following her. But her stalker wasn't a new fan like she wanted to believe, someone impressed with her reporting, someone who recognized her talent. No. This was someone threatening her.

You are being watched, and if you don't drop this story, you will die.

She really didn't have to wonder what story. Because she knew.

This threat wasn't for her to stop working on any of those fluff pieces. Nobody cared that she covered a gallery showing or the opening of a new restaurant; sometimes not even the owners cared because people didn't watch the news on TV. The read it on social media instead.

No. There was only one story of any interest that she had ever covered. The plane crash from five years ago, which had presumably taken the life of Jonathan Michael Canterbury IV and confirmed his family curse, that all of the Canterbury male heirs died much sooner than they should.

But Canterbury hadn't died. Other men had, though, except for one: Rory VanDam. Like Canterbury, he'd survived for a couple of months in the mountains before the two of them had been rescued. Because both men had refused to give her an interview, she wasn't sure how long each had been on their own before finding one other and then being rescued together. The wreckage of the plane and the pilot and a couple of other men, who'd just completed hotshot training and been on board, too, had never been found.

Nobody knew for sure why and how the plane had crashed. Or what had happened to the others. Canterbury claimed he didn't know for certain, but he'd suspected that it was because of him, because someone had been trying to kill him even before that crash.

But what if he was wrong?

The man who'd been trying to kill him, his brother-in-law, denied any involvement in the plane crash. Of course, he could have been lying, as people so often did. But why admit to everything else but deny involvement in the crash? It didn't make sense. If he wasn't the reason the plane had gone down, why had it crashed?

And what if Canterbury hadn't been the intended target after all?

Those were questions that Brittney had been asking herself ever since she discovered Canterbury alive and working with her brother as a hotshot out of Northern Lakes. She wanted to make sure that whatever had happened with that crash didn't happen again, with her brother as one of the hotshots who didn't survive.

Desperate to keep Trent safe, she'd tried asking other people about what had happened to that plane. Like the Federal Aviation Administration, who should have been able to locate the black box of the wreckage. She'd also tried talking to the director of the hotshot training center that the plane had left before the crash.

And she kept trying to talk to Jonathan Canterbury, who was still calling himself Ethan Sommerly. But he refused to give her a follow-up interview. She glanced at the note. Writing that didn't seem like something Ethan would do even if he wasn't best friends with her brother. He was more direct than this. He would just tell her, as he'd been doing every time she asked him, that he had no intention of ever talking about the crash again.

That left Rory VanDam. She'd seen him in passing when she'd been in Northern Lakes covering that story. The thought of him had her heart skipping a beat, but that was just in anticipation of getting more information out of him. Not because of how startlingly good-looking he was, with short blond hair and very pale blue eyes. She hadn't seen much of him, though, because he kept slipping away before she was able to ask him any questions. And both Ethan and her brother had refused to give her a contact number for Rory. Her brother was barely speaking to her after that story.

A twinge struck her heart with regret and with fear. She'd nearly lost him over the holidays when that person who'd wanted revenge against him had been trying to kill him. No, he'd been trying to kill someone close to Trent.

She still hadn't gotten the full story out of Trent yet, she only knew that person had been arrested. Detective Heather Bolton had made certain of that. She'd saved Brittney's brother's life and had stolen his heart in the process.

A tug at her lips curved them up into a slight smile even as a wistful sigh slipped through them. She wasn't jealous. Not really.

It wasn't as if she wanted a relationship for herself. Not right now. Maybe not ever. Despite everybody thinking she'd been too young when her dad died for her to be able to remember him, she did. She remembered that loss and pain not just for her but for her mom and her brother, too.

And every time her hotshot brother went out to fight a fire, she worried that she was going to lose him next. She nearly had, not to a fire but to someone holding a grudge against him.

Like he was holding one against her.

Would he ever forgive her for investigating his hotshot team? For exposing his best friend's secret and real identity and for, inadvertently, putting him in danger because of her exposé?

Hopefully Trent was out of danger now. But she didn't know for certain. Even though the detective had caught the person after him, Trent had stayed up in Northern Lakes.

Too many bad things had been happening there and not just because of her exposé. The Huron hotshots had been having a run of bad luck for a while now.

That was the reason she'd gone to Northern Lakes and had stumbled upon Canterbury, because she'd known something was going on with her brother's hotshot team, and she'd wanted to investigate all those unlikely "accidents." Too many of Trent's team members had been getting hurt or worse. One member of the team had died, and so many others had nearly died, as well.

Had something else happened?

Was that why Trent had stayed up there? And by doing so, had he put himself in danger yet again? But apparently she was in danger, too.

She glanced around that parking garage again, peering into the shadows. She couldn't tell if that person was out there yet, watching her. Or maybe they figured that leaving the note would scare her off.

If so, whoever had left it didn't know her well at all. Leaving that note only piqued her interest more as well as pissed her off.

Feeling a sudden urge to reach out to one of the people who knew her best, she pulled her cell phone from her purse. Before this whole mess with his hotshot team, she'd thought her brother knew her and would have known that she never intended for anyone to get hurt, least of all him. But she couldn't call her mom and stepdad, who probably knew her and her heart better than her brother did, because she didn't want to worry them. So she called Trent.

"Hey."

The quick reply startled her, making her nearly drop the phone. Trent had been declining her calls for so long that she hadn't expected him to actually answer.

"Brittney?" Trent asked, his voice a little louder with concern. "Are you there?"

She drew in a shaky breath and nodded. "Yeah, yeah. I just didn't expect you to pick up." Especially at this hour. Not that eleven was late for Trent when he so often pulled overnight shifts.

He chuckled. "Then why did you call?"

She froze for a moment. Why had she called? Was she going to tell him about the note? If she did, he would no doubt tell her to back off even though he knew that she wouldn't. Then he would worry about her and try to intervene, playing his usual part of overprotective big brother. And he might get hurt trying to protect her, which was her whole reason for wanting to discover the truth, so that he wouldn't get hurt like the other hotshots who'd been lost in that plane crash.

"Uh…"

"You're at a loss for words?" Trent asked. "That's so unlike my little sister."

"Stop teasing her," another voice chimed in on Trent's end. Heather's husky voice.

"You're back in Detroit?" she asked.

"Yes."

"Why did you stay in Northern Lakes for so long?" With the way he and Heather seemed to feel about each other, she was surprised he'd stayed away from the female detective for five minutes let alone two weeks.

"Ah, and now my little sister is back, too," he said. "Firing her usual questions at me."

Brittney felt another twinge then, of nostalgia, remembering how young she'd been when she'd started questioning everything and everyone around her. Trent had always been the most patient with her back then, even more so than their dad and her mom. He'd always been the best big brother.

But she hadn't always been the best younger sister. "I'm sorry," she said, her voice cracking a bit with the emotion overwhelming her, thinking of how close she'd come to losing him over the danger he'd been in. The danger he could be in again...

"Brittney?" Trent said her name as a question filled with genuine concern.

She forced a little chuckle. "What? Not used to me apologizing?" She had actually apologized a few times, over that story she'd done on his friend, but he hadn't been listening to her then.

Maybe that was because he'd known that she wasn't sorry at all about doing the story and would have covered it again. She was genuinely sorry about putting Ethan and Trent in danger, though.

And she definitely didn't want to do that again. But what if they already were in danger, either because of whatever had been happening with the team or something related to that crash?

And her story... That wasn't going away. It seemed to literally be following her around because, as she peered through her windshield, into the shadows of the parking garage, she noticed a little flicker of light.

The flame of a lighter?

The flash of a cell screen?

Or a camera?

Was someone not just watching her but taking pictures, too? For what or for whom?

She was tempted to grab her camera from her bag and take pictures of her own. Maybe she would be able to develop them with light enough to see who was out there, hiding in the shadows, watching her.

She always carried her camera with her because she preferred taking her own photographs. Hell, she would prefer to be a print reporter instead of a network one, but she'd taken the first job she'd been offered.

"Brittney?" Trent called her name loudly from her cell speaker, like he was trying to get her attention.

She nearly smiled again at the thought of all the times she'd tried to get his while they were growing up and most recently while he'd been ignoring her. Just like she intended to ignore that note.

And because she did, she couldn't tell Trent about it. She didn't want him in danger again and certainly not because of her. But if she didn't pursue the story, something could still happen to him and his other team members. She had to find the source of the threat and stop him or her; that was the only way she and the hotshots would be safe for sure.

Or as safe as hotshots could ever be given the hazards of their career.

"Sorry," she murmured again. Then she drew in a breath and forced a smile that, while he couldn't see it, he might hear in her voice. "So you're home?"

"Yes," he said.

And she could hear the smile in his voice.

"I'm home," he said.

But his home had burned down a month ago. So his home…

Was probably wherever Heather's was. His home was Heather now.

"Good," she said. She was happy for him, even as she felt that little bubble of wistfulness rise up from her heart again, as if she was yearning for what he had.

For love…

But she had no time for that now or ever. All she wanted was the truth despite the risk. But she didn't want it just for the sake of a story or her career.

She wanted the truth so that she was no longer being followed and threatened. After starting her van, she drove slowly out of the parking structure, and as she headed home, she continually checked the rear-view mirror to see if she was being followed again or still. There were other head-lights behind her, so that person was probably back there, watching and waiting to see what she would do.

If she'd heed that threat…

She couldn't do it, not if backing away let someone get away with murder. And if that plane hadn't crashed by accident, that was exactly what had happened five years ago. Murders and attempted murder, if either Canterbury or Rory VanDam had been the real target. And if they had been, that meant they were still in danger and could put anyone close to them, like her brother or the other hotshots, in danger, as well.

Superintendent Braden Zimmer should have been re-lieved that Rory was all right, that after two very long weeks he had finally awakened from his coma. But…

Braden's body shook a little as he leaned against the wall of the corridor outside Rory's hospital room. He wasn't sure it was Rory who'd woken up, at least not the Rory Van-Dam that Braden knew. The head injury was so severe, the mild-mannered man that Braden had known for the past five years had fought the medical staff that had been trying to save his life. He thought they were trying to kill him.

But maybe that was understandable after what had happened at the firehouse. Someone had started up all the engines and then struck Rory over the head when he'd stepped out of the bunk room.

Had Rory been the intended target? Or would whoever had walked into the hall been struck? And hit so hard that he could have died. That he might still have brain damage from what had happened.

Annie, that untrained, overgrown pup of a firehouse dog, had once again saved lives when her panicked barks woke up the other hotshots who'd been sleeping at the firehouse. If she hadn't woken up everyone…

They could have died, and Rory probably would have if he'd not gotten the medical attention he'd needed as quickly as he had. He might have bled to death or the swelling on his brain that had caused the coma might have killed him. As it was, he still wasn't himself. Not yet.

Maybe not ever.

Braden had to do more to protect his team from…one of his team?

The sabotage had started out harmlessly enough in the beginning. A piece of equipment or a vehicle was damaged, but it had been escalating in frequency and in severity to the point that someone was going to die if the saboteur was not stopped soon.

Chapter 2

The week since he'd awakened in the hospital ICU ward with a breathing tube down his throat he had spent trying to reclaim his memories. So much of the past had slipped away while he was in the coma.

Or maybe he had lost those memories when he'd been struck so hard.

Maybe that blow had knocked the memories out of his mind so that they returned to him only in his dreams. But having them come back to him that way confused him more because he didn't know what was real anymore.

If he was real anymore...

Hell, at the moment, he struggled even to remember his name.

Rory.

That was what everybody who'd come to visit him called him. Rory VanDam was the name on the hospital bracelet wrapped around his wrist. The chart he'd taken from the foot of his bed had called him the same thing while also chronicling all of his old scars and injuries. But a lot of those scars weren't from injuries *Rory VanDam* had received. Except for the blow to his head.

Had that been intended for him? Or would any other hotshot have been struck as hard had one of them stepped out of the bunk room when he had?

Rory, or whoever the hell he was, needed to figure that out, just as he had so many other things he needed to figure out. Like if it was even safe for him, or for his hotshot team, to stay here anymore. But he couldn't figure out anything from this hospital bed. He'd already spent too much time lying in it, the two weeks that he'd been unconscious except for those disturbing dreams.

Memories...

He had spent the entire past week stuck in the hospital because the doctors insisted on monitoring him, making sure that he was medically all right. He wasn't. His head certainly wasn't and neither was his heart. His blood pressure kept going up, probably as those memories had returned.

But he knew that if he intended to make any new memories, he needed to get the hell out of the hospital and figure out who had attacked him in the firehouse. And if they would try again for him or for one of his team members. Or had it been one of his team members who had attacked him?

The tubes were out of him now. The one down his throat and the IV in his arm were gone. So there was nothing but the blood pressure cuff tethering him to the bed. He slipped that off and swung his legs over the side of the bed. While he had some kind of socks on his feet, his legs were bare, as was his ass when he stood up and his gown flopped open in the back.

Where the hell were his clothes?

His legs shook a little beneath his weight as he stumbled across the room toward a cabinet. He jerked it open as the door opened behind him.

"Sheesh, man, have some modesty," a deep voice remarked.

"Hey, if you got it, flaunt it," he replied before turning around to face the man standing inside the door.

Ethan Sommerly's dark brows rose with surprise.

Rory usually didn't throw back smart-ass comments like the rest of the hotshots did. Usually he ignored any smart-ass comments directed at him. He'd learned, the hard way, that it was smarter to keep his head down and stay uninvolved. That way nobody got to really know him, and he didn't get to really know, or trust, anyone.

But that blow to the head had either knocked the sense out of him or maybe knocked his sense back into him. He really didn't know which.

"Everybody said you were acting a little off, a little less like your usual self," Ethan said, "but I didn't see it until now."

"Probably because you haven't been around," Rory replied, ignoring the little twinge of hurt that today was the first time he'd seen Ethan since the hotshot holiday party.

Pretty much every one of the twenty-member team of hotshots had checked in with him over the past week. Trent Miles had come that first day he'd regained consciousness; then he'd left for Detroit and Detective Bolton. But Ethan hadn't come around to visit.

But then the real Ethan couldn't come around anywhere anymore. He had died in that plane crash five years ago. Or so everybody assumed, since no other survivors and the wreckage had never been found.

But what if Rory and "Ethan" hadn't been the only ones who'd survived?

What if…

"You must have gotten whacked in the head harder than I thought," Ethan said, his tone a little defensive. "Because I've been around."

Rory narrowed his eyes to scrutinize his old friend. Ethan usually told the truth about most things, except for his identity that he'd kept secret for five years. Secret from everyone but Rory, who'd always known since the crash who Ethan really was. But Rory had kept Ethan's secret for the same reason he kept his own, because they would have been in danger had the truth ever come out.

That had certainly been proven when Brittney Townsend revealed Ethan's real identity as Jonathan Michael Canterbury IV. The minute everyone had known the infamous Canterbury heir, as the media had dubbed him years ago, was alive, someone had been trying to kill him.

"When were you around?" Rory asked him. And how could he have forgotten?

Ethan's face got a little pink above his beard, which had grown back but was neatly trimmed now unlike how bushy he used to wear it, as a disguise. The man shrugged. "It's probably been a week or so…"

"You were here when I was unconscious," Rory said. Even as his heart lifted a little with that knowledge, he added, "How the hell could I know that?"

Ethan shrugged again and chuckled. "I don't know. They say people in comas can still hear you talking to them."

"*They* don't know what the hell *they're* talking about," Rory said. "Because I didn't hear you. The last thing I heard, before waking up here with the tube shoved down my throat, was the sound of the engines running and Annie barking—"

"So she did save everybody again like Stanley has been swearing she did?"

His heart lifted even more. "If everybody really got out without getting hurt like Braden swore they did." That was the first thing Rory asked when he'd remembered Braden was his boss after he finally remembered who the hell he was supposed to be.

Ethan nodded. "Nobody else got hurt. Braden doesn't lie. Now, Stanley I wasn't so sure about…"

Did Ethan think that the teenager could be the saboteur? Since Braden had shared with everyone that he'd received a note warning him that someone among them wasn't who they'd claimed they were, everybody had been looking at everybody else with suspicion. But that anonymous note had referred to a member of the team and probably to either him or Ethan, not Stanley. And no matter how many memories he might have lost, Rory knew *he* wasn't the saboteur. He didn't think Ethan was, either. But Stanley?

He seemed like a sweet kid who loved his dog.

"I didn't make it across the hall to the alarm to pull it," Rory said. "So Annie must have woken up everyone else before the fumes got too bad. Stanley's right, then, she saved everybody who was there."

"But you."

"I'm alive," Rory said.

"The doctors weren't sure you were going to wake up again," Ethan said, his voice even gruffer than usual. "And after a week passed, your odds of recovering kept getting worse."

"Is that when you gave up on me?" Rory asked. "But that doesn't really make sense, because you, better than anyone else, should know that I'm pretty good at beating the odds."

Not only had they managed to parachute off the plane before it crashed, they'd also managed to find each other within a couple of days and had survived the next two months in the cold of the mountains before they were finally rescued.

Ethan rubbed his big hand across his beard, along the edge of his square jaw. "We both are good at beating the odds."

Rory nodded heartily in agreement, and pain radiated from the back of his head to his temples. Maybe he wasn't as recovered as he thought he was. But he ignored the pain and remarked, "You beat a curse."

"What did you beat, Rory? You've never told me what it was," Ethan remarked.

He sighed again, a heavier one full of all the pain from his past. "I beat a curse, too, of a sort..."

It hadn't been a family legacy of bad luck like Jonathan Michael Canterbury IV had beaten. It was more like the curse of someone who had sworn a vendetta onto him. Revenge for what he'd done all those years ago. But even knowing what he knew now, he would do it all over again. *The right thing.*

But he hadn't shared any of the details with Ethan because, as he'd told him when they'd been stranded in those mountains and had reiterated again a few months ago, the less he knew about Rory the better. The safer he was.

Ethan pointed toward Rory's head. "I don't think you've beaten it for good."

Had the blow to his head been about that or...

"You don't think it was the saboteur who started all those trucks and hit me over the head?" Rory asked. It had to have been. Nobody else knew he was alive.

Unless...

Had Brittney Townsend's exposé about the Canterbury heir got someone else checking out the plane crash more closely? Someone who now wondered if Rory was really someone else?

Ethan shrugged his broad shoulders. "I don't know. The saboteur hasn't been responsible for everything that has happened to the hotshots."

"No, they haven't been," Rory agreed. "Your past came back to haunt you."

"Is that what's actually happened here?" Ethan asked. "Has your past come back to haunt you?"

Rory VanDam's past only went back five years, to the moment, with the help of a US Marshal, Rory VanDam had been created. But the other man…

The one Rory barely remembered, the one he didn't want to remember, *he* had a past. And that was where it needed to stay, for so many reasons.

But instead of answering honestly, he just shrugged.

"The trooper has been trying to interview you," Ethan said, as if warning Rory.

"Gingrich?" His head pounded harder as a memory niggled at him, something about Gingrich…something sinister…

Ethan's dark eyes widened with concern. "You really have forgotten things. Gingrich is in prison now," Ethan reminded him. "He took a plea deal for trying to kill Luke Garrison and Willow and for his involvement in Dirk's murder."

Rory shuddered as he remembered Dirk's gruesome death. That was even worse than…

He shoved that memory back, unwilling to relive that once again, and focused on his friend. Drawing in a deep breath, he asked, "So what trooper wants to see me?"

"Trooper Wells," Ethan said. "She's been wanting to talk to you."

Rory had done his best to avoid having any conversations with any of the state troopers who had investigated what had been happening with the hotshots. He hadn't wanted to give anything away, any clue to his own past and his real identity. Though right now he wasn't even sure what that was…

"But at least it's just her wanting to talk to you and not that damn reporter," Ethan grumbled.

"Brittney," Rory said with a slight sigh.

Ethan grinned. "You haven't forgotten her."

Brittney Townsend, with her gorgeous eyes, deep dimples and curly dark hair, would be impossible to forget but more so for her indomitable spirit and determination than her attractiveness even.

"No," Rory admitted, "and I haven't forgotten that I need to avoid her."

For so many reasons…

The answers weren't wherever the hell that plane had crashed. The answers to Brittney Townsend's questions were in Northern Lakes, the small town out of which the Huron Hotshots operated. And where Brittney was driving to right now.

Ethan, aka Canterbury, had already told her that he thought his brother-in-law had caused the plane to crash. But if that was the case, why was someone threatening Brittney now to drop the story? Ethan's sister's husband was already in jail, heading to prison for a very long time. He had no way of leaving those notes or following Brittney and no access to funds to hire someone else to do his dirty work now like he had before.

So if it wasn't about Ethan, then…

Rory VanDam had to have the answers she was seeking. He had to know something more about the plane crash and about the victims of it. Had one of them been the intended target? Or had he been?

Unlike the last time she'd tried to interview him, she was not going to take no for an answer. No was definitely not the answer she was seeking. Nor was the second note she received after pressing Mack McRooney, the trainer for the US Forest Service hotshots, for information about the plane crash this past week. Well, she hadn't really pressed, she'd just left more messages for him. And then she'd received one herself:

You were warned. Now you'll suffer the consequences.

This note hadn't been typewritten on a piece of paper and shoved under her windshield wiper. This one had appeared on her cell phone as a text message with the contact's information blocked.

So the person had her number and knew about her questioning the US Forest Service. When Mack didn't return her calls, she'd tried talking to everyone who'd picked up the phone at the US Forest Service. Nobody had given her any answers, though. But somehow the person leaving her the notes had found out she was still asking questions. The hotshots worked for the US Forest Service.

Maybe one of them didn't want her asking questions about the crash. Ethan had no reason to threaten her—his secret was already out. But what about Rory? Was he hiding something about the crash? Or about himself?

She'd only met him a couple of times when she'd come to Northern Lakes to find out what was going on with her brother and his hotshot team. The twenty members were quite diverse in looks and personality. There were the younger crew members who were excited about their dangerous career, and there were older ones who were more blasé about it but were still incredibly fit because of the demands of the job.

Then there was the elite of the elite. Like her brother. And his friend Ethan. They were next-level fit and strong and muscular.

The new guy, who'd taken the place of the deceased team

member, Dirk Brown, was like Ethan and Trent. But Trick McRooney had been raised by the man who trained most of the hotshot firefighters to be as accomplished as they were.

She'd tried talking to Mack, too, since that plane had left his training center right before the crash. But he had yet to return any of the calls she'd left for him where he lived and worked in the state of Washington.

Maybe his son, Trick McRooney, or his daughter, the superintendent's arson-investigating wife, Sam McRooney-Zimmer, would be able to convince their father to talk to Brittney about that crash and about Rory VanDam.

Rory wasn't as big and muscular as Trent, Ethan and Trick. He wasn't as loud and silly as Brittney's brother and so many other members of the team. But there was something about him, something even more compelling than the others.

At least to Brittney.

Maybe it was just because he was so different than the others. He was muscular, too, but in more of a lean and chiseled way than the bulky muscular builds of the others. He was also quiet and watchful, with features as chiseled as his muscles. And with short blond hair and very pale, icy blue eyes, he looked like some kind of Nordic prince. Like royalty...

But it wasn't so much his good looks that were compelling to Brittney but what simmered beneath the surface. Secrets. She knew they were there, and that maybe he was so quiet because he was determined to keep them locked inside him.

How far would he go to keep his secrets?

Sending threatening messages? Carrying out those threats?

Instead of being scared off, as the notes had intended,

Brittney was even more fired up to learn the truth. And not just for her sake.

Trent worked closely with Rory. If the man was someone that her brother shouldn't trust or who would put him and the other hotshots in danger, they all deserved to know the truth about him.

And about that plane crash.

What the hell had really happened to that plane that someone was so desperate to make her stop pursuing her story about it that they had threatened her twice?

The closer she got to Northern Lakes, the more her anticipation grew. Not of seeing Rory VanDam.

She wasn't even certain he was still in Northern Lakes after the holiday party. She hadn't dared ask Trent about him because, just like the notes, if he knew about them or her intentions to interrogate Rory, he would try to stop her. To protect her?

Or to protect his fellow hotshots?

She still didn't believe he'd forgiven her for the last story she'd done on them. But while she felt badly about that, she couldn't let whoever was threatening her get away with it. The only way to stop the person was to find out who they were. Hopefully Trent would understand that this wasn't about furthering her career, she was doing it for her safety and for his and the rest of his team's.

Last time she'd come up to Northern Lakes, she'd intended to find out why bad things had been happening to the entire team, but the majority of her story had been about Ethan or, rather, Jonathan Michael Canterbury IV.

While she'd been hounding Ethan and following him and his family around Northern Lakes, Brittney had made a good friend and was looking forward to seeing her again. Tammy Ingles owned the salon in Northern Lakes. She was hip and sassy and genuine. With Brittney's career being so competitive, she hadn't made many genuine friends since becoming a reporter, and the ones she'd had from school and college had drifted away as they got married and started families. Or maybe she'd drifted away because she'd been working so hard, trying to move up to serious news from covering those fluff pieces, trying to be as successful as the rest of her family.

The only friend she'd had for long and that she really trusted was her mom. And now Tammy. They talked often on the phone through FaceTime and texts. But she hadn't told her about that weird sensation she'd been having of someone following her. And she hadn't told her about the note and the text, either. She knew that Tammy and Ethan had promised each other no more secrets. So whatever Brittney told Tammy, she would tell Ethan. And he would probably tell Brittney's brother.

But Tammy wasn't just open and honest with Ethan. She would tell Brittney everything she knew about that plane crash and what had been going on with the hotshots. And if she knew, she would tell Brittney where Rory was.

Even if he wasn't in Northern Lakes right now, Brittney would track him down wherever else he was. Hopefully, though, he was still in Northern Lakes. The roads began to curve more as they wound around all the inland lakes in this northeast region of the Great Lakes state. She was getting closer.

The weather was also getting colder. Snow still covered the road despite what had been proving to be a mild winter. At least in Detroit.

The weather wasn't the only thing that was going to be cold here—with the exception of Tammy, everybody else would probably be as chilly and unwelcoming toward her as they'd been the last time she'd visited Northern Lakes. But Brittney found herself smiling anyway. She was almost there.

Then something struck the windshield. Loudly. Like a gunshot blast. The glass spider-webbed, weaving together to stay intact, but obscuring her vision.

She couldn't see the road. Couldn't see the curve.

She stomped on the brakes and gripped the steering wheel tightly. But it was too late to stop the vehicle, as her van left the road and fell onto its side and then its roof, metal crunching as it rolled and rolled. And Brittney couldn't see where she was going.

If she was up or down…

And she had no idea if she was going to survive the crash, or if, just as that text had warned her, she was about to suffer the consequences of ignoring the threat. If she would die just as it had forewarned if she didn't drop her investigation. If she kept trying to find out the truth.

Was she dead?

The shooter stared through the scope of the long-range rifle.

Brittney Townsend had been warned. She'd just been too stupid to heed the warning. So another one had been sent. But she'd gotten in her van anyway and headed north. And without her even noticing, the shooter, who'd been following her on and off over the past few weeks, had followed her again before passing her.

Once off the freeway, the shooter had found the perfect spot, on the road between the freeway and Northern Lakes, to set up this ambush. Just as they'd set up something similar before.

Those other "ambushes" had proved successful.

Or so the shooter hoped. They kept studying the scene

through the scope, finger posed yet on the trigger. Would they need to fire again?

Was Brittney Townsend going to get out of that wreckage? Could she extricate herself from the crumpled metal?

Or was she, just as the note had warned her, dead?

Sirens began to whine in the distance. Had someone seen the crash? Or had the reporter, herself, called for help?

The shooter lowered the weapon and turned back toward their SUV. They had to get out of here now before anyone saw them. Before they were able to confirm if the reporter was dead.

And would it even matter if she was? Some stupid reporter wasn't the real problem. The problem was the past. It could not come back around, and it definitely could not be reopened all over again. Or too many secrets might finally be discovered and destroy the shooter.

The shooter couldn't let that happen, had to do whatever possible to keep the past in the past. So more people might have to die than one ambitious young reporter.

Chapter 3

After Ethan left his hospital room, with the promise that he would return and drop off Rory's truck, Rory found some clothes bundled up in a bag in the deep bottom drawer of the bedside table. They must have been what someone had brought him because he hadn't been wearing them that night. Those clothes had probably been cut off him in the ER.

Or by the paramedics who'd treated him at the firehouse. Two of the Northern Lakes paramedics worked with him. Dawson Hess and Owen James.

Someone must have raided his locker for the jeans, boxers, socks and deep green US Forest Service sweatshirt they'd found for him. Because the clothes were his. Well-worn and comfortable, so much more comfortable than that hospital gown he tossed onto the bed. He'd just done up the button of his jeans and pulled his sweatshirt over his head when the door to his room creaked opened.

Hoping it was the nurse coming back with the release papers she'd promised him, he turned with a smile only to let it slip away when he saw the trooper walk into his room. Trooper Wells. While he'd struggled a bit to remember her when Ethan had warned him about her earlier, the memories returned of her looking at him the way she looked at him now, with her green eyes narrowed with suspicion.

A lot of people had looked at him that way when he'd been growing up. Mostly because of the company he'd kept and his family than because of anything he'd ever done himself. For the past five years nobody had looked at him that way until recently. Until the bad things had started happening to the hotshots.

"Where do you think you're going?" the trooper asked him as if he'd been breaking out of jail.

After being in this room, tethered to that bed, for three weeks, Rory had begun to feel a little like he was being restrained in prison.

"The doctor told me that I can leave," he said.

"I haven't told you that yet," the trooper said.

"I didn't know you were holding me here," he said. "And on what charges? Is getting hit over the head some crime I don't know about?" Because he sure as hell knew about a lot of them, probably more than she knew.

"I need to talk to you about what happened that night," she said. "And you've been avoiding me."

He gestured back at the bed where his hospital gown lay crumpled on the tangled sheets. "I was right here this whole time."

"With a gatekeeper who kept insisting you weren't well enough to answer my questions," Trooper Wells said, her voice sharp with resentment.

"Well, for the two weeks I was in a coma, I'm thinking it would have been a little hard for me to hear you." Since he hadn't heard Ethan talking to him, or maybe he had and that was why he'd kept dreaming about the crash.

Or maybe there was something about the crash, something that he needed to remember. Some detail that had kept coming back to him in his dreams…

Only now he couldn't remember his dreams that well.

They were fuzzy and unfocused since he'd regained consciousness. He pushed those blurry remnants from his mind and focused on the trooper.

"And if I couldn't hear you, I wouldn't be able to answer you," he continued. "Though even now that I can hear you, I won't be able to help you. I didn't see anything. I just stepped out of the bunk room doorway into the hall and got hit. I didn't see what hit me, much less who did it." It had all happened so damn fast.

"Why did you leave the bunk room?" she asked.

He tensed. Had Braden not shared with her about someone starting the trucks? He knew at one point Trooper Gingrich had been a suspect in the sabotage. And as Trooper Wells's training officer, Gingrich had worked so closely with her that nobody was certain that they should trust her. That she might have actually been working with Gingrich when he'd gone after Luke and Willow Garrison.

Even if she hadn't been, Rory didn't trust her. He didn't trust anyone. Not anymore.

He'd trusted Ethan for the past five years because they'd both had secrets they'd wanted to keep. But now that Ethan's had been revealed...

Rory couldn't totally trust even him any longer. Hopefully he'd kept his word about dropping off Rory's truck in the hospital parking lot.

"Mr. VanDam," Wells prodded him. "Why did you leave the bunk room?"

He lifted his hand and pressed it against the back of his head while he grimaced. "Ahh, I don't really know. With this concussion I've lost so many memories."

Unfortunately, too many of them had returned. Maybe it would have been better if they'd stayed gone.

"You remember walking out of the bunk room," she pointed out. "You remember getting hit."

He shrugged. "Maybe it's my memory, or maybe that's just because of what people told me."

Braden had had to remind him when he'd first regained consciousness and been in such a panic, over the tubes down his throat and over his jumbled mind.

"So other people have been talking to you since you've regained consciousness?" she asked, her mouth twisting into a grimace.

He shrugged again and pressed his lips into a tight line. He was not about to give up any of the team members' names. He might have already put them through more than they deserved to endure. He could be the reason they'd been in danger.

"What is wrong with all of you?" she asked. "I know, thanks to Brittney Townsend's story, that a lot of things have been happening to your hotshot team. However, none of you have reported any of those incidents to the police. I don't think that has anything to do with some stereotypical rivalry between police and fire departments."

There was a reason that rivalry had become a stereotype. Rory had seen it play out, again and again, in his previous life and career. But he couldn't admit to that because that man, the one he'd been back then, needed to stay dead, or he would die all over again and this time for real.

He sighed and admitted, "No. It has to do with your old boss. With Marty Gingrich and his obsession with my boss and hurting him, and he wasn't above using other people to do that, to get to Braden." He'd slept with Braden's first wife and had an affair with another hotshot's wife, too.

Trooper Wells's face flushed nearly as red as the tendril of hair that spilled out from beneath her tan hat. "I had nothing to do with what *he* was doing."

Rory understood all too well how frustrating it was to be judged by the company you kept rather than who you really were as a person. But because he didn't really know her, he had no idea who she really was. She could be just as complicit and cutthroat as her former boss.

"I'm sorry, Trooper Wells," he said with some sincerity. "But I'm not going to be able to help you. There's still too much I don't remember."

"Then maybe you better not leave the hospital," she suggested.

It wasn't just the hospital he intended to leave, and maybe she knew that, too. "I'm sure they need the bed."

As it was, the door hadn't shut tightly behind the trooper, so he could hear voices raised with urgency and excitement. "The paramedics are on their way in with the patient. ETA five minutes."

Not a lot happened in Northern Lakes to keep the hospital very busy unless it happened to a hotshot.

"What's going on…?" he murmured, panic pressing on his heart. Had someone else been injured? Another member of his team?

Trooper Wells's radio began to squawk in her ear, loud enough that Rory could catch tidbits. *Possible gunshots heard. Crash.*

Something bad had definitely happened. He could only hope that it wasn't to another hotshot. He stepped around the trooper and jerked open the door to the hall.

The hospital was small enough that his room wasn't far from the ER. He had only to go to the end of the corridor. The doors to that restricted area opened as a nurse, probably the one he'd overheard talking, rushed through them. And he ducked between them just as they were beginning to close again.

"VanDam!" Wells called out to him.

He glanced over his shoulder, just as the doors closed on her, shutting her out. He turned back, following the nurse who hurried toward where the ambulance would pull into the bay at the rear of the ER.

The nurse wasn't Luke Garrison's wife. Willow was off on maternity leave, taking care of the beautiful, healthy baby she and Luke had. This was another nurse. Older. And vaguely familiar, probably from all the times Rory and his team had been in and out of the hospital.

They'd been getting injuries treated from things they'd thought were accidents. And also from things they'd known weren't. Like having their brake lines cut, nearly being run down and shot at…

Like the patient on their way to the ER now.

A crash…

Gunshots…

Had someone been shot?

Who?

As he joined the nurse in the bay, she glanced at him. But she didn't tell him to leave the restricted area. Just as he'd vaguely recognized her, she must have recognized him as a hotshot.

Oh, God…

So it probably was one of his team coming in the ambulance. Who?

The paramedic rig, lights flashing and sirens wailing, appeared on the road before careening into the lot. The tires squealed and brakes screeched as the ambulance rolled up to the ER entrance.

Rory drew in a breath, but it was shallow, his lungs compressed from the heavy weight of dread and guilt lying on them. He couldn't draw a deep breath. He couldn't slow his speeding pulse, either.

The rig stopped, and the back doors swung open. Owen James jumped out. The former Marine was a member of the Northern Lakes fire department and Rory's hotshot team.

"Owen, who is it?" Rory shouted to the blond-haired paramedic as the hospital staff rushed out to the rig.

Between them and Owen, they pulled a stretcher from the back. Owen didn't answer him. He was totally focused on his patient, firing off stats to ER residents and nurses.

Having been around paramedics a lot, Rory recognized the stats. The low blood pressure and pulse. The low oxygen level.

This person was potentially in trouble. Rory stepped closer, peering over the nurses to see who had been hurt. A woman lay on the stretcher.

She was neither of the female hotshots. She wasn't a hotshot at all. But Rory recognized her. The curly dark hair, the caramel-colored skin that her eyes would have matched if they'd been open.

But they were closed, her thick lashes lying over the dark circles beneath her eyes. She was unconscious. But even unconscious a certain vitality radiated from Brittney Townsend. She was so bright and brilliant, like a star whose light should never dim. Only get brighter.

"Oh, God, no…" Rory murmured.

While the reporter unsettled him and he'd hoped not to see her again because of her determination to get to the truth, he had never wished her any harm. In fact, he'd wished just the opposite…

Brittney squinted and closed her eyes against the lights that were so bright they threatened to blind her. And the pounding, it was so loud and intense that she flinched with pain.

Who was pounding? And where was it coming from?

Inside her head or out?

Earlier there had been the sound of a motor running.

Maybe her van's.

Maybe some kind of machinery.

There had also been voices yelling out to each other over that noise. Then someone had shouted her name, his gruff voice full of concern. "Ms. Townsend? Brittney?"

She'd tried to open her eyes. She'd tried to reply to him, but it had taken too much effort. Just as the last thing she'd done, grabbing her cell, calling for help, had taken too much effort.

Had she even managed to complete the call? With the way the van had been rolling, the metal crunching, hadn't she lost the phone?

She couldn't be sure now if she had called 911 or if her cell phone or vehicle had detected the crash and placed the call for her. Had she passed out? And why?

Was she hurt? Was that why the light affected her eyes so much? Was the pounding inside her head?

Her mom had gotten migraines from time to time, and until now Brittney hadn't understood how much pain Maureen Townsend must have endured. Probably because her mom had just powered through it as she had everything else in her life. The honorable judge Maureen Townsend was tough. Brittney tried hard to be as tough, as ambitious, as smart as her mother.

A little fluttery feeling passed through Brittney's chest, making her breathe faster, shallower, at the thought, at the realization that she would probably never measure up to the high standards her mother had set for life. Brittney worried that she would never make her as proud as Trent already had. And Trent wasn't even Maureen's son—he'd just come to live with them after his mother had died a few years after his and Brittney's father had already died during a deployment.

Tears stung her eyes, and she blinked, trying to chase them away and fight them back. She was tough, too. She'd had to be.

She drew in another breath and willed the tears away. As her vision cleared, her eyes focused on the man standing over her bed, his pale blue eyes intent on her face and filled with concern.

For her?

Or for himself?

Was he worried about her being hurt or being alive? And if it was the latter, would he try to do something about it, even right here, in what must have been the hospital?

Brittney opened her mouth to scream for help, but before she could get out more than a squeak, his big hand covered her face, cutting off her scream. And her breath...?

Trent's cell lit up with the name Owen James. And nerves tightened the muscles in his stomach. Sammy, the black cat lying on Trent's bare stomach, stood up, arched his back and sunk his claws into Trent's abs. "Owww..."

Sammy jumped off the bed and ran out of the bedroom. And for some reason Trent felt like running, too. He'd pulled a late shift at the firehouse here in Detroit—otherwise he would have been up already. For some reason, seeing this call come in, he wished he was more fully awake.

But maybe he was just overreacting. His fellow hotshots were friends. Just because one of them was calling him now didn't mean that something bad had happened. Except lately.

Every time one of them called, it was because something bad had happened. He drew in a deep breath, to brace himself, and accepted the call. "Hey, Owen, what's up?" he asked.

Silence greeted him. No. Not exactly silence. Other voices murmured in the background of wherever Owen was. Had the paramedic butt-dialed him?

"Owen," he called out, raising his voice. Maybe his friend couldn't hear him over the noise around him, wherever he was. "Are you there?"

The paramedic released a shaky breath that rattled Trent's cell speaker. "Yeah, I...uh... I..."

"What is it?" Trent asked. No. "Who is it? Who got hurt?" Because he heard just enough of the background voices to catch a medical term here and there, he figured out Owen was at the hospital. As a patient or a paramedic? "Are you okay?"

"Yeah, I'm sorry," Owen said. "She doesn't want me to tell you, but I think you should know. And I probably shouldn't tell you because of privacy laws and such..."

"She?" Heather had gone to work a few hours ago, but the area she covered as a Detroit detective was nowhere near Northern Lakes. And Trent was so close to the female hotshots, Hank and Michaela, that he doubted either of them would have asked Owen to keep anything from him. Then he groaned with another realization. "Brittney."

Damn.

He'd wanted her to leave his hotshot team alone, to stop hounding Ethan for that follow-up interview, to not shed any more light on the situation with the saboteur than she already had when she'd reported on their string of unfortunate events. He didn't want Braden losing his job as superintendent, and that was bound to happen if any other hotshot got hurt.

But a hotshot hadn't been hurt. His sister had. "What happened?" Trent asked, fear gripping his heart. "Is she all right?"

"Yeah, yeah, she's in the ER getting checked out, but I think she'll be fine. I didn't detect any broken bones. Probably just a concussion."

"*Just* a concussion?" he asked, his voice cracking. "Rory spent two weeks in a coma from just a concussion!"

"She was pretty conscious."

"Pretty conscious?" Trent asked.

"She was going in and out a bit, but seriously, she looks fine," Owen said. "So you don't need to freak out."

But there was something in Owen's voice, something he was leaving unsaid.

"What happened?" Trent asked.

"She got in an accident," Owen said. "Her van went off the road and rolled over. The roads are still snow covered up here. Icy—"

"That's bullshit."

Owen said, "You were up here just a few weeks ago and went off the road—"

"Because someone pushed me off the road," he said. And into a lake.

"There's no evidence that anyone had tried to force her off the road. There's no damage to the front or rear of her van, except for broken windows, and that probably happened when it rolled," Owen said, and he almost sounded as if he was trying to convince himself as much as he was Trent. "She must have just been driving too fast for conditions."

Even though Owen couldn't see him, Trent shook his

head in denial of the paramedic's claim. Trent had taught his little sister to drive, and she'd learned how in Detroit. Since she was fifteen years old, Brittney had had no problem maneuvering rush hour traffic or snow-covered roads.

There was no way in hell that her crash was an accident. Any more than his crash had been when his truck had been forced off the road and into a lake. He was lucky he and Heather hadn't died in the crash or frozen to death in the lake. His stomach flipped at the thought of Brittney going through something like that alone.

But she wasn't alone. Most of his hotshot team was still in Northern Lakes because they'd been worried about Rory and what had happened at the firehouse with all the engines being started up. Trent had stayed there as long as he could, but he'd missed Heather so damn much. At least he'd had a week with her before having to go back.

He jumped up from the bed that they'd spent a lot of time in over the past week. "I'm on my way up," Trent said.

"That's good," Owen said, his voice even gruffer.

"What is it?" Trent asked. "What aren't you telling me?"

"I don't know for sure. Like I said, nothing at the scene indicated that it wasn't just an accident…"

Trent cursed. "I knew it! You don't believe it was any more than I do. What is it?"

"Somebody said something about hearing gunshots," Owen admitted.

Panic gripped Trent's heart so tightly that he gasped.

"But like I said, there was nothing to indicate that. The tires were intact. Nothing had been shot out. If anybody was shooting, it was probably just some hunter. Maybe the sound of the gunfire startled her."

"She wasn't shot?" Trent asked, his heart beating so damn fast.

"No. No," Owen assured him. "She doesn't even have any lacerations."

He released a shaky breath. But he still wasn't entirely relieved. Something was going on with his sister, something he should have known about.

When she'd called him the other day, he'd heard it in her voice. It had been a little brighter than usual, like she was trying to cover up something. He'd just figured it was because she thought he was still mad at her over that damn story she'd done on the team.

"Can you keep an eye on her until I get there?" Trent asked. "Make sure nothing happens to her and that she's—" his voice cracked "—safe?"

"Rory is in with her right now," Owen said.

Trent snorted. "Yeah, right," he said. "He works harder to avoid her than Ethan does."

And if Rory hadn't already been in the hospital himself, Trent might have suspected he was the reason for Brittney winding up there. If anyone wanted to get rid of the reporter, it was probably Rory. The man was even more intensely private and antisocial than Ethan was.

When he wasn't working as a hotshot, he was a ranger on a mostly uninhabited island in the middle of one of the great lakes. Only campers and hikers ever visited the island, which was a national forest, and none of them ever stayed for long. Only Rory had, and that had been his ranger assignment for the past five years.

Ever since the plane crash.

Was Brittney right? Was there more to that story than had already been revealed? And was her pursuit of that story the reason Brittney had wound up in the ER?

Chapter 4

He shouldn't have touched her. He'd known that the moment he'd pressed his hand over her soft lips. But when she'd opened her mouth, he'd known she was going to scream.

And that damn trooper was hanging around somewhere.

Ready to finish his interview and probably start one with Brittney. And if Brittney screamed while he was leaning over her bed, the trooper was going to think whatever Brittney must have been thinking…

That he was going to hurt her.

"Shh," he said, peering around the curtained-off area of the ER where her gurney had been rolled. He couldn't see any feet beneath the curtains, at least none close enough that anyone could be listening to them. But because the walls were just curtains, everybody in the emergency room would hear her if she screamed.

And they would wonder what he was doing to her.

They weren't the only ones. He wondered himself what had compelled him to come check on her. Owen told him she'd been in a vehicle accident. But from what Rory had overheard from Trooper Wells's radio, it sounded like this crash might have been very much like the other *accidents* the team had been having. And not an accident at all.

Gunshots.

"Calm down," he cautioned her. "If you have a concussion, you're only going to hurt yourself screaming." And because she had been unconscious since she'd arrived at the hospital, he suspected she did have one. But at least she was breathing on her own. And she'd already regained consciousness.

"I'm not going to hurt you," he assured her. That must have been what she'd thought, or why else had she looked like she was about to scream?

Her beautiful topaz eyes narrowed in a glare.

"I'm not," he insisted, and he pulled his hand away, his palm tingling from the contact with her lips. She was so damn beautiful, which was something he was an idiot to even notice much less react to, like he was reacting with a quickening pulse and that damn tingling skin.

And he wasn't an idiot just because she was a reporter and his team member's younger sister…

He was an idiot because he should have known better than being attracted to another woman who would wind up destroying him. And she would…

It was no doubt why she was here.

"Trent left a week ago," Rory told her. At least that was what Braden had told him, that Trent hadn't left until after Rory had regained consciousness. But even after he'd woken up from his coma, Rory hadn't been exactly clear about who was whom. Hell, he hadn't even been certain about his own identity. "So if you've driven up to see him…"

"I drove up here to see you," she said.

His pulse quickened even more, and it wasn't just with attraction now but with apprehension. "Me? Why? Do you know about the…"

He didn't know what to call it. It hadn't been an "accident." Nobody had *accidentally* whacked him over the head hard enough to put him in a coma for two weeks.

Brittney's forehead furrowed beneath corkscrew curls of her chocolate-brown hair. "About the plane crash? Of course I know about it. I reported on it."

He shook his head. "No, I was—"

"There you are," a female voice said, the tone accusatory, and Trooper Wells jerked aside one of the curtains around Brittney's gurney. The woman was looking at Rory, though, before she turned toward the bed and added, "And there you are. I've been looking for both of you."

"Why?" Rory asked. "I already told you that I don't know anything about what happened in the firehouse—"

"What happened in the firehouse?" Brittney asked, and she struggled to sit up from the stretcher. But her delicate features twisted into a grimace of pain.

"Sit back," he said, and he touched her shoulders, trying to ease her onto her pillows again without hurting her. Then he peered around the trooper, out into the ER. "Where the hell is the doctor? Why isn't anyone treating you?"

The head nurse, Cheryl, must have been hanging around within eavesdropping distance because she popped up behind the trooper. "The doctor saw her and ordered an MRI, and we've just been waiting for an opening to use it. It's available now." She edged around Wells then to approach the gurney. "So I need to bring her downstairs to Imaging for it." She unbraked the bed and began to roll it toward Rory and the trooper.

The trooper stepped back but Rory hesitated for a moment. Seeing Brittney arrive in the back of the paramedic rig had affected him, had brought on all kinds of feelings he didn't know he had about her. Concern. Attraction.

Along with those unwelcome feelings had come the unwelcome memories of what happened to people who got too close to him. He didn't want to make any more memories like that.

Never again.

So with a slight shudder, he moved aside, but when the gurney started past him, Brittney reached out and grabbed his arm, stopping it and him.

"Don't leave me," she said, her voice cracking a bit with a vulnerability he wouldn't have expected her capable of feeling.

"I'm sure Trent will be here soon," he assured in case she was scared of being alone.

She shook her head and flinched at the movement. "I don't want Trent. I want you."

Despite knowing that she didn't mean it how it sounded, he felt a jolt like electricity and shock and something else, something he hadn't felt in a long time. A connection.

But she didn't want him. She just wanted his story. And the smartest thing he could do was get the hell out of there before she, or anyone else, could catch up with him again.

Brittney hadn't missed that look of panic on Rory's face when she'd said that she'd wanted him. But she hadn't meant that the way it had probably sounded. She hadn't, and yet when she'd said it, she'd felt this strange yearning for a connection, to not be so alone.

She'd been so focused on her career that she hadn't noticed how lonely she'd been, or maybe she'd noticed but just hadn't wanted to acknowledge it. Kind of like how she didn't want to acknowledge how damn good-looking Rory VanDam was in that conquering Viking kind of way, with his pale blond hair and pale blue eyes. But he had a shadow on his jaw for once, a dark shadow.

While she was closed in the MRI chamber, she focused on his image in her mind. She should have been focusing on her questions instead, about him and the plane crash and about what had happened on the road that had sent her van tumbling over and over.

But her mind shied away from that, from that fear she'd felt in the moment. When she'd heard…

What had she heard before the windshield metamorphosized into a spiderweb? A gunshot? Had someone shot at her? No. Nobody had known she was heading up north. She hadn't told anyone, not even at the station when she'd requested a few days off. But maybe her producer had figured out that she was determined to follow up on the plane crash story. Or someone had followed her…like they'd been following her.

The MRI didn't take long, and she was wheeled back up to the ER, to that cordoned-off area where she'd awakened to Rory leaning over her. Had he really been concerned about her or about what she might have learned?

And the trooper…

Why had she been looking for Rory? To talk about what had happened at the firehouse?

What the hell had happened?

The questions pounded inside Brittney's head like the pain. She probably had a concussion. With the way the van had rolled and the metal had crunched, she wouldn't be surprised if that was what the doctor told her once the results of the MRI came back.

The nurse pulled open the curtain to where a man sat in a chair that had been beside her bed. It wasn't her brother. Even if someone had called Trent, he wouldn't have been able to drive up within the time frame that she must have arrived at the hospital.

The nurse rolled her bed into place, next to that chair where the man was sitting, and asked Brittney, "Do you need anything?"

"Just answers," she murmured.

"The results should be back soon," the older woman assured her with a smile.

Those weren't the answers she needed, though. She just smiled at the woman and nodded.

The nurse was probably busy because she hurried away, stopping only to pull the curtains closed.

Brittney just glanced at those before rolling her head back toward the man sitting beside her bed. "You didn't leave..." she murmured, surprised that Rory had stayed like she'd asked.

He shrugged. "Trooper Wells probably wouldn't have let me. I feel like she's holding me here under house, er, hospital arrest."

"For what?" she asked. "For whatever happened at the firehouse?"

His lips curved into a slight grin. "Do you never not ask questions?"

"You set yourself up for those questions," she pointed out. But it wouldn't have mattered if he'd said nothing at all, she still would have had questions for him.

He sighed and nodded. "Yeah, I guess I did, but I've already been interrogated once today."

"So why did you stay?" she asked.

He sighed again, more heavily, and shrugged. "I really don't know..."

"No guess?" she teased.

"Because you asked me to," he said, as if he was reluctant to make the admission.

Something shifted inside her, making her heart feel

funny. Maybe she had an injury from the seat belt. The damn airbag hadn't gone off. But the seat belt had snapped tightly around her, holding her in her place while the vehicle rolled. She touched her chest then and drew in a shaky breath.

"You're not okay," he said. "Do you need pain medication? An IV? Why haven't they given you anything yet?" He jumped up from the chair then, but before he could stalk off, she caught his arm again.

"They're waiting for the results of the MRI," she said. "And I'm not in pain." To prove her point, she tried to sit up, but she flinched as her head pounded harder and her stomach ached.

"Liar," he said, but his deep voice was soft and the look in his eyes…

She couldn't be sure but it almost looked like admiration. She wasn't used to seeing that from any of the hotshots. Usually they looked at her with irritation. Especially him.

"Okay, maybe it hurts a little," she admitted.

"I'll get Cheryl or a medical resident," he said, and he started to tug his arm free of her grasp.

But she held tighter to him. "No. I don't need anything. It's not that bad."

He shook his head. "I still don't believe you. You trying to prove how tough you are?"

She flinched again, but the pain wasn't because of her concussion. It was because Rory was probably right. She kept trying to prove herself. No. She just wanted to be taken seriously. To be successful. But that wasn't the reason she was so determined to find out everything she could about that plane crash and about the hotshots; she just wanted to keep her brother safe, or at least as safe as he could be with his career.

"That's not it," she insisted. "I don't want to take anything that might knock me out again." She needed to stay awake and stay alert, so that threat wasn't carried out like it very nearly had been. The windshield hadn't shattered like that by accident. Something, and someone, had caused it.

Rory nodded. "I get that. I spent two weeks in a coma."

She gasped and tightened her grasp on his arm. "What happened?" And why the hell hadn't she heard about it?

"That's what I would like to know," another voice chimed in, and Brittney glanced up to see that Trooper Wells had returned, pulling back the curtain to peer in at them.

Rory's long, lean body subtly tensed next to her. Even though Brittney held only his arm, she could feel that tension in him and inside herself, as well. It was clear that the trooper was not done with them. But the hotshot shrugged and sighed. "I told you, Trooper Wells, I didn't see anything. And I barely remember anything."

"About that night or about anything else?" The trooper asked the question that was burning inside Brittney.

He shrugged again. "I have no idea what I forgot."

"Your boss said you barely recognized him or even knew your own name," the trooper remarked.

Rory glanced down at Brittney and then back at the officer. "Do you think this is a good idea? Talking about this in front of a reporter?"

The trooper's face flushed. But she lifted her chin as if powering through the embarrassment. Brittney recognized the gesture and the sentiment. She'd done it herself several times while she'd been covering something live and something had gone wrong.

But until this afternoon, until someone had tried to kill her, nothing had ever gone as wrong for her as this had.

She hadn't taken anything, but she felt strange, light-headed. Maybe with fear more than pain. She tightened her grasp on Rory's arm, deriving a strange comfort in his closeness. For the first time in a long while, she didn't feel so alone.

"I thought you two were more than acquaintances," the trooper remarked with a pointed look at Brittney's hand holding on to him.

Brittney would have jerked her hand away if she wasn't afraid that Rory would take off and leave her. And after what had happened with her van, she really didn't want to be alone. "He's a friend of my brother's," Brittney said. But she really didn't know Rory VanDam. She suspected nobody did. Yet, for some reason, she felt safer with him here with her.

"Who's your brother?" the trooper asked.

Figuring she could find out easily enough, Brittney replied, "Trent Miles."

The trooper's green eyes widened. "He just had an accident himself here recently. His truck went off the road and into a lake."

"That wasn't an accident," Brittney said.

"Was yours?" the trooper asked.

Brittney quickly nodded, grimacing as a sharp pain reverberated throughout her skull. "Yeah, snow-covered roads…all that…"

"Are you sure? There was a report of someone hearing gunfire in the area."

Brittney shrugged. "I don't know about that." And until she could figure that out for certain, she wanted to be the only one investigating her "accident." She knew that Trent and his team had reason not to trust their local police, after one of the troopers had tried to kill a hotshot.

"You didn't hear gunshots?" the trooper asked.

Brittney probably should have told her the truth, but she didn't know how close this trooper had been to the one who'd tried killing her brother's hotshot team member. Close enough to have helped him?

Clearly Rory didn't trust the woman because he had avoided her questions, but he had also avoided answering Brittney's. Until Brittney was certain she could trust the trooper, she had no intention of telling her about anything that was happening with her. About the gunshots.

About the threats.

"I don't know," she said. "I don't remember."

"But you know the roads are snowy? Is that why you went off in the ditch and rolled your vehicle?"

Brittney shrugged again. "I don't know. I really don't remember." It had all happened so fast. She'd always believed she would be better equipped to handle a situation like that. But that blast and the subsequent shattering of her windshield had startled and blinded her. And she hadn't reacted the way she'd wanted to, with the strength and calm that her mom or Trent would have.

She wasn't used to being in danger, not like the hotshots were used to it. And she didn't want to get used to it, so she had to figure out fast who was behind the threats she'd received.

The trooper stared at her, her green eyes hard. "I can't help you if you don't tell me the truth."

"I can't tell you the truth until I know what it is myself," Brittney pointed out. And that was as honest as she intended to be with the trooper.

"You better let the authorities figure that out," the officer advised. "And don't investigate on your own."

While the trooper seemed young, probably even a year

or so younger than Brittney, she was wise. Or maybe she'd simply heard about her.

Wells turned toward Rory again. "That goes for you and your hotshot team, too. Whatever is going on with all of you, you need to leave it to the police to handle. You might know what you're doing when it comes to fighting fires, but you don't know when it comes to fighting bad guys."

Rory's lips curved into a slight, almost mocking grin, and he chuckled. "Really, Trooper Wells. And being up here in Northern Lakes, you know a lot about fighting bad guys?"

There was something in his tone, something that made Brittney pull her hand back from his arm. He sounded like he knew much more about fighting bad guys than any firefighter should know.

Because he'd fought them? Or because he'd been one?

Chapter 5

"Where are you going?" Owen asked as Rory walked past him, heading toward the exit.

He wished he'd been able to slip past the paramedic undetected, but Owen had been hovering somewhere inside the ER since Brittney had been brought in. Just like Rory had been hovering, but now that he knew she was all right, he was free to leave.

He should have left before now, but he'd wanted to make sure that she wasn't in any immediate danger. So when the doctor had ducked behind the curtain and asked him and the trooper to leave, Rory had hovered, like Owen, but close enough that he could hear the results of her MRI.

No broken bones.

And just a slight concussion.

The pressure that had been on his chest since seeing her lying on that gurney finally eased. She was fine. Physically. For now...

But if someone had fired at her vehicle, if someone had caused her to go off the road, she was still in danger until that person was caught. And what if she was in danger because of him? Because she was so damn determined to find out everything about the plane crash?

The person who'd caused it wasn't going to want their secret getting out, that it wasn't an accident. Just like

Rory getting hit over the head hadn't been an accident. And maybe her going off the road hadn't been one, either, which meant that he might be, inadvertently, responsible for her being in danger.

"Rory?" Owen prodded him, his brow creasing with concern as he studied his face.

Everybody had been looking at him that way since he'd regained consciousness from the coma. With such concern and…confusion.

It was as if they didn't recognize him anymore.

Maybe that was because Rory had not recognized or remembered many of them or even himself when he'd woken up after two weeks of bad dreams and oblivion. But he remembered enough now to know that he was in danger and not just because of that whack on the head.

"I got released," Rory said. "And Ethan dropped off my truck earlier." Or at least he'd asked him to do it and Ethan had promised that he would, that he'd have Tammy follow him to the hospital to drop it off before they left for a much-deserved getaway.

Owen peered around him. "Ethan's here?"

Rory shook his head, and his stomach flipped with the pain radiating from the back of his skull. God, he hoped Brittney's head wasn't hurting like his. And if it was, she was damn tough. "No, Ethan and Tammy were taking off, going someplace warm for a couple of weeks."

Owen nodded. "Oh, that's right. I keep forgetting that he quit the ranger job to stick around Northern Lakes."

"Around Tammy," Rory said. "And it's not like he needs the money." The guy was the Canterbury heir no matter how hard his brother-in-law had tried to take him out.

As hard as someone had tried to take out Rory. And Brittney?

Had she been telling Trooper Wells the truth about the crash? Or was there more to it than she'd admitted?

He suspected there was, and that concerned him, way more than it should. But if she was in danger because of him...

"Somebody needs to stick close to Brittney until Trent makes it up here," Owen said. The radio in his hand squawked. "And I have to go out on a call."

Rory tensed. "Who's hurt?"

"Nobody's hurt," Owen said. "It's a transport from the hospital back to the nursing home for someone who is all right now."

Rory's tension eased. "That's good."

"Yes, and I put it off as long as I can, but Trent is still about an hour away," Owen said. "Can you stick around until he gets here?"

"Why me?" Rory asked, his pulse quickening with the thought of sticking close to Brittney Townsend. But that might be dangerous for both of them...

Owen glanced around. "I don't see anybody else here."

"But somebody else would show up if you'd called them," Rory said. "Or if Trent had called them."

"But you were here at the hospital when she got hurt."

Rory narrowed his eyes and studied his friend's face. "What are you saying?"

Owen held up his hands. "I'm not saying anything. But I think we both know that we shouldn't take any chances right now. You should know that better than anyone else after what you've been through."

Rory sucked in a breath. "What...what do you mean?"

"You were in a coma for two weeks, man," Owen said. "Because someone put you there."

He shuddered. Who had done that? A stranger? Or someone he knew and should have been able to trust?

"That's why we have to be extra careful."

"We have to," Rory agreed. "But her..."

"She's Trent's sister," Owen reminded him.

Rory groaned. "You know how I feel about her."

"I thought I did, but now I'm wondering if you know how you feel about her," Owen replied. "Or did you forget that like you've forgotten some other things?"

"What do you mean?" How badly had he slipped up in those first days after regaining consciousness?

"You've been sticking close to her since I brought her here in the rig, which surprised the hell out of me since you were so pissed off the last time she came up to Northern Lakes. You were trying so hard to avoid her then that you spent most of the time she was here hiding out in the woods."

"I like the woods," Rory said. "That's why I'm a forest ranger."

"You remember that," Owen said. "But you seem to have forgotten how much you dislike the reporter."

"I don't dislike her," Rory said.

"I see that," Owen said with a wide grin.

"I just don't trust her." She was determined to further her career with a story that might have already put her in danger and would certainly put him in danger if the truth came out. But then he already was in danger and apparently so was she...

"You don't have to trust her to keep an eye on her until Trent gets here," Owen said. "And I need you to do that because I have to go."

As if on cue, the driver from the rig called out to him.

"Owen! Mrs. G. wants to get back to the home before *Judge Judy* starts."

Owen smirked. "She wants to get back to Mr. Stehouwer."

The names vaguely rang a bell with Rory. The older couple had been in a fire at the boarding house that hotshot Cody Mallehan's fiancée had owned. They'd been her boarders until the Northern Lakes arsonist had burned down her house.

Everyone had survived, though. But it was just one more reminder of how precarious life was, probably why Mrs. Gulliver didn't want to spend any more time than necessary away from her Mr. Stehouwer. While being alone was the safest option for him and people around him, Rory missed being around other people, being close to them. He hadn't realized how much until Brittney had grabbed his arm and said she'd needed him.

And if she was in danger because of him, he had an obligation to protect her that went beyond even his duty to his fellow hotshots. Rory sighed. "Damn it. Go."

Owen slapped his shoulder. "Thanks. I appreciate it and Trent will, too."

Rory wasn't so sure about that. As pissed off as Trent had been at his sister, he was still protective of her, protective enough that he hadn't wanted her left alone. But if Trent knew what Rory really thought about his sister, he probably wouldn't trust him to watch over her. She didn't just unsettle him with her questions but also with her attractiveness.

And her touch…

Rory didn't entirely trust himself to watch over her and not want more of a connection with her. But he drew in a breath, to brace himself, and turned back toward where he'd left her behind that curtained-off area.

But the curtains had been pulled back. And her gurney was empty.

His pulse quickened with fear. Where the hell had she gone? He started forward, but someone grabbed his arm. And from the way his skin tingled, even through his heavy sweatshirt, he knew who it was.

She chuckled. "You're not much of a babysitter," she remarked.

Obviously she'd eavesdropped on his conversation with Owen. "No, I'm not," he agreed wholeheartedly. And she didn't even know the half of it. She could never know the half of it or she might wind up like the last woman he'd been attracted to.

Dead. He had to make sure that didn't happen, that he kept her out of danger somehow. He couldn't carry any more guilt than he already did.

"Good thing for you that I don't need a babysitter," Brittney said. "But I do need a ride."

Rory narrowed his eyes.

"Ethan dropped off yours," she said, revealing just how much of his conversation with Owen that she'd overheard.

"I'm not driving you back to Detroit," Rory said.

"I don't want to go back to Detroit."

"You should," he said. "You should go back." If not for her sake then for his. Because if she stuck around Northern Lakes, Rory had no doubt that this wasn't going to end well. For either of them.

Brittney suspected that Trooper Wells had underestimated her. She wasn't the first one who'd made that mistake. And she probably wouldn't be the last.

The person who'd left her that note and sent her the text

hadn't underestimated her, though. They knew that if she kept investigating she was going to discover the truth.

On her own.

But she wasn't alone right now. Albeit grudgingly, Rory VanDam was giving her the ride she'd requested. To the body shop that the state police used as an impound lot in Northern Lakes. Brittney already knew which one it was from when Ethan Sommerly's truck had been blown up.

Hers hadn't blown up, but it didn't look much better than Ethan's burned-out truck had looked.

Rory's breath whistled out between his teeth as he pulled his truck up to the fence behind which the mass of crumpled metal sat. He looked from the wreckage to her. "Are you sure you're all right? Did the doctor actually release you?"

"You really don't trust me," she remarked. She'd overheard most of his conversation with Owen. "You think I would do anything for a story." Only a console separated her passenger seat from his driver's seat, and she was tempted to lean across it, to tease him, about just how far he thought she would go. But she was already all too aware of how close he was to her, and something inside her, that she'd ignored for a long time, was reacting to that closeness.

"Wouldn't you?" he asked. "Isn't that why we're here?"

"I would do anything for the truth," she said. And she hoped like hell she wasn't risking her life for it. But if she stood around and did nothing, that didn't mean the danger would go away. The only way she could control the danger was to find out who presented the danger.

While she'd had a few doubts about Rory when she first got that note, Owen had verified that Rory had been in the hospital when her "accident" happened. That was why he'd trusted Rory, over other hotshots, to protect her. She wanted to trust him, too; she needed someone she could turn to…

But she didn't want to put him in danger, either, although it seemed like it was already too late for that.

"When did you get hit over the head?" she asked.

His mouth curved into a slight grin. "Why? Do I need an alibi for something?" Then his grin slid away, and he focused on her face. "This isn't the first thing that's happened to you, is it?"

"Just tell me when you got hit and went into that coma," she persisted. He didn't need his coma for an alibi, though. She just wanted to know if the same person might have hurt him who'd been threatening her.

"The night of the hotshot holiday party."

She sucked in a breath and nodded. "That's why Trent didn't come back to Detroit with Heather."

He shrugged. "He stayed before that happened. He was here that night that…"

"You got struck over the head," she finished for him. "Something else happened that night, didn't it?" And was the person who'd left the note on her van the same one who'd hit him? Or was someone else after him? Or just after any hotshot they were able to hurt?

He grinned that slight grin. "My getting whacked wasn't enough for you?"

He was teasing her, trying to be funny, but she couldn't laugh, not at him getting hurt so badly. Instead, she was tempted to reach across the console and touch him, to run her fingers over his head to find his wound. And…what? Kiss it better?

A sudden urge burned inside her to lean closer, to brush her lips across his. Maybe her concussion was worse than she'd thought. "You were in the hospital for weeks, then?" So obviously his concussion had been much worse than the one she'd gotten in the crash. Maybe that was why he wasn't avoiding her like he previously had.

"You didn't check my medical records while you were in the hospital?" he asked. And he probably wasn't teasing now.

"I would have tried," she said, "but Trooper Wells might've caught me with the way she kept popping up like she was lurking around…" She peered out the windows, looking for a state patrol vehicle. The concrete and metal body shop building and the fenced-in yard behind it were on the western outskirts of town, farther from Lake Huron. Trees surrounded the area, blocking it from the highway and even the driveway that led back to it.

"She didn't follow us," he said.

Maybe she hadn't, but Brittney suspected someone else might have. She had that uneasy feeling again, goose bumps rising on her skin with the sudden chill that rushed over her. And she shivered.

"It's not her you're worried about," Rory said.

She glanced back at him to find him staring intently at her, his pale blue eyes narrowed with suspicion.

"What's going on, Brittney?" he asked her.

"Which one of us is the reporter?" she fired back at him with a smile.

His mouth twitched, as if he was fighting against the urge to smile back at her. His blue eyes sparkled.

Her pulse quickened, and not because of some unknown person watching her but because he was. And he was so much better looking than she'd even remembered. She'd been curious about him before, for the sake of her story, but now she was just curious about him. About how his lips would feel against hers…

How he would kiss her…

How he would touch her...

She blinked, trying to break that connection and focus again on what mattered. On finding out why they were both in danger. "I'll answer one of your questions if you'll answer one of mine," she offered.

If he'd been fighting it, the smile won, curving his lips up at the corners. He chuckled and shook his head.

"Chicken," she taunted him with a smile of her own.

He nodded now. "I am definitely afraid of you, Ms. Townsend."

"Why do I scare you?" she asked. Was he feeling what she was? This sudden attraction? This strange connection?

Was it because they'd both recently survived attempts on their lives? Or maybe whoever had caused their accidents hadn't meant to kill them...

Just what?

Scare them away?

"I'm scared," he said, "because I'm not stupid." Then he sighed. "No. I take that back. If I was smart, I would have taken off and left you alone in the hospital."

"Why didn't you?" she asked.

"It's tough to get an Uber in Northern Lakes at this time of year," he replied.

"And you were worried about me hitching a ride?" she asked. "Or were you worried about my brother? Is that why you agreed to babysit me until he gets here?"

"I thought you didn't need a babysitter," he reminded her.

"I don't," she said. Then she glanced around again and muttered, "Maybe a bodyguard..."

"What's going on, Brittney?" He repeated his earlier question.

She dodged it this time by opening the passenger door and jumping out. But when she approached the fence, she

noticed that a chain, secured with a heavy padlock, held
the gate together. She turned toward the building, but no
lights shone inside, although it was kind of hard to tell
with the only glass being in one panel of each of several
garage doors.

"It's after five," Rory said. "It must close then."

The sky was already turning gray with a pink rim just
below the thick clouds.

She cursed. "I need to get in there. My overnight bag
is inside the van." That wasn't all. Her purse was in there,
too. She rattled the gate, trying to push the sides of it far
enough apart to squeeze between, but she couldn't even
get her arm through the narrow opening. She cursed again.

"Even if you could get into the fence, I'm not sure we
could get inside the vehicle."

She pointed toward where part of the metal had been
peeled back like the top of a tin can. "They got me out that
way," she said. "I can get back in that way." She rattled the
gate again, but the chain was too thick to give her any more
room to squeeze through. So she moved farther down the
fence and jammed the toe of her boot into part of the chain
links while she locked her fingers into another part. Using
her arms, she tried pulling herself up.

Rory chuckled.

"Give me a boost!" she ordered him.

"Yes, ma'am."

Then big hands wrapped around her waist, pushing her
up. As she went higher, his hands went lower, over the
curve of her hips, along the outside of her thighs and finally, where she'd intended him to boost her, her boots.
Her whole body tingled in reaction. She swung her leg over
the top of the fence and turned to stare back down at him.

"That wasn't what I meant by a boost." But she wasn't

really complaining. Her skin had heated up everywhere he'd touched her. And as the sun set, the temperature was dropping along with it. The wind kicking up tangled her hair across her face, blinding her.

But then Rory was there, close, as he climbed up the fence to her. He swung his leg over, too, and jumped down, landing lithely on his feet in the yard on the other side, with all the grace of a gymnast landing a somersault.

Brittney hadn't been a very good gymnast. She wasn't all that flexible. She struggled to swing her other leg over the top. But when she did, she lost her foothold with her other boot and dangled from way too close to the top and too far from the ground.

"I'll catch you," Rory said.

"I'm not like a cat or a baby being tossed out the window of a burning house," she said. "I'll flatten you."

"Ouch," he said. "You must think I'm pretty weak."

"Don't say I didn't warn you," she murmured. Despite her words, she tried to hang on and find footholds for the toes of her boots. But her fingers slipped from the chain links and she dropped, not to the ground, but into some strong arms.

It wasn't like catching a baby, though. He didn't cradle her easily in both arms. He caught one of her legs and just half her body, while the other half of her dangled forward, nearly hitting the ground. Then they both hit the ground as he stumbled back and fell. But she was sprawled across him, not the dirt, while he lay flat on his back.

"I warned you," she reminded him as her breasts pressed into his hard chest. His heart pounded fast and hard beneath hers, which probably matched its frantic pace.

"I guess I am pretty weak," he said in between pants for air.

She must have knocked it out of him. She wriggled around, trying to get off him. But his hands caught her hips, gripping them like he had when she'd been trying to get up the fence.

"Give me a sec," he said gruffly.

"Are you hurt? Broken bones?" she asked.

"No. Just that damn concussion."

"Did you hit your head on the ground?" she asked, and she stretched up his long body that was so very tense beneath hers and ran her fingers along his jaw to the back of his head. His spiky-looking hair was surprisingly soft, but then she felt what must have been a ridged line of stitches or staples. Her stomach lurched over how badly he'd been hurt, and how lucky he'd been to survive such a violent blow. "You really were hit hard. That was definitely no damn accident."

"And neither was yours," he remarked.

"How do you know?" She hadn't admitted to hearing those gunshots, but she was damn sure that she had.

He reached out, running his hand underneath her van. And he pulled out a bullet. "It must have fallen out of the wreckage."

She let out a shaky breath.

"You're not surprised," he said. "You did hear the gunshots. What the hell is going on, Brittney? And this time I want an answer out of you."

"I'll give you one," she said. "Just not here."

Because she had that feeling again, that sick, not sixth, sense that she was being watched. Her stomach churned with the fear gripping her. If that person was out there and armed again, she wasn't the only one in danger now. Rory was, too.

He'd already survived what must have been an attempt on his life. Would he survive another?

* * *

Braden Zimmer sometimes got this strange feeling, a forewarning, when a fire was about to start. That feeling had helped his wife catch the Northern Lakes arsonist the year before. Sam McRooney-Zimmer had caught Braden, too, when he'd fallen so deeply in love with the arson investigator. Sam had taken a little more convincing to give him and Northern Lakes a chance.

But since there, fortunately, weren't a lot of arson fires in Northern Lakes, Sam traveled frequently, and she was out of town now. Instead of hanging out in his empty house, Braden usually spent more time at the firehouse.

If only he'd been here the night after the holiday party...

But Sam had been home that night.

Despite all her help and her brother's help, Braden still couldn't figure out who the saboteur was. Or why.

Why do all these things to the hotshots, especially if he or she was one of them? Why hurt one of their own like Rory had been hurt? So damn badly.

He'd been released from the hospital, so Braden expected him to come back to the firehouse, which was another reason he was here. And that feeling...

It wasn't the one he got about fires. It wasn't a forewarning, it was certainty and dread, twisting his stomach into knots. Because he didn't need a sixth sense to know that something bad was bound to happen again. Until the saboteur was caught, bad things would keep happening.

His office door creaked open and Trick, his brother-in-law, poked his red-haired head through the opening. "Did you hear about that reporter?"

Braden tensed, and that dread in his stomach got heavier. "What reporter?"

"Trent's sister. Brittney Townsend."

Braden groaned. "What about her?"

"She's back in Northern Lakes."

He groaned again. "Do you think she heard about Rory getting hurt? Is she here about the saboteur?"

Trick shrugged. "I don't know."

"Is she here now? At the firehouse?"

Trick shook his head again. "She was in the hospital last Owen knew. He brought her there in his rig. She was in a crash."

Braden sucked in a breath. "Does Trent know?"

Trick nodded. "Yeah, Owen called him. He's on his way up. He wanted Owen to keep an eye on her but he had to go out on call."

"Then why aren't *you* watching her?"

"Rory is. He was just supposed to watch her at the hospital until Trent got there. But I checked in on them and they were both gone."

Braden groaned.

"It's not like Rory is going to tell her anything about the sabotage," Trick said. "He wants less to do with her than the rest of us do."

Braden dropped back into his chair, but he wasn't really relieved that Rory wouldn't talk to her. "Maybe we should talk to her."

"About what? Her crash? The roads are still pretty slippery. Even though Trent told Owen it wasn't an accident, I figure it probably was."

"Probably." Braden shook his head. "After everything that has happened, I struggle to accept that anything is an accident anymore."

Trick released a ragged sigh. "Me, too."

"We should talk to her," Braden said. "About what happened to her and maybe even about what's been happening around here."

"But Braden, that could cost you your job," Trick warned him.

He shrugged. "I'd rather lose my job than lose one of the team. Again."

"Dirk's death wasn't your fault. That had nothing to do with the team."

But that didn't make Braden feel any better about the loss of a good man. And he'd nearly lost another one when Rory had been assaulted.

With an axe handle.

A firefighter's axe.

That didn't mean that it had to have been a firefighter who'd attacked Rory, though. Stanley often forgot to lock the doors. Really anyone could have gotten inside that night. And once inside, it would have been easy enough to find the keys for the rigs. But Braden still had that sick feeling in his stomach, that dread that the saboteur was one of his team.

Chapter 6

Rory had wondered before if that blow to his head had knocked the common sense out of him or back into him. He had his answer now as he followed Brittney Townsend through the door she'd just unlocked to a room at the Lakeside Inn in Northern Lakes. He'd lost all his common sense and all sense of self-preservation, as well. Or he would have dropped her off and run away.

No. He would have left her at the hospital until Trent got there. But she hadn't wanted to wait for her brother or to even let him know where she was.

But no matter what was going on between Brittney and Trent, Rory shouldn't be here. He should be somewhere else, anywhere else where nobody could find him. Hell, he should have stayed missing five years ago instead of coming out of the mountains with Ethan, but if they hadn't banded together during those two months, neither of them would have survived. They'd struggled during the long hours it had taken them to find each other.

And now he kind of felt the same way about Brittney as he had when he'd found Ethan on that mountain. Like they were both in danger and wouldn't make it if they separated. That, together, they were stronger and safer. But Brittney wasn't Ethan. He wasn't sure he should trust her, or if she would take chances that would put them both in more danger than they already were.

"This is a bad idea," he said, hesitating on the threshold to her room.

She reached out and grasped his arm like she had in the hospital when she hadn't wanted him to leave her. And this time, instead of holding him in place, she tugged him inside the room and closed the door behind him. Then she locked both the handle and the dead bolt and leaned back against the wood of the door.

"You're not going to keep out a bullet like that," he said. And another of those old memories surfaced even as he fought to force it back down, to drown it out for good. "You need to call Trooper Wells."

"Do you trust her?" she asked.

He sighed.

"So why do you think that I should?"

"It's the hotshots who can't trust her," Rory said. "You should be able to."

"My brother is a hotshot," she said. "So why would I be able to trust her if my brother can't? If she has something against him, she might use me to get to him."

"I don't think she's had as much to do with Trent as she has other hotshots, the ones who live up here," he said.

"What about you?" she asked.

He shook his head. "The most interaction I had with her was today." Because he didn't technically live in Northern Lakes.

"You didn't seem to enjoy that very much," she pointed out. "Are you sure you want me to call her here?"

"I'll leave." He took a step toward the door, but she hadn't moved away from it.

Now he wondered if she had locked and leaned against

the door to keep out whoever she thought was after her or if she'd done it to keep him inside with her. Was it that she didn't want to be alone again? Was she more scared than she would admit? Or was she feeling the same thing he was? This strange draw to her...

"I'm not going to call Trooper Wells," she said. "You don't have to run off."

"You should run," he said. And he meant it. "After finding that bullet, you know that was no accident." Just like so many of the things that had happened to the hotshots had been no accident, either.

"How can I leave?" she asked. "You saw my van. I'm not driving out of here in that wreck."

"You can take a bus," he suggested. "Or have Trent take you back to Detroit when he gets here. You'll be safe there." He hoped.

She shook her head.

He hesitated to ask the question he'd already asked her twice, the question she'd promised she would answer once they left the impound lot at the body shop. But once they'd extricated her suitcase from the back and her purse from beneath a seat, he'd realized that he might be better off not knowing the answer to this question.

Because if he knew, he might not be able to walk away like he should. No. He should run. Every instinct he had was screaming at him to do that, to run.

But to run away, he had to get closer to her. And when he stepped closer, the ground seemed to shift beneath him like it had when she'd dropped from that fence into his arms. He'd fallen for her then.

No. He'd fallen *with* her.

He could not fall *for* her. Or for anyone else. Not ever again.

* * *

Brittney waited for him to ask that question again. She needed him to ask it, or even just to say something, because the way he was staring at her unnerved her. But it wasn't like that sensation she felt whenever someone else watched her.

She wasn't chilled by Rory's stare. Instead, heat rushed through her, and her pulse quickened. Then he closed his eyes, as if staring at her unnerved him, as well. Could he feel this, too? This attraction that was beginning to overwhelm her with its intensity.

His long, lean body tensed, and he asked, "What's going on, Brittney? Why did someone shoot at you? What the hell has been happening?"

For some strange reason she trusted him and not just because he'd been in the hospital when someone had shot at her van. Because he was obviously in danger, too, and he understood what she was feeling…all the fear and frustration and maybe even the determination to find out who the hell was after them.

"Someone's been following me," she told him. "At first I thought it was just my imagination, or maybe someone who'd recognized me." She shuddered now. "Or even my creepy producer."

His eyes opened, filled with concern. "Your creepy producer?"

She shrugged. "I can handle him. And there's no way he would have shot at me or even followed me up here to Northern Lakes." She creased her brow. "No. They might have already been here because the shot came from the direction I was going, not from behind me."

"Who knew you were coming up here?" he asked.

"Nobody."

"Not even Trent?"

"Especially not Trent," she said. "He's barely been talking to me since I did that story about Ethan."

"About Jonathan Canterbury…" he murmured.

"Did you know?" she asked. "Did you always know who he really was?"

He shook his head, but she didn't know if that was in reply to her question or in denial of answering it. "Ethan's refused to do a follow-up interview with you," he said. "And I refused to do one at all."

"I'm well aware of that," she said. "So when I got this note…" Her handbag was slung across her body, so she reached inside and pulled out the piece of paper and showed it to him.

"'You are being watched, and if you don't drop this story, you will die,'" he read the note aloud, his voice gruffer with each word. "What story?"

"It has to be the one about the plane crash," she said. "Because when I tried talking to Mack McRooney about it, this text came through…" She pulled out her cell, but the screen was black. The battery must have died after the crash, just like she might have died in the crash. She'd been damn lucky. "The text said something like, 'you were warned, now you'll suffer the consequences.'"

He shuddered. "And then you were shot at. Damn, Brittney. You need to report this."

"To whom?" she asked. "Trooper Wells? Why should I trust her when you don't?" And why did she feel like he was the only one she could trust? She didn't know him well or really at all. But since waking up to find him with her in the hospital, concerned about her, she had connected with him on a whole other level.

He sighed. "I don't trust anyone, Brittney. Not anymore."

"Why not?" she asked.

He touched the back of his head, where she'd felt those stitches. And she understood why. "Well, you can trust me," she insisted. "When you were getting hit over the head, I was in Detroit. And you were already in the hospital when I found that note on my windshield."

"When did you find that note?" he asked.

"Two weeks ago," she replied.

"And when did you get that text?"

"Earlier today."

His breath hissed out between his clenched teeth. And he shook his head. "Damn, Brittney. Instead of listening to these threats, or at least reporting them, you headed up here. Why?"

"Because I know the only way to make sure this person stops following me and threatening me is to find out who they are and stop them," she said.

"I hope you don't think it's me," he said.

She had briefly considered it but not now, not when she'd seen how concerned he'd been about her in the hospital and now. He was a good man. Like her brother. And she wanted to keep him safe, too. "Like Owen said, you're one of the few with an ironclad alibi," she said. "You're probably the only person I really can trust."

"That doesn't make it safe to be around me," he muttered the words.

But she'd caught them. "What do you mean? These threats are about you? About the plane crash?" That was her suspicion, especially after the text had come after she'd tried talking to the hotshot trainer. But there had been things that had happened to the hotshots since that plane crash. Many things.

He shook his head. "No. I don't know. I'm talking about that night at the firehouse."

"What happened that night?" she asked.

"Trent didn't tell you?"

She shook her head.

"He was probably worried about you reporting about it, about the hotshots again," he said. "So I shouldn't say anything because maybe that's it, maybe that's the story someone wants you to drop."

"If you don't tell me, I'll find someone who will," she said.

He smiled faintly. "I don't think any of the other hotshots are going to tell you about it, either."

She smiled widely. "Tammy will."

"Damn it."

Obviously Ethan must have shared that Tammy and she were friends. "Does that surprise you?" she asked.

He shook his head. "You saved her life. She owes you."

"Is that why you kept Ethan—Canterbury's secret?" she asked. "Because he saved your life?"

"You ask so many questions," he murmured. "Occupational hazard?"

"I just have so many questions," she said. "I always have."

"So that's why you became a reporter?"

"You ask a lot of questions, too, Mr. VanDam," she pointed out.

He shrugged. "I usually don't," he said. "But I'm interest—no, I'm curious."

She was amused that he'd stopped himself from saying interested. So to tease him, she batted her eyelashes and stepped a little closer to him. "About me?"

"About why someone would threaten you and force you off the road," he said.

"I'm curious about that, too," she said. "It has to be related to the plane crash."

"You ran that story months ago," he said. "And you already covered it. So why would anyone be trying to back you off from what you've already done?"

"Because they know what I know, that there's more to that story," she said. "That there's more to the plane crash."

He shook his head. "It was Ethan's brother-in-law. He was behind everything."

"He swears he wasn't," she reminded him.

"Yeah, because people died in that plane crash," he said. "So of course he's not going to admit to that."

"He's already in prison," she said. "And will be for a long time. So what difference does it make? And how would he be following me and leaving me these threats?"

"He hired people to go after Ethan," Rory said. "Maybe he hired someone to go after you."

She shook her head. "That doesn't make sense, and you know it. You're the one who wants me to leave that plane crash story alone."

"I have an alibi. I was in a coma," he reminded her.

She didn't really believe it but she felt compelled to throw his words back at him. "Maybe *you* hired someone."

He snorted. "With what money and how? I'm not a Canterbury."

"Are you a VanDam?" she asked. "Or did you take somebody else's name like Ethan did?" That hadn't really occurred to her before, but if Ethan had pulled it off, maybe he could have, as well.

He expelled a ragged sigh. "You need to stop, Brittney."

"Why? Am I on to something?"

"You must be *on* something," he said, "if you think there's any more to the story you already covered about Ethan. You must be working on something else that put you in danger."

She snorted. "Gallery and restaurant openings? I doubt that anybody wants me to drop those."

"Maybe the competition to those businesses," he said. "Or maybe the competition for your job."

She nearly snorted again. She didn't even want her job, but she once had. She'd once been desperate enough to take any position that would get her screen time, that might get her noticed by a bigger program or network like her mentor, her idol, Avery Kincaid. Avery had worked at the station Brittney worked at; Brittney had been her intern. Then Avery had covered a story about the hotshots when an arsonist had targeted them and Northern Lakes. Avery had gotten her big break after that article and a relationship with a hotshot. All Brittney had gotten from her story about the hotshots was resentment and the attention of someone who had sent her those threats. Who? And why?

Maybe it was about that, about what had been happening to the hotshots. Obviously someone was after them or Rory wouldn't have been hit over the head.

He clearly wasn't going to talk to her about the plane crash. At least not yet. So she circled back around to another question he had yet to answer. "What happened that night you got hit over the head?"

He shook his head.

"Tammy will tell me," she reminded him.

"Since she and Ethan left town for a romantic getaway, I think you'll have to wait until she gets back," he said.

And she groaned. "That's right." Tammy had texted her a screenshot of a plane ticket that Ethan had bought her for Christmas. "They're going on a cruise."

So she wouldn't get to see Tammy this trip. And if she didn't find out who was after her, she might not be alive to make another trip north.

"Damn it, Rory, please," she murmured, and tears of frustration and probably exhaustion stung her eyes. But she blinked them back.

He stepped closer to her now, so less than a foot separated their bodies. "I got hit when I stepped out of the bunk room to find out why someone had started up all the fire engines."

"Was there an alarm? Why would someone start up all the fire trucks?"

He shrugged. "I don't know. A prank."

"Hitting you over the head wasn't a prank," she said. And she reached up to run her finger over that spot on the back of his head, over his spiky, soft hair and the stitches beneath it. "It must have been bad."

"I really don't remember much about it," he said. "I had no idea what happened. And Trent never said anything to you?"

She bit her lip and shook her head. "He doesn't trust me anymore. Not after I did that story."

"Were you and him that close before the story?" he asked. "He never mentioned you before you showed up in Northern Lakes. And then he didn't even admit you were his sister until after you helped saved Tammy's life."

Had he been ashamed of her even before that story? Or hadn't he wanted her to make a nuisance of herself like she had at the firehouse in Detroit? As she probably had the entire time they'd been growing up, when she'd trailed him everywhere, firing questions at him.

She closed her eyes against a sudden rush of tears.

"God, I'm sorry," Rory said. "That was so damn insensitive. I'm sure he had his reasons. He probably didn't want any of the guys hitting on you."

She shook her head. "I'm sure that's not it."

"None of his coworkers in Detroit have hit on you?" he asked.

Thinking of the catcalls and whistles whenever she'd stopped by the firehouse, a smile tugged at her lips and she opened her eyes. Most of them only made those noises to irritate Trent, but there were a couple of them who had made serious attempts to get her to go out with them. "But that's Detroit."

"What does that mean?" he asked. "You're only hot in Detroit?" he asked.

Feeling that pull, that attraction between them, Brittney gave in to the urge to flirt. "What do you think?" she asked. "Am I hot in Northern Lakes?"

"So damn hot that there won't be any snow left on the ground or ice on the lakes," he said. "Yeah, that must be why Trent didn't mention you. He didn't want any of the hotshots hitting on you."

"You wouldn't hit on me," she said. "You would be more likely just to hit me to get away from me."

"I would never hit you," he said. "And I know I should get far away from you, but for some reason I just can't." He stepped closer now and slid his arms around her waist. His chest touched hers, his thighs brushed against hers, and his body was so hard, so muscular.

She sucked in a breath as that attraction turned to desire. To *need*.

"Rory…" Her hand, almost of its own volition, reached for the back of his head again, to pull it down to hers.

But he resisted, his body going all tense.

"See," she said, releasing a shaky breath. "You wouldn't hit on—"

He pressed his hand over her mouth again, like he had in the hospital. Then he leaned close and whispered, "Listen."

And she heard the heavy footsteps in the hall, too. Then the door handle rattled behind her. Someone was out there, trying to get in.

So she'd been right. Someone had been watching her at the impound lot. And they must have followed them back here, to the hotel. To do what?

Finish what he'd tried to do when he'd shot at her van? Kill her? And was Rory going to get hurt along with her? She'd wanted to stick close to him for protection, but she hadn't realized that she was putting him in danger, too. She didn't want him getting hurt any more than she wanted her brother getting hurt. She couldn't lose anyone else she cared about.

Damn it, Brittney.

Why wasn't she answering her cell?

Was it payback for all the times that Trent had ignored her calls? Her texts? Her?

He wished now that he could go back. That he could take every call, answer every text.

The only spot he'd still draw the line was with her questions. He didn't want to answer those because he had a feeling that asking them was what had put her in danger.

Because she hadn't gone off that damn road on her own. The roads weren't even as bad as they'd been that day weeks ago when his truck had been forced off the road.

Brittney wouldn't have crashed like that, not without some help. And she wouldn't have disappeared out of the hospital without some, too.

Rory.

Owen had left her there with him.

"What are you worried about?" Owen had asked when he'd called to yell at him after discovering that they were both gone. "Rory couldn't have had anything to do with her accident. He was in the hospital."

"She didn't have an accident, and neither did he," Trent had told the paramedic. "And because they're both in danger, they're in even more danger when they're together."

And Owen had cursed in acknowledgement that Trent was right. He'd offered to look for them, too.

They hadn't been at the firehouse. Or at the impound lot where her van sat all crumpled up like a wad of paper that had missed the wastebasket.

She could have died. And knowing that, that she was still in danger, Trent had headed next for the hotel. Thanks to her mom and stepdad, Brittney had money. So she'd probably check into the Lakeside Inn.

But the front desk refused to tell him if she had. And so he'd sneaked upstairs to check out the rooms.

As he started down the hall on the third floor, he heard something. Not her voice, like he'd been listening for at every door.

But a soft creak. Before he could turn around, something struck him, knocking him to the ground. He could only hope it wouldn't knock him out like Rory had been knocked out for weeks.

Chapter 7

Rory had hoped that the bullet might have dropped out of some other pile of wreckage in that impound yard. But he'd seen right away that the windshield had spider-webbed out from a hole in the middle of it. She could have been killed. From that bullet. Or from the crash.

It definitely hadn't been an accident. Then there was the note and the text. The threats.

Was it really about the plane crash? Was that why someone had struck him over the head that night?

Had someone else already figured out the truth that Brittney was so determined to uncover?

So determined that it could cost her her life? He wanted to make sure that didn't happen, especially if it was because of him. So he'd driven her back to the hotel and followed her inside, and then he'd been the one in danger.

With the way she'd looked at him…

The way she'd touched him…

He'd wanted to kiss her so damn badly that there had been a buzzing noise inside his head. So he was surprised that he'd heard the heavy footsteps.

But then there had been no mistaking the turning of that doorknob.

Someone was out in the hall. And, since the old hotel had

doors with no peepholes, he'd headed out the window onto the fire escape. He'd only gone down one floor, in through another window and out into the hall. Then, worried about leaving her alone up there, he'd run up the steps, slowing his pace only to quiet his approach.

He'd drawn in a breath before pushing open the stairwell door to the hall. A big man, his back to Rory, stood near another door, listening.

He was definitely looking for someone, and Rory had a pretty good idea who.

Knowing that the man had been armed out there on the road, when he'd fired those shots at Brittney, Rory didn't take any chances. He snuck up and tackled the man, knocking him to the floor. Then, desperate to knock him out before he could draw his weapon, Rory swung his fist toward the man's face.

His knuckles connected with flesh and bone before his eyes focused and he saw whose face he was striking. Trent's.

His hotshot team member shoved him back, knocking him against the wall. Fortunately his shoulders struck first, but the back of his head followed, hitting the thick wainscoting of the hallway, too. Rory grunted as pain radiated throughout his skull. And he flinched and closed his eyes for a moment.

"What the hell!" Trent yelled.

"What the hell, exactly," Brittney said.

Rory opened his eyes and reminded her, "You were supposed to stay in the room."

Before going out the window, he'd told her to do that, and he'd been so damn tempted to kiss her then. But he'd been more worried about her life than how her lips would taste. And as distracted as he'd been, he hadn't realized she hadn't agreed to stay put.

She stood over them now, a lamp grasped in her hands. "And let you get shot or worse?"

"Shot?" Trent asked the question, his eyes wide with shock. They were the same light brown as his sister's, but now his gaze moved from Rory back to Brittney. "Are you all right?"

"I'm fine," she said.

Rory shoved himself up until he was standing, but when he did, the ground seemed to tilt like it had when she'd fallen off the fence onto him. And he staggered. He might have fallen again if Brittney hadn't rushed forward to slide her arm around him.

She pointed the lamp, which she held with just one hand now, at her brother. "What did you do to him?"

"To him?" Trent repeated, and he stroked his jaw. "He hit me."

"What were you doing sneaking around the hotel, trying to get into rooms?" Brittney asked.

She must have assumed what Rory had, that Trent had been the one trying the doors. Rory hoped he'd been, and since he'd kind of caught him in the act, chances were good that it had been him.

But what if it hadn't been…?

He slid his arm around her and peered down the hall in both directions. No doors had opened. Probably because it was still the offseason in Northern Lakes. Too cold for regular fishing and water sports and too warm for ice fishing and snowmobiling. Or was someone behind one of those doors, watching them?

"You should get back into the room," he advised her. She'd left that door open behind her.

"Why?" She looked around then. "Do you think someone else is out here?"

"It was just me," Trent assured them. "The front desk wouldn't give me your room number. And you wouldn't pick up your damn phone or text me back—"

"Frustrating, isn't it?" she interjected with a glare at her brother.

Trent ignored her and continued, "So I kept calling you and listening at the doors…"

"To see if you could hear her phone," Rory finished for him, and his apprehension eased. Since it had just been Trent, she should be safe in the hotel.

Unless whoever was watching her had followed them back to it.

He was torn. Trent was here now. So he had no reason to stay. Except…

What if she was in danger because of her story on that damn plane crash? Because if that was the case, it was all his fault. So he had a duty to protect her, and maybe she was right, that the best form of protection was to find out who was behind the threats and stop them.

So even though he knew he should take off and get far, far away from her, he let her guide him back into her room, as if he needed her support.

As if he needed her.

And he'd learned long ago that it was too dangerous to need anyone. It was better to rely only on himself, except for those two months in the mountains with Ethan. After the things that had happened to him, the blow to his head and her crash, he felt kind of like he was parachuting out of a plane again and that he needed Brittney to survive.

Brittney was furious with her brother. For so many reasons.

So when he came back into the room with the bucket of ice she'd sent him to get, she glared at him again as she took it from him. Then she wrapped some of the ice into a towel and pressed it against the wound on Rory's head where blood had begun to seep through the stitches. She'd guided him to a chair once she'd gotten him into the room. He'd seemed a little unsteady after hitting the wall, and she wondered if he should return to the hospital.

Concerned and irritated, she asked, "What the hell were you thinking?"

The two men looked at each other, as if uncertain which of them was supposed to answer her. She'd tried asking Rory already, but he'd gone out the window so fast she hadn't been able to say anything or stop him.

But she'd been so damn worried.

When he'd rushed onto the fire escape to find out who was in the hall, he could have confronted a stranger with a gun. But Trent wasn't a stranger. Or he hadn't been until lately, since she'd come up to Northern Lakes. No, even before that he'd been keeping things from her. That was why she'd come up to Northern Lakes, to find out what was going on with him…because she'd known it had something to do with his hotshot team.

While she'd known about them, they hadn't known about her. Why?

"I was talking to you," she told her brother.

"And I already told you, I was worried about you, especially when you didn't answer my calls or texts," he explained.

She snorted. "So now you want to play my protective big brother after weeks of ignoring me? And even before that, you denied my existence."

"What are you talking about?"

"Here in Northern Lakes, with your hotshots, nobody knew I was your sister or that you even had a sister."

Trent turned toward Rory, glaring at him. Obviously he knew who had ratted him out to her.

She stepped in front of Rory, not wanting Trent to hurt his friend for just telling her the truth. "Don't blame him. He's not the one who denied knowing me. What was it? Three times before a cock crowed?"

"It wasn't like that—"

"Not exactly," she conceded. "But it sounds like it was close."

"I didn't deny it, but…"

"You didn't claim me, either," she said. "Why? Are you ashamed of me?"

He flinched.

And she felt a pang strike her heart. "Oh, you are."

"Brittney, it's not you, it's your job—"

"My job is who I am, just like yours is who you are," she said.

Trent snorted. "You can't compare fighting fires to reporting on the stories that you have."

Heat rushed to her face with embarrassment, especially with Rory listening to this whole exchange. But then a surge of self-righteous indignation chased away the shame. "I haven't always covered the most compelling stories," she admitted. Not until she'd found the missing Canterbury heir. "But I am good at what I do, and I'm going to prove it to you and everyone else."

Obviously she was on to something significant, or someone wouldn't have threatened her like they had. But the story wasn't as important as discovering who was behind the threats and stopping them. Then she would prove to Trent that she was good at what she did and she could take care of herself and even protect him and his hotshots, as well. As long as she made sure Rory didn't get hurt in the process.

"You're going to get yourself killed," Trent said.

She snorted now. "You could have died that night that Rory got hurt. You were in the bunk room, too. You could have been the one who got hit over the head and put in a coma. And *you* never said anything to me about it."

"I was fine," Trent said. "Nothing happened to me."

But it had to Rory, and knowing now that he'd been hurt affected her for some reason, some reason she wasn't willing to even acknowledge. Yet. "It could have happened to you, if not getting hit then the fumes from the trucks could have hurt you. I still should have known about it."

"I didn't want you reporting on it," he said. "If there's any more scandal around the hotshot team, Braden will probably lose his job."

She sucked in a breath and nodded. Apparently he cared more about his relationship with his hotshot superintendent than with his sister. "So that's how it is."

"After you did that story on Ethan, how can you expect me to trust you?" he asked.

Tears stung her eyes, but she closed her eyes to hold them in. "I need you to leave right now."

"Britt—"

"Go," she said. "Or I'll call hotel security—"

"The only hotel security here is Rory," Trent said with a chuckle.

She opened her eyes to glare at her brother. "Even with a concussion, he knocked you on your ass." But she didn't want him fighting her brother again, not for her or for any reason. "I'll be safer with him than with you right now." Because Rory understood the danger just like she did, and Trent had already been through too much recently. She didn't want him involved in this, and she didn't want to drive a wedge between him and other members of his hotshot team.

"I would never hurt you, Brittney," Trent said. "You know that."

She shook her head. "You already have, Trent. Just leave, or I'll call Trooper Wells to throw you out."

"Something's going on with you," Trent said. "And I want to know what it is."

She shook her head again. "Nope. You can't ignore me for weeks and weeks like you have and then suddenly try to play my big brother again like—"

"I am your big brother."

"Right now you're trespassing in my hotel room," she said. "And I will call the police—"

Trent sighed heavily. "Damn it, Brittney."

"Just go."

She wasn't sure that he would. But he knew her well enough to know how stubborn she was. Even more stubborn than he was, so he sighed again and turned and walked out the door. She waited until it closed behind her to let out the breath she'd been holding. While she was relieved that her brother had left, that meant that she was alone again with Rory.

And the last time they'd been alone, she had nearly kissed him. Maybe Trent skulking around the hallway had saved her from making a big mistake. But now that she'd made her brother leave, she was worried that she might make that mistake yet. Or one that was even worse...

Feeling as edgy as if he was battling a blaze with no equipment, Ethan paced the airport terminal, walking up and down the wide aisle between the gates. He had been looking forward to this trip until Rory got hurt.

But now everything had changed.

Except his feelings for Tammy. He didn't want to disappoint her. She'd been looking forward to this cruise. But she stepped into his path, and he nearly collided with her.

"You're not this upset about a delayed flight," she said. "What's going on?"

He shrugged. "I don't know." But it felt like something was wrong, and it wasn't just that the saboteur had struck again. It was who they'd struck...

Rory.

Ethan had been through so much with that man, but there was so much he still didn't know about him.

"You've been quiet and tense ever since you dropped Rory's truck at the hospital for him."

He hadn't said much during their two-and-a-half-hour trip from Northern Lakes to Detroit, where they were supposed to catch this flight. If the plane ever arrived.

His stomach pitched as he thought of another plane that had never arrived at its destination. The plane he and Rory had been on, the plane that Rory...

"Ethan?" she repeated his name with a question in her voice and concern in her beautiful hazel eyes. "Are you okay?"

Trying to reassure her, he forced a grin. "I'm always quiet, remember?"

She shook her head. "No. You might have been quiet before, but you haven't been since..."

Since they'd become lovers.

And since Trent's sister had revealed Ethan's secret, he no longer had anything to hide. Except for what he knew about Rory.

"Since you," he said. "You make me want to share everything with you." But he couldn't share this, and not just for Rory's sake, but for hers. The way Rory had told him that it was better that he not know…

"So tell me the truth," she said. "Do you really want to go on this trip?"

"I do," he said. "So badly, especially after seeing those bikinis you packed…"

"But?" she prodded. She knew him so well, so well that she answered her own question. "You're worried about Rory."

"I'm worried about the whole team," he admitted. But specifically Rory.

If it was the saboteur who'd whacked Rory over the head so hard he'd put him in a coma, then that person was getting more and more dangerous. Which meant that everyone was in greater danger than they'd been before.

"And you feel like you're deserting them when they need you most," she finished for him, articulating that sick feeling he'd had in his gut since driving away from Northern Lakes.

That sick feeling that something was going to happen to the people he loved like family.

Chapter 8

Rory shouldn't have stuck around at the hospital. He should have hopped in his truck and driven off without checking on Brittney Townsend, without ever talking to the ambitious reporter. He understood her ambition a little better now, after being a witness to the tense conversation between the siblings.

And while Trent hadn't slammed the door on his way out of the room, it felt like he had because the room was eerily silent after he left. So eerily silent that Rory felt awkward clearing his throat.

He felt awkward about more than that, though. Like that almost kiss...that kiss that he wanted to happen now. But that was crazy. They both had too damn much going on, were in too much danger, to entertain an attraction of any kind. But he was attracted to her. Too attracted.

He adjusted the makeshift ice pack against the back of his head. The concussion had definitely messed him up. That had to be why he was still here, why he hadn't gotten as far away from the reporter as he could get, why he'd started to believe that she was right, that it was best for them to stick together like he and Ethan had stuck together.

The person who'd put the threat on her vehicle could have been the same person who'd struck him over the head that night. Or maybe they'd hired someone. Like Ethan's brother-in-law and so many others in Rory's life had proved, a lot of people would do anything for money.

The towel was wet, the ice melting inside it. With a sigh, he pulled it away from his now damp hair and head.

"Are you okay?" she asked him, and she reached out with a slightly shaking hand and took the towel from him.

"Are you?" he asked with concern.

She nodded. "Yes, but I hate fighting with Trent."

"I'm sorry that you did," he said. "I shouldn't have told you what I did earlier—"

"It was the truth," she said. "And I deserved to know."

"Not when it upset you," he said. "And I am sorry about that." He didn't want her hurting emotionally or physically, and because of that, he had to make himself leave. So he stood up with the intent of heading toward the door. But the room spun for a moment, his head so light that spots danced in front of his eyes.

She grabbed him like she had in the hall, sliding her arm around him, using her body to steady his.

Except the heat and softness of her body unsettled him more. He wanted her for more than support. He wanted her.

He dragged in a breath. "I'm fine."

"You should go back to the hospital," she said. "Hitting the wall like you did might have done more damage than reopening your stitches."

"I'm fine," he repeated. "I just need to get some rest." After three weeks of being in that hospital bed, two of those weeks in a coma, he shouldn't need any more sleep for a while. But being active for the first time in three weeks had taken more energy than he'd thought.

Too much energy to fight this attraction to Brittney. So

he had to leave. Fast. Before he did something incredibly stupid…like kiss her.

"I need to leave," he said more to himself than to her. He had to remind his body that it had to move away from her, not closer. He stepped away from her, and her arm dropped back to her side. His legs heavy with reluctance, he headed toward the door. When his hand closed around the knob, he started to turn it, intent on making his escape.

Though he wasn't sure if he wanted to escape from her or from the temptation of her.

"Wait," she said. "Don't leave."

She hadn't touched him, like she had at the hospital when she'd grabbed his arm more than once. But she didn't have to touch him to stop him.

Just her words did that.

Or maybe it was his own desire to stay that stopped him from leaving her. He could give himself an excuse. That he had to stay to protect her, and he fully intended to protect her…after he got some rest. And he had no doubt that Trent was lurking around outside somewhere. Probably back in the hall, intent on making sure nothing happened to his sister. She didn't need Rory.

She might actually be safer if he left, unless she was right, like that instinct inside him that had had him searching for the other parachuter five years ago. That sticking together was their best chance of survival…

But he wasn't going to be any use to her or himself if he didn't get some rest. So he drew in a breath and forced himself to finish turning that knob. But he couldn't quite bring himself to open that door and walk away.

Brittney curled her fingers into her palms, so that she wouldn't reach for him, so that she wouldn't pull Rory back from that door. While someone had threatened her and apparently tried to shoot her, Rory could have been killed in the firehouse. He was in just as much if not more danger than she was.

"Don't leave," she repeated with concern for him and with something more, that desire for him that made her want to kiss him so damn badly.

His long lean body tensed even more than it had when she'd slid her arm around him to steady him. "It would be a very bad idea for me to stay."

He wasn't wrong about that. If he stayed, Brittney was pretty sure she would give in to that desire to kiss him and maybe in to her desire for more. And he was the last guy she should get closer to, because of that feeling she had, about how much danger he was in.

She wasn't going to fall for someone and lose him like her mom had lost her dad. Sure, she'd found love again with Brittney's stepdad. But Brittney remembered the pain her mom had tried to hide from her. Late at night when nightmares had woken her up, she'd heard crying.

Her mother crying.

And she had been so afraid to hear a strong woman like her mom sobbing with such pain and such heartbreak. Brittney wasn't as strong as her mom was. She couldn't love and risk the loss.

Not that she was at risk of falling for Rory VanDam. She didn't really know anything about him, except that he kept, albeit reluctantly, coming to her rescue. At the hospital he'd made sure she was all right, and he'd taken her to the impound lot. And he'd just taken on her brother in the hallway. But he hadn't known it was her brother.

It could have been the man with the gun. Hell, the man with the gun could be out there now. She sucked in a breath at the frightening thought of that. But surely whoever had fired at her wouldn't take a shot at Rory. Unless Rory was as involved in all of this, because of the plane crash, as she'd previously suspected he was. Maybe his getting hit over the head and the threats she'd received were related because someone didn't want him to tell her what had really happened.

"Where are you going to go?" she asked him. "Back to the firehouse?"

He moved as if a sudden chill had passed through him, his body shuddering slightly.

"You know you're not safe there," she said.

"Because of your brother?" he asked, and he turned back toward her then, touching the back of his head.

She shook her head. "As big an ass as my brother can be, he wouldn't have intentionally hurt you. I believe him, that he didn't know it was you when you jumped him in the hall. And he just instinctively shoved you off."

"I wasn't talking about then," Rory remarked.

And she bristled defensively. "There's no way it was him who struck you at the firehouse. Trent's hotshot team members mean everything to him. He would rather hurt me than hurt any of you."

"He would never purposely hurt you," Rory said. "He loves you."

She sighed. "I know. But just because you love someone, it doesn't mean you like them. And I don't think my brother likes me or respects me very much."

"Is that why you're so determined to report on something big, to earn his respect?"

Her face heated with embarrassment as she remembered what he'd overheard, her conversation with Trent. Replaying it in her head, it all sounded so pitiful now. "I want to report on something big because the truth should always come out."

"Why?"

"Because people deserve to know what's really going on." Instead of hearing her mother cry at night, when she thought Brittney was sleeping, she should have just told her what was going on. How much she'd missed Brittney's dad...

"Not if it puts them in danger," Rory said.

And now she knew, without a doubt, that her suspicions had been right. There was more to the story about the plane crash and about Rory VanDam than he wanted anyone to know.

"It's not the truth that hurts people," she said. "It's the people who are trying to keep the truth from coming out, who are trying to keep secrets, that are the threat. But once the truth is out, there's nothing for those people to try to protect anymore. Getting the truth out is the only way to eliminate the danger."

He expelled a ragged sigh and turned back to her, his pale blue eyes intense. "People don't kill just to protect their secrets," he said. "They kill for revenge. For passion..." As he said that, his gaze lowered to her mouth.

Her pulse quickened. The passion was there, burning so hotly between them. She stepped closer, irresistibly drawn to him and wanting to connect in a way she'd never connected with anyone else. And not just sexually.

This attraction between them seemed deeper than desire. But the desire was there. Too strong for her to not act on it, to not rise up on tiptoe and skim her lips along his jaw. "Tell me your secrets," she urged him in a whisper.

And he grinned, his eyes sparkling now with amusement as he stared at her. "You are..." His breath shuddered out, and then he lowered his head so that his mouth brushed across hers.

It was just the briefest of kisses, just his lips sliding across hers. Once. Twice. But she was suddenly aware of every nerve ending in her body, feeling as if she'd been jolted by something like an electrical current.

But he pulled away and stepped back and said, "You are right about one thing. It's not the truth that hurts people. It's people who hurt people." Then he opened the door and stepped out, pulling it closed behind him.

Leaving her alone with that thought and with her body tingling everywhere from just that brief kiss. Was he leaving because he was afraid that he was going to hurt her? Or that she was going to hurt him?

Or did he know who was behind everything?

The threats, the gunshots, someone hitting him so violently over the head?

But if he knew, why wouldn't he report that person? Even if he didn't trust Trooper Wells, surely there had to be someone he could trust.

Another police officer. Or at least his superintendent at the firehouse.

It would never be her. Since her own brother didn't trust her, she doubted that Rory VanDam ever would. He would never willingly tell her his secrets.

Trent didn't trust this strange alliance between his fellow hotshot and his sister. What the hell were they even doing together? Owen had said he'd had to leave for a call, so he'd asked Rory to keep an eye on her.

But the already injured hotshot had done more than that. He'd brought her here and stayed with her.

Trent didn't care how pissed his sister was at him, he wasn't leaving her alone. But she wasn't alone.

From the shadows of an alley across the street, Trent studied the hotel. Not many of the windows were lit up besides that one. The one that had to be hers, or had Rory booked the room?

After what had happened at the firehouse, he probably wouldn't go back there. And there was no way he could be medically cleared to resume his duties as the ranger on that small island.

But if it was Rory's room, why had he invited Brittney to stay with him? The last time she'd come to town nobody had worked as hard to avoid her as Rory had. Not even Ethan, whose whole life Brittney had blown up. After that, Trent would have expected Rory to avoid her even harder. And yet…

Rory was with her. And he'd done his damn well best to protect her. Trent raised his hand to his jaw, which was beginning to swell from where the guy had struck him. Hard.

Then instead of being mad at Rory, Brittney had gotten mad at him. Like a brother trying to find his younger sister was a crime or something.

The only crimes that had been happening lately had been the work of other people. Billy.

That poor kid who'd gone after Trent and Heather. But Billy was behind bars. He hadn't tried to hurt Brittney to get back at him.

But someone had.

She hadn't driven her vehicle off the road on her own or she and Rory wouldn't have been so damn edgy about hearing him in the hallway.

Something was going on, and Trent wasn't going to learn

about it when everyone else did, when Brittney did her damn story about it.

He was going to learn about it now because Brittney might not get the chance to do that story if someone wanted to harm her.

He lowered his gaze from that window then to the street around the Lakeside Inn. It was the offseason right now, so there weren't many vehicles parked near the building. It had been pretty empty, almost eerily so, like the hotel from *The Shining*.

He shuddered at the thought of that horror film. And the horror he would feel if anything happened to his sister or to Rory.

And that was when he noticed the shadow behind the wheel of one of those vehicles, a long black SUV. He was surprised he could see that much through the heavily tinted windows, but he was pretty damn sure someone was there.

And that he was watching the hotel for the same reason that Trent was.

Because of Brittney...

Chapter 9

Rory was amazed that he'd been able to walk away from Brittney after that kiss. For one, his legs were shaky, and he couldn't blame it on his concussion. His head hadn't hit the wall all that hard, but it must have knocked some sense into him because he had walked away from her. Even though he'd wanted to stay so damn badly.

He'd wanted to be with her in every way. To protect her and to get even closer to her. For the past five years he'd done his best to keep his distance from people, even from his team, and he hadn't realized until today in the hospital with her just how damn lonely he was. How much he craved to be close to someone...

But Brittney Townsend?

Could he trust her?

He needed time to think about what she'd said as well as the thoughts that had gone through his own head. And he couldn't think when he was close to her. Well, he couldn't think about anything but wanting to be closer to her, to be inside her. Maybe a little distance would clear his head.

But once he stepped out of the lobby doors onto the dimly lit sidewalk, Rory had that strange feeling that Brittney had talked about earlier at the impound lot. That sensation that he was being watched.

But was *he* being watched? Or was *she* the one someone was waiting for out in the shadows? Those threats she'd received might not have had anything to do with him or even with the plane crash. But it might involve the hotshots…

Like whoever the hell had struck him over the head…

He glanced uneasily back at the lobby, making sure that she hadn't followed him out. She hadn't wanted him to leave, but she had to know it wasn't a good idea for him to stay with her. He wasn't exactly great protection for her, especially if that damn plane crash was the reason that someone was threatening her.

No. They'd done more than threaten when they'd fired those shots at her vehicle, when they'd caused her to go off the road and her van to roll over and over. She'd been trapped inside that wreckage until Owen and his crew had used the Jaws of Life to extricate her from the van. Whoever had fired that bullet at her vehicle could have finished her off then, before help had arrived.

So maybe they'd only intended to frighten her away. If that was the case, they didn't know Brittney. All that had been accomplished, with the threats and that gunshot, was her resolve to find out the truth being strengthened. She was even more determined to get the story than she'd been before. She seemed to really believe that it would stop whoever was threatening her from hurting her. But he knew, all too well, how the truth coming out could cause more damage.

Was this really all about the plane crash?

And if it was, then it was his fault.

So he'd been smart to leave her. He would be smart to leave Northern Lakes, too. Maybe even Michigan.

"Rory…"

He barely heard the whisper. Where had it come from?

He glanced back at the lobby again to see if Brittney had followed him out. She hadn't, which was good because Rory had a feeling that the person calling his name was trying to lure him into danger.

"Rory…" the whisper echoed back, as if it was coming from between buildings. It was definitely too deep to be Brittney's.

But it sounded vaguely familiar. And Rory realized who it probably was.

"Trent?" he called back. Of course Brittney's protective older brother would have stuck close to her. Despite her unwillingness to share anything with him, he obviously knew she was in danger.

"Shh…" Trent whispered back from somewhere behind Rory.

He turned and saw the gap between buildings, the alley where Trent was waiting for him. He gestured out of the shadows, waving Rory over toward him.

Why? To pay him back for jumping him in the hallway?

To warn him to stay away from his sister?

Trent had probably never figured he'd have to warn Rory away from her. Neither had Rory. But Brittney had made sense about them sticking together in order to protect each other while working together to find out who was after them. Was it the same person? If it was, catching that person would definitely keep them safe and make sure they and the rest of the team stayed that way. Or, while they tried to catch him or her, that person got rid of both of them instead. It was a risk either way, and maybe not just to their lives.

Rory expelled a slight sigh of frustration and resignation, then he walked toward the alley. "Hey," he began. "I'm sorry. I really didn't know that was—"

Big hands reached out of the shadows and yanked him

between the buildings. He clenched his fists. Despite just apologizing to his team member, he was ready to fight him again. If he had to.

"Shh…" Trent said again.

"What the hell is going on?" Rory asked.

"I think there's someone sitting in that SUV over there."

Rory glanced around them. There weren't many vehicles parked on the street, but there were a couple of SUVs. "Which one?"

"The black one with the tinted windows."

The description brought one of his jumbled memories into sharper focus. The last time he'd ridden in one of them…

He shook his head, at the memory and at Trent. "How can you see anyone inside?"

"The windshield looks darker on the driver's side, like there's someone behind the wheel," Trent said, and he pointed a finger toward the vehicle.

So there was probably only a driver inside, not a passenger, unless the passenger was already out and maybe inside the hotel.

He let out a soft curse. "We should go back inside, make sure Brittney is okay." She was right—they were safer together.

Trent sucked in a breath. "What the hell is going on with my sister, Rory?"

"I don't understand what you mean." And he didn't know for certain. Was Trent talking about his sister's crash or about what he'd interrupted when he'd messed with the door earlier?

But Trent couldn't know what he'd interrupted. Rory wasn't even certain Brittney had intended to kiss him then.

But he had damn sure wanted her to, and when she had just now…

Rory had had to force himself to stop at just that brush of his mouth across hers, even though he'd wanted to deepen the kiss. Hell, he'd wanted to do a lot more than kiss her.

But she was off-limits and not just because she was Trent's sister. She was off-limits to him because Rory couldn't let anyone else get hurt because of him.

"You know what I mean," Trent insisted. "Or at least you know more than I do or you wouldn't have jumped me in the hall. You were expecting trouble."

"These days every hotshot should be expecting trouble," Rory pointed out.

"Damn saboteur," Trent murmured. "You don't think that's who's going after Brittney…"

Rory tensed. He hadn't considered it. He wasn't even sure that was who had gone after him. But he actually hoped it had been. He preferred to think they were both in danger because of the saboteur and not because of…

He turned back to focus on that long black SUV, and that sensation raced over him again like a cold wind. Someone was inside. Someone was watching them.

Or watching for Brittney? She'd said she'd felt that way before, like someone was watching her back home in Detroit and at the impound lot. The person must have followed them back here.

How the hell had Rory missed that long black vehicle following them? How had he missed it at the impound lot if it had been parked somewhere in the area? Because the person was a professional…either assassin or…

"You should go back into the hotel," Rory told Trent. "Make sure Brittney is okay."

Just in case that driver hadn't always been alone, just in

case someone else had already gone inside the hotel to try to find her like Trent had.

"Damn it, Rory, what's going on?" Trent demanded to know.

"I don't know." He couldn't be sure. But maybe if he got closer to that vehicle, if he could see who was inside it, he would know if Brittney was in danger because of him, because of the man he used to be. The man he had never wanted to be again.

Guilt hung heavily on Brittney, pulling her shoulders down as she hurried downstairs to the lobby. She shouldn't have let Rory leave. He was still suffering from his concussion, which her brother had probably only made worse when he'd knocked him into that wall.

Rory had bled quite a bit on the towel. She hadn't noticed it until after he'd left. She'd thought the reason the thick terry cloth was wet was from the ice melting. But it was more than water…

It was blood. Rory's blood had stained the fluffy white towel a deep crimson.

He needed to go back to the hospital for a CT scan and maybe more stitches if he was still bleeding. If the towel hadn't staunched the worst of it…

She shouldn't have let him go, not in that condition when he was so hurt and vulnerable. And yet he'd taken down her brother who was a big guy. Trent had always intimidated the hell out of the boyfriends she'd had in the past. Not that she'd had many.

She'd always been more focused on her family and her career. She'd never realized that she might have to sacrifice one for the other. When she'd done the story about the hotshots, she hadn't realized what it might cost her.

Her brother.

And maybe her own life…

And Rory's.

He'd handled Trent with ease. Even hurt, Rory was strong and fast. Not fast enough to avoid a bullet, though. But maybe fast enough that he was probably gone by now.

But when she started across the lobby, she could see his truck parked on the other side of the street, the US Forest Service logo on the door.

He hadn't left yet. Where was he?

Had he fallen? Was he lying facedown on the sidewalk?

She hurried through the lobby, past the night clerk who didn't even glance up from his phone. If something had happened to Rory, the young clerk would not have even noticed.

Brittney pushed open the glass door and stepped onto the sidewalk, which was illuminated from the light from the hotel. Nobody lay there. There wasn't even any blood.

Had he fallen on the other side of the street?

She couldn't see beyond the two lanes to the sidewalk on the other side. The businesses over there had closed for the night and the streetlamp was farther down the block, casting no light onto the sidewalk over there.

Her heart pounding fast with fear for him, she started across the street. And then suddenly light came on. Two headlights, the beams so bright that they blinded her.

And an engine revved.

It wasn't Rory's truck. That was still dark. But another vehicle, one just as big or bigger because the headlights were so high. It pulled away from the curb, tires squealing, and steered straight at her.

"Brittney!" someone yelled her name.

But she couldn't move for a moment, frozen in the beam of those lights. Frozen with shock and fear.

* * *

That reporter wasn't going to stop. That was clear enough now that the warnings weren't working. She wasn't backing off. She'd kept making calls, asking questions, and the more interest she showed the more someone else, like the authorities, might get interested.

She wasn't going away. And if she wasn't going to go away on her own, the driver had to make her go away.

Forever.

The SUV had been parked just far enough down the street to be away from the lights of the hotel and the streetlamps but close enough to watch the entrance. Two men had come out before the woman.

And both of them had slipped away into the shadows.

But as the SUV bore down on the woman, the men were suddenly there in the street with her. She was the only one who had needed to die. But the driver had no compulsion against taking out a couple of more.

Chapter 10

Rory's heart seemed to stop for a moment as he stared at Brittney standing in the beam of those harshly bright lights, frozen, as the SUV bore down on her. While Trent yelled her name, Rory started running toward her, as fast as he could. He jumped in front of those lights and caught her around the waist. Then he propelled her out of the way, rolling across the asphalt with his arms locked around her just as the SUV passed them.

The SUV was so damn close that Rory's clothes rustled and Brittney's hair blew across his face. With as big as the vehicle was, it probably would have killed her. And maybe him and Trent, too.

Maybe Rory was dead. But if he was dead, his heart probably wouldn't have been beating as hard. And he wouldn't be able to feel the asphalt of the road beneath his back and the softness of Brittney's body lying stretched out on top of his.

"Are you all right?" he asked between pants for breath. His lungs burned with the need for air.

The breath that she must have been holding whooshed out in a ragged sigh, warming the skin of his neck where her face was tucked between his chin and his collarbone. Then she lifted her head, her hair brushing across his cheek, and stared down at him. "Are you all right?"

He closed his eyes for a moment, silently evaluating whether anything hurt more than it should. His head ached, like it had since he'd woken up from his coma, and now his shoulder and hip ached, too, but not so much that anything was broken.

A groan emanated from the darkness, and Rory opened his eyes with surprise. That hadn't been his groan.

"Trent!" Brittney called out with concern as she scrambled up from Rory and the ground. "Oh, my God!"

Rory rolled to his side and looked across the asphalt to where Trent lay a short distance from him. "Damn!" He shoved himself up, nearly dropping back down as his head got too light and his vision blurred. He drew in a breath, steadied himself and rushed over to where Brittney knelt beside her brother's prone body. "Trent, are you all right?"

"We need to call an ambulance," Brittney said. "But I left my cell upstairs."

"Mine's dead," Rory said, and he started toward the lobby. "I'll have the clerk call—"

"No!" Trent shouted. "I'm okay. Just knocked the damn wind out of me."

"It knocked you down," Brittney said. "You might have broken bones." She glanced over her shoulder at Rory. "You, too."

"I don't have anything broken," Rory assured her. He wasn't as certain of Trent's condition. He stepped closer and peered down at his hotshot teammate. "Maybe you shouldn't move—"

"I'm fine," Trent insisted, and he shoved himself up from the ground. "I'm just getting damn sick of nearly getting run down."

"Then you shouldn't have run into the street!" Brittney exclaimed. "Either of you!"

Trent shuddered. "You were just standing there, and it started straight for you…" He shuddered again. "I thought you were going to die. You wouldn't move."

She moved now, throwing her arms around her brother. She hugged him tightly for a moment. And Trent held her just as tightly, and over her head, he mouthed words to Rory.

He narrowed his eyes, trying to tell…

"Thank you," Trent said aloud. "Thank you for saving my sister."

Rory shook his head. "I didn't…"

"You did," Trent insisted. "I couldn't get there as fast as you did. I couldn't save her."

While Brittney had escaped injury this time, Rory suspected there would be another time. And what would happen if he wasn't around to save her? Would she survive?

Or was she only in danger because of him? Would she be safer if he left town, like he'd intended when he'd awakened in that hospital bed?

But even if he left, Brittney wouldn't be safe because he knew there was no way she was going to stop pursuing her story. Whatever story the person threatening her wanted her to drop…about the plane crash or about the saboteur or something totally unrelated…

Some story that she'd done in Detroit. And if that was the case, then Rory hadn't put her in danger, but maybe he could help protect her from it. And if it was the saboteur, Rory had no idea how to handle it. This person had pulled dirty trick after dirty trick on the team and yet nobody had figured out who it was.

Could Brittney? Or would trying to find out get her killed?

Brittney was shaking so badly that Trent and Rory escorted her back into the lobby of the hotel. She wasn't shaking because she was cold, even though the temperature had dropped a lot when the sun had.

But even standing near where gas logs glowed in the lobby fireplace, Brittney couldn't stop shaking, at least on the inside. On the outside, she was trying to act tough. She was trying to be as strong and brave as her big brother had always been ever since they were kids. They'd both lost their dad, but Trent had lost his mom, too, a few years later. And he would have wound up in foster care if not for Brittney's mother and stepfather taking him into their home. They were wonderful, generous people, but they'd probably done it more to appease Brittney's fears than anything else.

Trent had been in the vehicle when his mother was killed, and Brittney had been terrified that she would lose him like they'd lost their dad and him his mom. That terror rushed over her now, threatening to overwhelm her. This was why she'd come up to Northern Lakes the first time, to find out what was going on with the hotshot team, to make sure her brother was safe. But now she was the one who'd put him in danger.

"We need to call the police," Trent said. "To report someone nearly running you down."

"Call who?" Rory asked the question. "Trooper Wells?"

Trent cursed. "I'll call Heather."

"Your detective girlfriend has no jurisdiction in Northern Lakes," Rory said.

"But she brought back that kid who followed you up here, who ran you off the road," Brittney pointed out.

Trent sighed. "She brought him back for the crimes he committed in Detroit. And she had to get special authorization to do that."

Brittney really didn't want Heather involved, anyway.

Because Heather was good enough to get the truth out of her about the notes and the gunshot. But as good as she was, she and Trent had nearly died too many times just recently. Brittney couldn't count on their luck holding out. She couldn't risk losing her brother.

Then she turned around and realized she'd lost someone else. Only she and Trent stood in front of the fire. "Where did Rory go?" she asked with alarm.

Trent turned around then, too. "He's leaving…"

Vehicle lights flashed on again as, across the street from the hotel, Rory started his truck and pulled away from the curb. She couldn't let him leave, not when he was probably hurt. She started toward the lobby doors, but Trent stepped in front of her and caught her shoulders.

"You're not going anywhere," Trent said. "Until you tell me what's going on."

"I have to check on Rory," she said. "You hurt him upstairs, and just now…" She shuddered, thinking what could have happened to him. What could have happened to them both…

Maybe she should let him leave, though. She'd thought he was the reason she was in danger because of whatever he'd kept from her about the plane crash, but now she realized it might be the reverse. But who had struck him over the head?

"Rory's tough," Trent said. "He's survived a plane crash and a coma. I think he's indestructible."

Brittney wasn't so sure about that. Eventually his luck was going to run out. If it hadn't already…

"What if that person who nearly hit us goes after him and he's alone?" she asked.

"I think that person was after you," Trent said. "That vehicle didn't move until you stepped out of the lobby."

She shivered.

"Damn it, Brittney, you need to tell me what's going on," Trent insisted.

"Just like you told me what was going on with you a few weeks ago when your house burned down with the body of a murdered woman inside it?"

"I had received that Christmas card with the threat inside," Trent said. "Warning me that I was going to find out how it felt to lose someone close to me. At that time, the person closest to me was you."

Now it was Heather. Brittney felt a little jab of jealousy over that. Not that Heather had replaced her but that her brother was as strong as her mom, strong enough to love somebody that they could lose.

She also felt a little jab of envy that he'd received a card for his threat, and all she'd gotten was that sheet of paper stuck under her windshield wiper. The thought struck her as funny, but she couldn't share it with him despite being tempted. Gallows humor was how she and Trent had dealt with their losses. And she knew it was how his hotshot team dealt with loss and fear.

The humor fled, her fear for Rory's well-being chasing it away. "Where do you think Rory is going?" she asked. Hopefully back to the hospital, but she doubted that.

"Probably the firehouse."

"The firehouse, of course."

"You're not going there until you and I talk," Trent said, his hands tightening on her shoulders.

"Just like how you didn't want me involved in your drama, I don't want you involved in mine," Brittney said.

"You're trying to protect me?"

She gestured toward the street. "You could have gotten run down just now."

Lights flashed in the street as a police SUV rolled up outside.

"Did you call them?" she asked Trent. He was the only one who had his cell on him. Hers was on a charger upstairs, and Rory had claimed his was dead. Unless...

He'd lied, and he'd called after he'd left the scene.

"I called them," the clerk spoke up from behind the desk. "I saw what happened."

Brittney turned toward him, shocked that he wasn't still engrossed in whatever he'd been watching on his phone. "You called? That wasn't necessary."

Or appreciated.

"That dude deliberately tried to run you down," the kid remarked.

"You saw who it was? You saw the driver?" Brittney asked, her pulse quickening.

He shook his head. "No. The windows were too dark. But it definitely didn't look like an accident."

Brittney was pretty damn sure it wasn't, just like her crash earlier hadn't been an accident, either. Somebody wasn't just trying to scare her off now. They were trying to kill her.

Trent had always known his younger sister was stubborn. But he hadn't realized how stubborn until now. The state trooper who'd shown up at the hotel to take the report hadn't gotten much more out of her than shrugging and head shaking.

If Trooper Wells had shown up, she probably wouldn't have gotten anything else from her. Since he wasn't able to...

As much as Brittney liked asking questions, she disliked answering them even more. And he had so many damn questions for her.

But she'd insisted she was tired and needed her rest.

"You're not getting rid of me," Trent had informed her as he'd booked the adjoining room to hers. And he'd made her open the door between them because he knew her too well.

She was probably going to sneak out the minute she thought he was sleeping. So he wasn't going to sleep.

Not now.

Probably not until he knew she was safe. So he sat up against his headboard, peering through the crack in the door between their rooms. He had a good view of her door to the hall. She wasn't getting past him. Just as she very nearly hadn't gotten past the person who'd tried running her down.

Who the hell could be after Brittney?

His stomach churned with the thought that had occurred to him, the thought he hated to even entertain. It could be a member of his team…if that was who the saboteur actually was. But it almost had to be because he couldn't see how anyone else would have been able to get close enough to sabotage their equipment without being noticed.

He'd always felt like his team was his family. But his real family might be in danger because of one of them. At least he knew it wasn't Ethan or Rory.

But who else could he trust?

He called the one person he trusted the most in the world right now.

"Hey, babe," Heather answered, her voice husky either with sleep or the desire that shot through him at just the thought of her. "How's your sister?"

He sighed.

"Your text said she was okay enough to leave the hospital," she reminded him. "Didn't you find her?"

He wasn't sure if he had. The Brittney who'd turned on him in the hall, yelling at him for shoving Rory into the wall, who'd berated him for not claiming her as family on her first trip to Northern Lakes, that Brittney didn't seem at all like the adoring little sister he knew.

That he'd probably taken for granted for too damn long. He could have lost her. Not just once but twice in one day.

"Trent, sweetheart?" Heather called out to him. "Is everything okay?"

He drew in a deep breath before replying. "For the moment…"

But he had a feeling that moment wouldn't last.

"But?" Heather prodded. "What happened?"

"I cheated on you," he said.

She laughed, and he smiled, loving how much she trusted him, how secure she was in his love and devotion to her. Just as he trusted her and felt so damn safe with her. "How's that?"

"I nearly got run over with someone else," he said.

She sucked in a breath. "Damn. Are you all right?"

"Yes."

"And the other person?"

"People," he said. "Brittney and Rory."

"They're okay?"

"Brittney is," he said. "Rory took off so fast that I'm not sure…"

"I didn't even know he was out of the hospital yet."

He'd told her about Rory's concussion, how he hadn't left Northern Lakes until he knew his fellow hotshot was out of the coma and on the mend.

"He just got released, and Owen had him watching Brittney until I got up here."

"The guy just woke up from a coma," Heather said. "How much protection could he be?"

"He saved her life tonight," Trent said. And he stroked

his fingers along his jaw. "He took me down when he caught me lurking around her hotel room, too."

"You were lurking?" she asked. And he could hear the smile in her voice.

"Damn clerk wouldn't tell me which room she was in or call it for me," Trent said.

"But you found her," she said.

"Yeah."

"So why is Rory protecting her?"

"Owen figured Rory was the only one he could trust since he was in the hospital when her van went off the road."

"So he's assuming the worst about that crash, too?" she asked.

"Because I told him that there is no way Brittney would have gone off the road unless it was the same way we did…"

"Because someone forced us off."

"And tonight, with her nearly getting run down in the street outside the hotel…" Emotion choked off his voice for a moment, making him hoarse as he remembered the horrifying moment that Brittney had frozen in the beam of those bright lights.

"And you don't think that was an accident, either?"

"It's what she told the trooper who came for the report," Trent said.

"But you think she was lying."

"She's definitely hiding something," he said. "She won't answer any of my questions. She won't tell me what's going on."

Instead of commiserating with him, Heather chuckled again. "Payback's a bitch, huh?"

He sighed. "That probably is why she's not sharing anything with me. She's still mad that I didn't share anything with her. But I was just trying to protect her."

"And maybe she's doing the same for you," Heather pointed out.

He tensed with the realization. His baby sister was trying to protect him. "But what is she protecting me from?" he asked.

"I'll see what I can find out from her television station here," Heather offered. "I'll talk to her producers and co-workers, see if they have any idea what's going on and who might be after her…unless you want me to come up there?"

"I don't even know if she's staying here," he said. "So no. Focus on Detroit, on finding out what you can there. And I'll see what I can get out of her."

"You be careful," she said.

He smiled. "Of my sister?"

"She is fierce," Heather reminded him. "She's strong and smart."

He knew that in his head. But in his heart, she was that sweet little girl who'd followed him around, firing endless questions at him, confident that he had all the answers. She'd worshiped him then. Now she had to know that he had no more answers than she did.

Actually she had more than him because she knew what was going on, no matter how vehemently she kept denying that she did. Or if she didn't know for certain, she at least had a better idea than he did.

Because he could think of only one reason. His hotshot team. Why else would she have come up to Northern Lakes? Whatever she was investigating was here…

The plane crash? Or the sabotage?

He had to get her to back off for her sake now. For her safety.

"And, Trent," Heather said, her voice even huskier than

usual as it emanated from his speaker. "No more cheating on me. You know defying death is our thing."

"Yes," he said, and he smiled. "Tell Sammy not to steal my spot next to you in bed."

"Nobody can steal your spot," Heather assured him. "And I'll talk to the people at the station right away and let you know what I find out."

"Thank you. I love you."

"Love you, too."

Love was their thing now, but their relationship had started as a ruse to flush out a killer. Or at least they'd thought whoever had sent Trent that card was a killer.

But there had been more dangers in his life than he'd even realized then. So pushing Brittney away had been the right thing, to keep her safe.

He'd known what to do then. He had no idea how to protect her now. Because he had a bad feeling that the biggest danger she faced was herself and her dogged determination to find out the truth no matter the cost.

Even if it was her life...

Chapter 11

When Rory had first been cleared to leave the hospital, he had had no intention of staying in Northern Lakes. He'd just intended to stop at the firehouse and grab whatever he'd left in his locker before leaving for good. Or at least for the island where he was the ranger on duty.

Would he be safe there?

Was he really even the one in danger?

Would it have mattered who'd stepped into the hall that night the engines had started? Would whoever had walked out of the bunk room been hit as hard as he'd been?

No. He couldn't be sure that he specifically was in danger or if his entire team was, with maybe the exception of one person...

If the saboteur was one of them...

He hated to think that, though.

Just as he hated to think of Brittney in danger. And she definitely was. All night that image of her standing in those high beams had flashed through his mind like those lights had flashed on—suddenly, sharply, sinisterly. If he hadn't been there, would Trent have gotten to her in time?

Or would they both have gotten hurt or worse?

He'd known Trent had stayed with her after that, and he would have made damn sure that nothing else happened to her. So he'd probably been more protection for her than Rory would have been after that last near miss.

He'd been so exhausted last night that when he'd sat down on a bunk to talk to Stanley, who'd been snuggled up with Annie in another bunk, he must have fallen asleep.

But those dreams…

That nightmare had kept waking him up. And he must have woken up Annie, too, because at some point the massive sheepdog/mastiff mutt had crawled into bed with him. He didn't know if she had needed comfort, or if she'd been comforting him.

Or protecting him?

If only Annie could talk…

She could probably tell them who the saboteur was. She must have seen whoever had struck Rory that night.

He stared at her now from where he was pretty much jammed between the wall and mattress since she was hogging the narrow bunk. "So who was it, girl?" he asked. "Who hit me?"

She whimpered and moved her head closer to his. Then she rolled out her big tongue and swiped it across the side of his face.

He chuckled. "Your kisses do not make it all better," he told her.

But he had an idea whose kisses might make him feel better. Brittney's.

Was she okay? She'd seemed so last night, and after what had happened, how close a call she'd had not once but twice, Trent would not have left her unprotected. He might have been irritated with her for reporting about the team and Ethan, but he loved her.

She obviously loved and idolized her big brother, too.

But she was also proud and determined to take care of herself while getting the truth she was looking for.

Was that his truth?

He knew what had happened to that plane. And why.

And it had nothing to do with Ethan and the Canterbury curse, or even the greedy brother-in-law.

No. That plane had gone down because of him. And guilt had weighed so heavily on him ever since it had happened. But that wasn't the only thing he felt guilty about...

Amelia. Not that she deserved his sympathy after what she'd done. But he'd hurt her.

Annie whimpered again and bumped her massive head against his. The dog was incredibly empathetic, which was probably why Stanley had bonded with her so much. The kid had aged out of foster care with nowhere else to go when Cody Mallehan had convinced their boss to hire the teenager to help out at the firehouse. Stanley had had a rough life, but he seemed happy now.

Rory looked around Annie to the other bunk, but it was empty, the bed already neatly made. "I thought you were the kid's shadow," he told Annie.

She whimpered again and swiped her tongue across his cheek.

"Hey, no more kisses," he said with a chuckle.

"Clearly you're not much of a kisser," a female voice remarked.

"Annie? You can talk?" he asked, joking because there was no mistaking to whom the voice belonged.

Brittney.

Annie jumped up from the bunk and barked, as surprised by the reporter's sudden appearance as he'd been.

"Down, girl," Brittney said. "I'm not trying to steal your man. I can see that what you two have is true love."

Rory chuckled, but Annie's barking probably drowned it out. He had to raise his voice to tell Brittney, "I don't know about that. She didn't save me from whoever hit me over the head."

"Shh," Brittney told the dog. "The two people in this room with you both have concussions."

Rory realized that maybe for the first time since he'd awakened from the coma that his head didn't hurt that much. It was just a dull ache now, like the aftereffects of a migraine or a hangover.

He might have preferred the hangover, though he barely ever drank. He had to make sure that he didn't lose control or get confused and talk too much.

Reveal too much.

Brittney had tilted her head to study the door. Her topaz eyes were narrowed with speculation. "Did she bark like this before you got hit in the head?" she asked.

"Not loud enough to wake everybody up," Rory said. "That's why I went out into the hall. To pull the alarm and to shut off the damn trucks."

Brittney nodded.

"What?" Rory asked uneasily.

"Annie knew whoever hit you over the head," Brittney surmised.

No. Speculated. That could be all that it was. She had no proof that one of his hotshot team members had tried to hurt him. Or kill him?

He didn't want to think that someone he knew could want him dead. Again.

But he shouldn't have been surprised. He was just so damn sick of having no one he could trust. No one who really cared about him.

But to want him dead, that was more than disinterest or distaste. That was hate. Or greed.

Because anyone could succumb to greed, he knew that all too well.

Had someone been hired again to try to kill him? Someone he knew. Someone he should have been able to trust...

He slid his hand around the back of his head, to where the skin had been pulled together with stitches and staples, leaving a thick ridge of flesh beneath his hair.

"How are you?" she asked. "That's why I left my hotel room last night. After I saw how much blood was on that towel that I wrapped the ice in..." She stopped and swallowed, as if she'd been choking on something.

Emotion?

For him?

She swallowed again and continued. "I wanted to make sure that you were okay."

"That's why you were out there? In the street?" he asked. And he rolled off the bunk then to stand in front of her. Annie stayed between them, though, as if trying to protect him from Brittney.

But Brittney was a stranger to the dog.

She must have been right, that Annie knew whoever had hit him.

"I'm the reason you came outside last night?" he asked again.

She nodded. "I wanted to make you go back to the hospital to get checked out."

His stomach pitched at the thought of her getting hurt because of him. He reached out to touch her cheek, sliding his fingertips along her jaw. She was so beautiful. And he wanted so damn badly to kiss her again, to really kiss her this time.

But he couldn't afford that kind of distraction now and neither could she.

"We both nearly went back to the hospital…" he murmured, thinking of how they'd rolled across the asphalt. "And Trent?" He glanced around her then. "Where is he? Is he really all right?"

Her lips curved into a slight smirk. "He's going to be pissed when he wakes up and finds me gone," she said. "He booked the adjoining room and tried staying awake all night. He lasted until about an hour ago."

Rory fought the smile curving his lips and shook his head. "It's not safe for you to go out on your own, not after what happened yesterday."

"What happened yesterday?" Braden asked.

Rory jumped and dropped his hand from Brittney's face. She whirled around to the doorway where his boss was leaning against the jamb.

Braden's dark eyes studied them both, and his forehead was slightly furrowed beneath a lock of dark brown hair. Clearly he wondered what was going on between Rory and Brittney.

Rory wondered himself.

Was she just flirting with him to get him talking? To get the story she was so determined to get that two threats and two attempts on her life hadn't scared her off?

In fact, those threats had just made her more determined to find out what was going on because she thought the truth would protect her, that it would lead to the arrest of the person threatening her. But the truth didn't always lead to justice.

Rory could have corrected that misapprehension. The truth hadn't saved him, it had nearly killed him. But know-

ing his truth would put her in danger, too. If it hadn't already...

"What happened yesterday?" Braden asked the question.
"Owen said you were in an accident. And then something
happened at the hotel."

"You heard about that?" Rory asked.

"The police were there," Braden said. "I heard the call
over the scanner."

"The police were there?" Rory asked Brittney now.

She nodded. "The desk clerk called them. I didn't think
the kid was even paying attention to the lobby, let alone
out—"

"What happened?" Braden repeated. "From how you're
evading my question, I take it that these things weren't really accidents?"

Brittney shook her head. "Not any more than the things
that have been happening to your hotshot team have been
accidents."

Braden's face flushed slightly. "Is that why you're here?
To report some more nonsense?"

She sighed a heavy sigh as if she was disappointed in
the hotshot superintendent.

Rory was a little disappointed, as well. Braden had kept
a lot of things from them for a while. The note he'd received
that had warned him that someone on the team wasn't who
they said they were.

Had that note been referring to Ethan really being Jonathan Michael Canterbury IV? Or had it been referring to
Rory? Not many people should have realized that he wasn't
who he said he was...

Just him and maybe Ethan. But even Ethan didn't really
know for certain.

And there was someone else...

Trick appeared in the doorway behind their boss and his brother-in-law. Trick wasn't just the brother of Braden's wife, but he was also the son of the man who'd trained most of them. Mack McRooney knew the truth. But Mack was the kind of guy who knew what secrets needed to be kept. And why.

So Rory doubted that Mack's son or daughter knew anything about him beyond that their father had trained him five years ago along with Ethan Sommerly and Jonathan Canterbury. The real Ethan hadn't survived that crash. He wasn't the only one who'd died in it, though.

Rory felt that jab of regret for the lives lost. Too many… He couldn't let Brittney become another casualty.

One minute Brittney was standing with Rory in the bunk room, wondering if he was about to kiss her again. Then his boss showed up with another giant of a man following closely behind him. Within minutes of their sudden appearance, she'd been escorted to the superintendent's office.

And the red-haired man leaned against the door, as if blocking her inside with him and the superintendent. His body was so big that she could barely see the door around him. There was no way she was getting out with him there.

"I thought you guys were going to escort me off the premises," Brittney said.

"We probably should have," the red-haired man said with a pointed look at his boss.

Braden Zimmer smiled. "How did you get onto the premises, Ms. Townsend?"

"Call me Brittney," she said. "We're all friends here."

The red-haired man snorted. He had to be Trick McRooney. Braden's brother-in-law. Mack's son. She actually needed to be his friend, so that he could convince his father to talk to her. She suspected that Mack had to know something more about the plane that had just left his training facility in Washington state before it crashed.

Braden smiled. "Okay, Brittney, how'd you get in?"

"The door was unlocked."

Braden groaned.

"The kid with the curly blond hair had just walked out."

"So you let yourself in," Trick said.

She nodded.

"Why?" Braden asked. "Who or what were you looking for?"

Heat rushed to her face. Rory. She'd been looking for Rory, but not for the reasons Braden might have thought when he'd come into the bunk room and found them standing so close together with Rory's hand touching her face.

She'd wanted to kiss him so damn badly then. She still did. But that wasn't why she'd sought him out.

"I was concerned about Rory," she said.

"Why?" Trick asked. "You don't know him. He's barely spoken to you."

She smiled. "That was last time I was here. This time... he's different." He wasn't avoiding her as hard as he had last time. In fact, he'd saved her life last night in the street.

But only she and Trent knew that. The clerk hadn't realized that Trent wasn't the one who'd pushed her out of the way of that speeding SUV, so he hadn't mentioned a third person to the trooper who'd taken their statements. And neither had she nor Trent.

Rory had already been through too much that day. That month...

And five years ago...

He had survived a plane crash. One that Trick's dad had to know more about.

"I've been trying to get ahold of your father," she told Trick.

He just arched a red eyebrow. "You want to train to become a smoke jumper or hotshot?"

"Maybe I should," she said. "I might get more respect..." At least from her brother.

"But that wasn't your real reason for contacting Mack," Braden stated. He knew.

"No. I want to ask him more questions about that plane crash that happened, the one Ethan and Rory survived."

"Why?" Braden asked. "You know everything about it already."

"I'm not so sure about that," she said. She also wasn't so sure that she knew everything there was to know about Rory VanDam. Could Mack tell her more?

Would he?

Or should she just try harder to get the man himself to speak to her?

"So that's why you're really here?" Trick asked the question. "To get me to talk my dad into talking to you?" He was smirking at her.

And she knew the likelihood of him ever doing that for her was pretty damn low. "That and to talk to Rory," she admitted.

"And he's talking to you?" Braden asked. "About the crash?" He exchanged a quick glance with Trick.

Did they think there was more about the crash to discover? Or was it Rory they were worried about? She was worried about him, too.

"What the hell is happening in your firehouse?" Brittney wanted to know. "How does one of your own almost get killed here instead of fighting a wildfire?"

Braden sucked in a breath and shared another glance with Trick. "I wish to hell I knew."

"You have no idea who's been behind all these things happening to your team?" she asked.

Braden shook his head. "They wouldn't be happening if I did."

A little chill passed through her. Was he saying that because he would have turned the suspect over to the police or because he would have dealt with him or her himself?

"What about that story?" Braden asked her. "Are you working on it?"

"About the sabotage?" she asked. "I've tried, but I haven't gotten any of the hotshots to really talk to me about it." Not even her own brother.

But if these guys thought she was working on it, the saboteur might, as well. Was that who had actually left her the notes? Who'd taken a shot at her van?

And last night...

Was it a hotshot behind everything? Was it another hotshot who had struck Rory so hard that he might have died? Brittney needed to find out for her sake and safety, as well as for the sake and safety of the entire hotshot team, including her brother and Rory.

Or someone could die...

Braden's uneasiness intensified during his impromptu meeting with the reporter.

After letting her out of the office, Trick closed the door behind her and leaned back against it again. "She's still working on the sabotage story."

"I know." And that might have been what had put her in danger if Trent was right and she hadn't just had an accident when her van went off the road.

And what about last night?

Someone trying to run her down?

"Maybe you should follow her," Braden suggested.

"You don't think Trent is following her?" Trick asked. "He rushed up here to make sure she's okay. I doubt he's letting her out of his sight."

"That means he's probably in danger, too, then."

"We're all in danger until the saboteur is caught," Trick pointed out.

Braden's stomach churned with that dread. "I know." He released a heavy sigh. "Maybe it's a good thing she's working on this story. Maybe she'll figure out what we haven't been able to…"

"Who the saboteur is," Trick said. But then he wrinkled his forehead and scrunched up his nose. "That's not the only story she's working on, though."

"The plane crash." Braden shrugged. "That was all about Ethan."

"Ethan wasn't the only one in that crash," Trick said. "Rory was, too." He straightened away from the door. "Maybe I should give Mack a call."

Mack's kids rarely referred to him as Dad. He'd been much more than their father, he'd been their mother, too, after theirs had taken off. He'd also been their mentor and their best friend.

Braden nodded. "I'm going to call Trent," he said. "Make sure he's around and keeping an eye on his sister. I don't want anyone else getting hurt."

But he knew all too well that the chance of nobody getting hurt was extremely low. He could only hope they didn't get hurt badly. Or worse…

Chapter 12

Rory hadn't stopped Braden and Trick from whisking Brittney away from him. He knew that neither of them would hurt her. She was safe with them.

And yet he'd followed them. He'd waited outside the office, listening to as much of the conversation as he'd been able to hear through the door and probably Trick's body. Trick was close to the door, so Rory had heard everything he'd said.

Brittney had tried contacting Trick's dad about the plane crash. God, she was smart. So smart that she was probably going to figure out the truth. And that would undoubtedly get them both killed.

Unless...

He had some insurance. Insurance he'd been holding on to in case this day ever came. He just wasn't sure how to use it because he'd never known who he could trust with it.

Or if he should trust anyone at all.

Could he believe Brittney that she was really looking to stop whoever was threatening her? Or was she just looking for a story? Trying to further her career as if that would earn her brother's respect...

Where the hell was Trent?

He should have woken up by now and discovered that she was gone.

Before the conversation finished in the office, Rory slipped away. He hurried upstairs to the locker room, intent on cleaning out his and leaving town.

But every time he had that intention, something came up. Like Brittney. She was in danger, like he and Ethan had been alone in the mountains. But together they'd protected each other, they'd kept each other alive. Could he and Brittney do that for each other?

She stood in the doorway, watching him. "Where are you going?" she asked.

"I need to get back to work," he said.

"There's no wildfire," she replied. "No reason for the hotshot team to go out."

"That's just part of my job," he said. "I'm a forest ranger."

"You're recovering from a head injury," she said. "You shouldn't be out in the woods on your own."

"An island," he said. "But it is heavily wooded."

"Does anyone else live there?" she asked.

"There are a few cabins on it. But mostly it's national forest land."

"You shouldn't be alone," she said.

"There are plenty of animals on the island," he said. And there they were all of the four-legged variety, not the two like where he'd grown up.

"An animal can't call for help if you need it," she said.

"I probably won't need it since there are no other humans on the island this time of year," he said, and he touched the back of his head and that ridge.

"You should get your stitches looked at," she said. "Make sure the wound didn't open back up last night. You bled quite a bit on that towel."

"Sorry," he said. "Hopefully the hotel won't charge you for it."

"Hopefully they won't evict me," she said, "after the clerk called in that incident with the SUV."

"The trooper didn't come to talk to me," he said.

"Trent and I didn't give him your name."

"Him? It wasn't Trooper Wells?"

She shook her head. "She probably would have realized you'd been there, too."

So it was probably only a matter of time before the trooper came to question him again. "I really need to get out of here," he said.

"Why? You want to avoid the police?"

"I want to avoid being asked things I can't answer," he said.

"Can't or won't?"

His lips twitched with amusement over her persistence. "I can't say who was driving that SUV. The windows were too darkly tinted. And I didn't see a license plate. So can't."

"I wasn't talking about that."

"I didn't see who hit me the night of the holiday party, either," he said.

"If only Annie could talk…"

He smiled then. "We've all wished that."

"She could tell you who the saboteur is." She tilted her head then and murmured, "But I wonder if she would…"

"What do you mean?"

"Maybe she would protect him."

"What are you talking about?"

"Stanley," she said.

Rory shook his head. "Nope. No way. And don't you dare interrogate that kid. He was once suspected of being the Northern Lakes arsonist and it nearly killed him." He'd been hit over the head, too.

"Then tell me who you suspect," she prodded him.

"I don't." And that was the problem. He had no idea who the saboteur was. Which was another reason he needed to get away from the firehouse. He could hardly believe that he'd managed to sleep there the night before. But it had been just him and Stanley and Annie in the bunk room.

And he'd been so damn tired.

Still was. But that was her fault. He'd kept thinking of her last night, and not just that horrific moment when she'd frozen in the path of that SUV. But the moment before that, when they'd kissed. It had been such a light kiss and so brief, and yet so damn powerful, too.

"Where's Trent?" he asked.

She shrugged. "Probably still sleeping."

"He should be awake by now." Rory needed him awake and alert enough to watch over his sister so that Rory could get the hell away from her. She'd already messed with his head more than the concussion had.

Or maybe the concussion was the reason she was getting to him so much, making him want her so badly.

"Trent's not going to tell me who he suspects, either," she said.

"That's not why I asked where he was," Rory said. "And I really don't suspect anyone, least of all Stanley." He was a good kid. Everybody on their twenty-member team seemed like good people. But he knew better than to trust that anyone was really who they seemed to be.

Even Brittney. Maybe most especially Brittney.

The way Rory had looked at her just before he closed his locker door had unnerved Brittney. It was like he wasn't sure what he was looking at. Or whom...

Once he closed the door, he grabbed up his duffel bag and stepped around her, heading toward the exit.

"Where are you going?" she asked, and she stepped in front of him, blocking him from leaving like Trick had blocked her. Rory couldn't be serious about going back to some deserted island, not when he was still recovering from a head wound.

"I'll make sure you get safely back to Trent," he said. "And then I'm leaving."

Something about the way he said it, with such finality, made Brittney wonder if she would ever see him again if he left. Not that she should expect to...

She had only been to Northern Lakes once before, and after what had happened to her since her arrival this time, she would be crazy to want to return.

Crazy to want to see Rory again, too. No. She wanted to do more than see him. She really, really wanted to kiss him and to really kiss him this time, not just brush their lips across each other's. But she wasn't about to do that here, in the firehouse, where anyone could walk in on them like Braden had earlier in the bunk room.

And the way he was looking at her now, with such tension and almost suspicion, Rory didn't look at all attracted to her now. If he'd ever been...

Maybe she'd only imagined that it was mutual. But even if it was, she had no time for this attraction she felt for him. She needed to focus on her story...whichever one the person threatening her didn't want her to do.

Was it about the plane crash?

Or the saboteur?

"I should go back to Braden's office," she said. "And see if he'll give me a list of every member of the team." She knew her brother wouldn't give her one. But Braden...

He hadn't seemed as upset about her reporting about the

saboteur as he'd once been. He might even welcome her help in figuring out who it was.

Or he would if he wanted to keep anyone else on his team from getting hurt like Rory had been hurt. But some of the other hotshots who'd been hurt hadn't been because of the saboteur. The dead man's wife had killed him. And a state trooper had tried killing another...

Then there was Trent, who had someone come after him for revenge.

"What about you?" she asked Rory, voicing her thought aloud.

"I won't give you a list," he said.

"What about your past?" she asked. "Anything or anyone in it that might be coming back to haunt you like it came back to haunt my brother?"

His long, lean body tensed even more than it had already been, and all the color drained from his face, leaving him deathly pale, like he had seen a ghost.

"What is it?" she asked. "Your head? What's going on?" And did she need to call a doctor for him?

Or Owen?

Where the hell was the paramedic?

Rory released a shaky breath. "I'm fine. I'm just...talked out, Brittney. If you want that list of team members, ask Braden."

"So you're not going to make sure I get safely back to Trent?" she asked. She was just teasing him. Really.

But she also wondered...did he care about her? Or would he just try to protect anyone he thought was in danger?

Probably. That was undoubtedly the reason he'd become a hotshot, to protect people from fires.

She wanted to ask him about that and about so many other things. But she could feel the opportunity slipping away from her. She wasn't even sure what island he was talking about let alone how to get to it.

Was there a ferry to it?

Since it was largely uninhabitable, probably not.

"We have to leave now for me to take you back to Trent," he said. "Because I can't stick around any longer."

"Why not?" she asked.

His forehead furrowed as if he was confused. "How can you ask me that after everything that's happened?"

"How can you just run away after everything that's happened?" she asked. "That's not going to stop things from happening, you know? The saboteur keeps doing things, and he or she isn't even making them look like accidents anymore."

"It'll stop things from happening to *me*," he said.

Shocked, she sucked in a breath. "And you only care about yourself?"

He hadn't come across that way to her. He'd seemed like he was genuinely concerned about her safety and about his team. Or else why the hell had he run out in front of that SUV last night? He could have let Trent get to her first.

But Trent hadn't.

Rory was the one who'd saved her. Who'd risked his life to do so. So he certainly didn't care only about himself.

Maybe he didn't care about himself at all. Or he would have gone back to the hospital last night. Maybe that was why he was deathly pale. Maybe he needed to go back there now.

"Before you rush off to the middle of nowhere, you should get a medical checkup," she suggested. "You were bleeding again last night."

He shook his head. "I'm okay. And I'll be even better once I'm out of here."

"Away from me and my questions?" she asked, her pride stinging. And maybe something even more vulnerable than her pride.

Her heart.

"Brittney, you need to look out for yourself," he said.

"Don't worry. I'm not your responsibility," she assured him. "You don't have to walk me back to the hotel. I can take care of myself."

"That's not what I meant," he said, his voice gruff with frustration. "I'm just… I can't stay…"

She stepped aside, out of his path, and repeated, "Don't worry about me. Just go. Run away."

Because no matter what he'd done last night, that was what he was doing now. Running away instead of facing the situation and trying to solve the mystery of the saboteur and whoever the hell was after her.

Were they one in the same?

She intended to find out, but she was disappointed that he had no interest in discovering the truth. She'd been such a fool to be attracted to him at all. And now she was damn glad she hadn't kissed him as deeply and passionately as she'd wanted to. Hell, she'd wanted to do more than that, but she was glad she hadn't, especially when he walked right past her and out the locker room door.

Brittney Townsend hadn't been easy to scare away from the story she was after. And now she wasn't easy to kill. She should have died in the wreckage of that van of hers when it had rolled over and over, trapping her inside it.

Miraculously she'd survived that.

But last night…

It hadn't been a miracle that she'd gotten out of the path of the SUV just in time.

That had been interference of another kind. It certainly hadn't been divine intervention. It had been a man. Brittney's white knight wouldn't be able to save her again, though.

Because the next time he was going to die with her, like he should have the night before. The killer wasn't going to make the mistake of trying to use a vehicle again, especially one that had probably been described to the police.

So that vehicle was hidden for now...

Leaving the driver with nothing to drive at the moment. But that hadn't stopped them from following the reporter when she'd left her hotel earlier that morning.

She was at the firehouse now. Probably asking more of her damn questions.

The killer raised their weapon, peering through the scope into some of the windows. Who was in the three-story concrete building with her?

Her white knight?

The gun barrel focused on the door she'd entered. It would probably be the one she exited.

And when she did, she was going to die.

And if she wasn't alone, whoever was with her would die, too. But the killer would have to wait until they were far enough out of the building so that neither could take cover and avoid being hit, like they'd avoided it last night. This time they had to die.

Chapter 13

Damn her!

Damn her so damn much…

Fury coursed through Rory, making his pulse pound as his blood pumped hotly through his veins as he ran down the firehouse stairs to the main level. But he wasn't mad at her. Not really.

He was mad that she'd spoken the truth.

He was running away again, just like he had more than five years ago. And then after running away, he'd hid out here in Northern Lakes and on Bear Isle.

But if he hadn't hidden like he had, he would probably already be dead. And hiding out hadn't just kept him from getting hurt, it had kept the people around him from getting hurt.

Or so he'd thought…

Maybe the saboteur was after the team because of him. Because of that damn note someone had sent Braden…

Someone on your team isn't who you think they are…

Sure, that could have been referring to Ethan, but who, besides Rory and Ethan, had known who he really was?

Nobody had recognized Jonathan Canterbury after those months they'd spent in the mountains before they'd been rescued. He had truly looked like Ethan Sommerly, the hot-shot who'd trained with them in Washington state.

That man was gone now. And so was another man…

Rory felt that pang in his heart, that guilt and regret. It was all his fault. And instead of bringing their killers to justice, he'd hid to save his own life. And maybe he'd put other people in danger.

Brittney.

Was it his fault that someone was after her? Was she right, that the only way to stop the bad guy was to find out the truth once and for all?

That wouldn't necessarily protect him from the vendetta against him. From the hit sworn out on him…

But maybe the truth would protect her, like he had to protect her. He stopped at the door to the outside, his palm against the metal. And he closed his eyes and sighed.

A nose rubbed against his other hand, the one wrapped around the straps of the duffel bag. Annie whimpered.

"What's up, girl?" he asked.

She must have been waiting by the door for Stanley to return. The kid had probably gone back to Cody's, and he couldn't bring the dog with him there since the child Cody and Serena was fostering was allergic to her.

"I'm sure he'll be back soon," he assured the dog.

"What about you?" Brittney asked as she stepped off the last step of the stairwell. "Are you running away for good or just until I'm gone?"

"I need to get back to the island," he insisted.

"Why?"

He wanted to go back for that insurance. He hadn't been able to figure out exactly how it would help him, though, or he would have used it long ago. And because he didn't know for certain if it was of any use, he replied, "Because I work there."

"Doing what?"

"Monitoring wildlife, the woods, stopping poachers and trespassers. And enjoying the quiet…"

"You really want to go back there for that?" she asked.

He touched the back of his head. "Seems like a good treatment for a concussion. Silence."

But he really needed to retrieve that other thing, the thing that might be able to protect Brittney at least, if not him. But that was only if the person threatening her to back off wanted her to leave the plane crash story alone. If it was actually the saboteur after her, Rory had no idea what to do about him or her. Or he would have done that long ago.

Like he probably should have used his insurance long ago. But he'd never been able to figure out how to use it because he hadn't known whom he could trust with it… because the insurance itself had proved to him that he could trust no one.

"Why haven't you left already?" she asked, and she pointed at the door he had yet to open.

"Why are you leaving?" he asked. "Aren't you going to ask Braden for that list?"

"We both know he's not going to give it to me," she said.

Rory wasn't so certain. Braden was desperate to find the saboteur, which was why he'd hired his brother-in-law as one of the team, thinking Trick could be more objective than he could. But then Trick had fallen for Henrietta…

And for Northern Lakes. He wasn't going back to his life as a floater for other teams. He was here to stay. Or so Rory hoped, for Trick's and Henrietta's sakes.

"It's not like you to give up that easily," Rory remarked.

She narrowed those topaz eyes and stared at him. "You don't really know me."

"I know you're determined." Too determined. It was probably going to get her killed.

She smiled. "I can't deny that."

"Then why are you leaving?"

She held up her cell. "Tammy texted me. She and Ethan decided not to go on that cruise."

"Did she say why?" Rory asked. Ethan had been looking forward to that trip. Hopefully he hadn't canceled it because of him.

"I'm going to find out now," Brittney said. "I hope Trent didn't ask him to cancel, so he could be my babysitter. I don't need one."

"I'll go with you," Rory said, and he reached for the door handle again. He cared about Ethan, about Trent, about his whole damn team. And he cared about Brittney, too. Too much to leave her unprotected.

"I just said I don't need a babysitter," she reminded him.

"I'm not babysitting."

Annie whined.

"She wants to go, too," Brittney said. "She hasn't been barking at me now."

"She tends to get used to strangers pretty quickly," he said. "Except for Ethan. It took her a while to get used to him without his beard. I really shouldn't let her out. She tends to run off."

"Hmm... Wonder where she gets that from?"

Rory resisted the urge to smile. "I'm not running," he said.

"You did. Last night. To save me," she said. "I shouldn't have said what I did upstairs about you only caring about yourself. You jumped in front of an SUV for me."

And he would do it all over again. He didn't want anyone getting hurt, especially if it was because of him and especially her.

"You're not wrong about me," he admitted. "I have been

a selfish jerk." He'd had to be, or he wouldn't have survived as long as he had.

But maybe survival wasn't enough, not when you had to give up so damn much for it.

"And I am going back to Bear Isle," he said. To get that insurance...

Maybe with her help, he could figure out who to trust with it. But should he trust her? Should he get her any more involved than she already was?

"I thought you were walking with me to Tammy's salon," she said. "That you wanted to talk to Ethan."

"I'll walk you over there," Rory said. "But I don't need to talk to Ethan." He knew what he needed to do.

He pulled open the door just far enough to try to keep Annie from squeezing out. But the dog was fast despite her size. And despite her size, she managed to squeeze through the opening and out.

"Annie!" he called to her, and he jerked the door open the rest of the way. And when he did, gunshots rang out, bullets pinging off the concrete building and the metal door. He dropped, pulling Brittney down with him.

She'd been in the doorway, too. Had she gotten hit?

"Brittney?" he whispered into her hair, which was soft beneath his cheek. "Are you all right?"

"Shh..." she whispered back at him. "The shooter might still be out there."

Rory was pretty damn certain that he or she was. And so was Annie. "Stay in here," Rory advised her. "Lock the door behind me and go get Braden and Trick." He pushed her farther inside so he could get out the door. Then he pulled it shut behind him.

More gunshots rang out, echoed by Annie's barks. She

was going after the shooter. Trying to save everyone like she kept saving them…

But who would save Annie from a bullet?

Brittney screamed, "Braden! Trick!"

They were already running down the stairs, heading toward her. "Who's shooting?" Braden asked.

"Where is it coming from?" Trick asked.

She pointed toward the door. "Rory went after him or after Annie…" She didn't know which, just that once again he'd run toward danger instead of away from it. And he had nothing with him to protect him.

Not a gun. No armor. He'd just rushed off with no thought of his own safety.

Tears stung her eyes as fear for him overwhelmed her. And remorse…

If something happened to him, she would regret so many things. Most of all that she hadn't kissed him like she'd wanted, with all the passion she felt for him. She hadn't really showed him how much she appreciated that he'd risked his life for hers last night, either.

And now…he was risking his again.

Some noise, far-off but familiar, pulled Trent from his dream. Or maybe the sound had been part of his dream.

Or the memory he had of gunfire…

Of someone shooting at him and Heather…

Heather dropping through the fire- and water-damaged floor of his burned house. And him not knowing if she'd been shot…

Was someone getting shot now?

The sound faded away then. It must have just been his dream. Or memory.

But then the sharp wail of sirens jerked Trent fully awake. He should have been awake all along.

He'd never intended to fall asleep.

"Brittney!"

His heart pounding, he jumped up from his bed and headed toward the connecting door. It was closed. She must have closed it. When he touched the knob, it didn't turn. She'd locked it on her side. To keep him out or to keep him from seeing that she'd taken off?

Hell, she might have even checked out. But he doubted that. She wasn't leaving Northern Lakes without her story. But what was it going to cost her?

Those sirens…

He was sure she was wherever the police were heading. He pulled open the door to his room and rushed out into the hall. He didn't wait for the elevator, taking the stairs instead. But he knew that no matter how fast he ran, he might be too late. Like he would have been last night…

Rory was the one who'd saved her then. Was he with her now? Had he protected her again?

But at what cost?

His life?

Chapter 14

Despite her size, Annie must have been part cat because she certainly had more than one life. Maybe even more than nine. Rory could relate. He'd had more than one himself.

Somehow both he and the dog had avoided getting hit despite all the bullets that had been initially fired at the steel door to the firehouse.

Someone must have called the police, though, and the gunfire stopped with the wail of sirens in the distance. The shooter didn't want to get caught.

So why take the chance of firing at them in broad daylight? How determined was he or she to kill…?

And who was the target?

Brittney or him? He'd been hit over the head, but nobody had shot at him and tried to run him down, at least not recently, like had been the case for Brittney.

He needed to make sure that Brittney was safe. He'd left her back at the firehouse when he'd run after Annie. The dog had kept running into the woods behind the firehouse. Was that where the shooter had been standing?

"Annie!" he called out.

Maybe the would-be killer was still out there. Waiting until he got closer to fire again.

Where had the dog gone?

Despite the unseasonably warm winter they'd been having, there were large patches of snow in the woods yet. There were also big sections of mud where the snow had melted and the ground had begun to thaw. If the shooter had been out here, maybe they would be able to track him through the snow and mud.

"Annie..." He lowered his voice now.

While she'd ignored his shouting for her, she turned now, at his whisper, and rushed back to him. Probably as scared as he'd been, she jumped up on him with her paws on his chest. The sudden weight of her body pushed him back, and he slipped and fell into that mud. At least it was mud and not wainscoting or asphalt like the night before.

But then he heard a gun cock, and he realized the fall and the mud wasn't what he should have been worrying about. And that he damn well shouldn't have assumed that the shooter had taken off with the sound of the sirens.

Because above Annie's big head, he could see the barrel of a gun pointing directly at him.

"Where is he?" Brittney asked, her heart hammering so hard with fear that her chest was starting to hurt. She paced by the door of the firehouse, the door that Trick and Braden were blocking as if they realized she would have run out after Rory by now if they hadn't stopped her. "Where is he?"

Braden shook his head. "The police are here," he reminded her. "They're searching the area."

"For the shooter," she said.

Braden said, "They'll find any victims—"

She gasped and slapped a hand over her mouth to hold back the sob that threatened to escape.

"I don't mean that they will find any, that Rory is one..."

"But he was a victim, not that long ago, in this very firehouse," Brittney reminded him. He'd been hurt so badly that he'd spent two weeks in a coma. He'd had no business running off like he had. After Annie or the shooter? "He doesn't have a gun. No way to defend himself..."

The door handle turned, and everybody whirled toward it. A trooper had been standing on the other side of it, so nobody could get inside to them. And probably so that they couldn't get out. She suspected she wasn't the only one who'd been tempted to run out to find Rory.

The door opened, but it wasn't the trooper who entered. Trent walked in instead. "What the hell happened?" he demanded to know. Then he rushed over to her. He clasped her shoulders and stared down into her face. "Are you all right?"

She nodded. "Thanks to Rory. He saved my life again." Even after how terribly she'd spoken to him...

He definitely cared about more than himself. He probably cared about everyone and everything else more than he cared about himself.

Trent peered around the garage area. "Where is he?" he asked.

She shrugged, knocking his hands from her shoulders. "He went after Annie."

Trent groaned. "I love that dog, but she doesn't have the sense to hide from shooters. Instead she races right toward them."

"Shooters?" Then she remembered the professional assassins that Jonathan Canterbury's brother-in-law had hired to kill him. They'd shot at the firehouse, too.

She shuddered. That had been her fault for revealing Ethan Sommerly's real identity. Was this her fault, too?

Had that shooter been after her or Rory?

"It shouldn't be taking this long to find him," Brittney

said, her voice cracking with the fear that overwhelmed her. Unless they'd found him and were working on him because he'd been shot.

Braden nodded. "We should have gone out after him," he said to Trick.

Trick pointed at her. "She would have gone out there, too."

"Brittney," her brother said, his voice gruff with emotion. "You've got to stop putting yourself in danger."

She held up a hand to stop his lecture. "Don't start. Just don't…"

"This isn't getting us anywhere," Braden said, and he opened the door to the trooper standing outside. "We can help you search—"

The guy touched the speaker in his ear. "Trooper Wells found someone."

Someone. Brittney wanted to demand to know what he meant. The shooter? A victim? The dog?

Who the hell had Trooper Wells found?

Ethan had heard the gunfire and the sirens. And he knew he'd done the right thing. He'd come back for his team. They'd been there for him and for Tammy when his greedy brother-in-law had taken her hostage. Ethan had to be there for them now. But he wasn't allowed anywhere close to the firehouse.

He wasn't the only one being held away from the area, though. Pretty much everyone else had showed up at the scene. Stanley was sobbing.

"I don't hear Annie barking anymore," Stanley said.

Donovan Cunningham, who had two teenagers just a little younger than Stanley, wrapped his arm around his shoulders. "That dog is lucky, Stanley. She'll be fine."

"She's been good luck for all of us," Howie Lane said.

He was one of the newer hotshots and was probably just a few years older than Stanley, in his early twenties.

Howie and Bruce Abbott had shown up together. They were young and worked in the area, when they weren't working as hotshots, as arborists.

Sometimes just being around them made Ethan feel old. They were so young and full of energy.

Carl Kozak slapped Ethan's shoulder. "I thought you were gone on a cruise."

Carl was the old man of the team, but with his bald head and muscular build, it was hard to tell his age.

"I didn't feel right taking off when Rory isn't one hundred percent yet."

"He's the one who went chasing after Annie," Howie said.

"You saw him?" Ethan asked. "You were here when the shooting started."

Bruce nodded. "Yeah, we were just about to go to the Filling Station for lunch when we heard the gunshots. Then we saw Annie and Rory running toward the woods."

Stanley gasped. "Was that where the shooter was?"

Ethan and Donovan exchanged a significant glance over Stanley's curly-haired head. The dog had probably gone after the shooter.

And Rory had gone after her.

Had they gotten hit?

Where the hell were they?

Chapter 15

Rory wasn't sure how he'd gone from lying flat on his back in the mud, staring up into the barrel of a gun, to here…

The shower in Brittney's hotel room.

The gun, fortunately, had belonged to Trooper Wells. Although he'd had a long uneasy moment of staring into the barrel before she'd finally turned it away from him.

Despite the warmth of the water washing away the mud, he shivered. Could *she* have been the shooter? Annie hadn't barked at her, so she could have even been the one who'd hit him over the head.

But why…?

Her former boss, Marty Gingrich, had hated the hot-shots, but she had no reason to, even though she had spouted off at a few back at the firehouse. She'd warned them all to stop trying to investigate on their own or they were going to get hurt.

"Is that a threat?" Brittney had asked the question, of course, probably because it wasn't possible for her to not ask one.

She hadn't asked him back to her hotel room, though. She'd told him he looked like hell and that he needed to come back with her.

With everyone else at the firehouse, he'd been happy

to get away from the noise that had had his head pounding again. Or was his head pounding for another reason?

With fear and guilt?

Annie was fine. She hadn't even gotten as muddy as he had. She wasn't hurt.

But Brittney could have been. Those bullets had come so close to her. And to him…

Instead of coming back here with her, he should have headed where he'd intended earlier. To the island…

To his insurance.

But Brittney, and her quick talking, had gotten them both away from the trooper and her questions. She'd insisted that Rory was too weak yet from his concussion to answer any more questions and that she needed to drive him to the hospital.

But she'd driven his truck back to her hotel instead. Then she'd pushed him into the bathroom. "You need to wash off that mud," she'd insisted. "You're not making me lose my room deposit."

He'd chuckled but complied. The hot shower felt really good. But thinking about walking back out there to her had him cranking the faucet to Cold. He needed the blast of icy water to bring him to his senses. To remind him of all the reasons why he couldn't get involved with anyone. As if getting shot at and nearly run down with her weren't good enough reasons…

After turning off the water, he grabbed a towel and then looked around the steamy bathroom for the duffel bag he'd brought in with him. Hadn't he?

Where was his bag?

His clothes?

After drying off with the towel, he tucked it around his

waist and opened the door to the room, peering out through a crack. "Have you seen my duffel bag?"

He'd dropped it at the firehouse before rushing out the door after Annie. But he'd picked it up before rushing out the door after Brittney when she'd given them the means to escape from more of the trooper's questions.

Wells had already interrogated him when she'd found him in the woods, as if she'd suspected he was the shooter. And when he opened the door and found Brittney going through his duffel bag, he wondered if she suspected the same.

"You were with me when the shots were fired," he reminded her. "You're not going to find a gun in there."

"I'm not looking for a gun," she replied without even looking up at him, without looking at all embarrassed for getting caught rummaging through his things.

"Then what are you looking for?" And he was so glad that he'd stashed his insurance somewhere safe.

"Your cape," she replied.

"Cape?"

"You must be some kind of superhero since you keep saving me," she said.

He shook his head. "I'm no hero. Super or otherwise…" Or so many other people wouldn't have died.

"You've saved me," she said.

He gestured at her going through his duffel. "And yet you still don't trust me. What did you really expect to find?"

She shrugged. "I don't know. Maybe a bunch of passports with different names but your picture on every one of them."

"Now I'm a spy?" he asked, and he managed to keep his voice even so he didn't give away how damn close she was getting to the truth.

"Spy or superhero?" she asked. "Which is it?"

"You didn't find a cape or any passports, so I'm not either of those things," he said. And he wasn't. "But I am getting a little cold." The towel was damp from him using it to dry off, though he hadn't dried off completely. Droplets of water still streaked down his back and chest.

Her gaze seemed to track one of those drops sliding down his chest, and he wasn't cold anymore. Not when she looked up again and her topaz eyes had gone dark, her pupils dilated.

"Can I have my clothes?" he asked, reaching out for the bag with a hand that shook slightly. The way she was looking at him was testing his self-control.

Could he contain the attraction he felt for her?

"You are cold," she murmured, but instead of handing over the bag, she reached over it and touched his chest, pressing her palm flat against where his heart was beating so hard and fast.

He shook his head. "This is a bad idea, Brittney."

"Why?"

"You and those damn questions," he murmured before gritting his teeth.

Her hand still on his chest, she stepped around the chair where she left his duffel bag, and she laid her other hand on him, on his abs. "Give me a reason this is a bad idea," she challenged him.

He couldn't hold back a slight grin at her audacity. "Uh, let's see. We won't have to worry anymore about who hit me over the head, tried to run you down and took shots at you and at us. That's because your brother will kill me. My team members will help him. And yeah, the police could show up anytime."

"The police?"

"Yeah, what do you think Trooper Wells is going to do when she checks with the hospital to see if we're really there?" he asked.

"Well, hopefully the police show up before my brother and the rest of the team kill you," she said, and she was smiling now, her topaz eyes sparkling.

"You are probably more dangerous than whoever is after us," he said. Because she was making him forget all the reasons why he couldn't have a relationship, why he couldn't care about someone...

But it was already too late for that. He cared about her.

He groaned, his body aching with the need for hers. And he hadn't even kissed her. He wanted her so damn badly. But he wanted even more to keep her out of the mess that was his life. He didn't want her getting hurt or worse.

Either the man wasn't attracted to her or he had incredible willpower. Because, despite her hands on his bare chest, Rory didn't wrap his arms around her and pull her close. He just reached around her for his duffel bag.

So she drew in a shaky breath and stepped back, letting her hands drop away from him. "Guess I'm not as cute as my producer tells me I am..."

Rory turned back to her then, and his pale blue eyes were intense as he stared at her. "You're not cute."

"Ouch."

"You're beautiful," he said.

She'd been called that before. Beautiful Brittney. She knew she was attractive, but apparently to a man like Rory VanDam that wasn't enough to attract him.

Then he sighed and added, "Stunning, smart, stubborn, infuriating..."

She smiled. "I'm infuriating?"

He nodded. "And that's why. You can't stop asking questions."

"There are things I want to know," she said, "I won't find out unless I ask…" So she drew in a breath and asked him, "Don't you want me?"

He groaned and closed his eyes. "So damn badly…"

"Then why aren't you kissing me? Touching me?"

He grimaced. "More questions…"

"And you're not giving me any answers."

"I don't want you to get hurt," he said.

"I'm not going to fall madly in love with you," she assured him. Not a firefighter. Not a hotshot…

Not someone she could lose like she'd lost her dad while he'd been deployed.

He grinned. "Good to know. That still doesn't protect you."

"You've been protecting me," she said. "And if I didn't already know how damn short life can be, I would have realized it after the close calls we've had. I don't want to regret not doing this…" She closed the distance between them again and looped her arms around his neck, guiding his head down to hers. Then she kissed him.

The second her lips touched his, her skin tingled and her heart started racing. It was like she was coming under fire again and the vehicle she was in was starting to roll over, to spin out of control. But she wasn't inside anything. There were no airbags to protect her and nothing to hold on to but him.

Then he was holding on to her, too, but he just didn't wrap his arms around, he lifted her up. And she wrapped her legs around his lean waist.

His body was so strong, so hard…so hot.

He kissed her back, his lips nibbling at hers, the tip of

his tongue teasing hers. She parted her lips for him, and he deepened the kiss, making love to her mouth.

Then she was spinning again, or at least moving, as he carried her over to the bed. She pulled him down with her, clinging to him. She hooked her finger in his towel, loosening it until it dropped.

And she whistled in appreciation of all his muscles. The man was perfect. Or he would have been but for a scar here and there, scars like the one on the back of his head. "Rory..." She touched her finger to one on his shoulder.

The bullets had missed him earlier today, but she suspected that one hadn't. At some time...that he had been shot. "Rory—"

Before she could ask the question, his mouth covered hers again, kissing her so deeply that she breathed him in, that his breath was her air. And their hearts beat in a frantic rhythm.

He pulled back and panted for breath. "Let me ask a question," he said, his voice gruff.

Unable to speak for the desire overwhelming her, she just nodded.

"Are you sure?" he asked.

She reached between them and wrapped her hand around his erection. It pulsated against her. "Very sure."

"Then you're overdressed," he said.

And the man moved fast, undoing buttons, lowering zippers, pulling off her shoes until she lay as naked on the bed as he was.

But his gaze covered her, moving over every part of her body. "You are so beautiful..." Then his hands and his mouth moved over her, kissing the side of her neck and the curve of her collarbone.

His hands moved to her breasts now, caressing them,

cupping them. Then he lowered his mouth and kissed one taut nipple before turning his attention to the other one.

She arched against the mattress, her body writhing inside with the tension he was building. The demand for release.

"Rory..." She didn't want to wait.

But he took his time, flicking his tongue across her nipple. Then his hand moved lower, between her legs, and his thumb pressed against the most sensitive part of her body.

Pleasure shot through her with a sudden and small orgasm. It had been too damn long since she'd been with someone. Too damn long since she'd felt this kind of pleasure.

She touched him, sliding her fingers over his muscles and his scars. She would save her questions for later because right now there was only one curiosity she wanted to satisfy. How he would feel inside her...

"Rory..." She wrapped her legs around him again.

"I—I don't have anything..."

"No diseases?" she asked.

He chuckled. "No protection. But yeah, it's been a while, so no nothing else, either...and no control if you keep..."

She rubbed against his cock again. "I have an IUD," she said. "And it's been a while. We're good..."

He parted her legs, lifting them up, over his shoulders as he guided himself inside her.

And she nearly came again at just that, that feeling of him filling her. Then he moved, thrusting his hips against her. She arched up, meeting his thrusts, and they found a fast, frenetic rhythm, one that drove them both to panting and grunting and groaning and madness.

Then finally the tension broke, and her body quivered inside and out. The pleasure was so intense, so unending...

Then his body tensed, and he shuddered as he found his release. And her name slipped through his lips. "Brittney..."

He sounded awed.

She was, too, awed by the intensity of the pleasure and the feeling. Of the connection...

But she knew all too well that it couldn't last. That they only had these stolen moments to enjoy each other because whoever was after her wasn't about to give up.

But she wanted these moments to last, so Brittney reached up and kissed him again. Deeply, passionately, and she felt him move inside her.

He groaned and then chuckled. "Brittney..." He definitely sounded awed.

How the hell had every bullet missed? Sure, the shooter had fired too soon, the minute the door had opened. But with the dog rushing out, running toward them, there hadn't had a choice.

If there had been any hope of hitting the target, the shooter had to shoot fast and then get the hell out of there before someone saw where they'd been standing in the woods.

Did anyone see them now? Where they stood in the shadows outside the hotel?

The shooter might have tried to take them out when they'd left the firehouse, but there had been so many police there. And while the shooter had followed them back here, other people had, as well.

The shooter wasn't the only one watching them. They weren't even sure if they were the only one who wanted them dead. And now the shooter wanted them both dead.

Him even more than her...

Chapter 16

Rory knew Brittney was dangerous. To his secret…and to the life he'd built in Northern Lakes with his hotshot team. But he hadn't realized how dangerous she was to him personally until now.

Even as she lay sleeping next to him, he felt as if he couldn't escape her, that he was connected to her in a way he had never been to anyone else.

Not even Amelia…

Which was strange because he'd trusted Amelia and he knew he couldn't trust Brittney. She cared more about getting her story, or the truth, than anything else. She didn't really care about him.

At least Amelia had pretended to. Maybe she even had, but in the end her greed had been greater than her love. And that greed had proved the end of her…

The twinge in his shoulder wasn't just because of how he was holding Brittney but from an old wound. One that tended to remind him of all the reasons he shouldn't take another chance on a relationship.

Brittney didn't want one any more than he did, though. Maybe less than he did. But instead of reassuring him, that had him panicking now. He wasn't about to fall harder for someone than they'd fallen for him. Not again…

He'd intended to stick with her, to protect her and to figure out the truth together. If the saboteur had come after both of them or if someone else had.

But if it was someone else, someone from his past, then he might get sucked back into it. And she might, too. She deserved to know the truth, but would she believe it…?

Without proof?

He could bring her with him to get his insurance, but he needed some distance, some room to breathe, or he might lose his head and his heart completely. So he slipped out of the bed with the tangled sheets and the sleeping woman. But as he did, he felt a twinge in his heart, and he wondered if it was already too late.

If he was already starting to fall for her…

He had to protect himself now, but he wanted to make sure she was safe, too. Who else would stop Brittney from getting hurt? He dressed quickly and quietly and grabbed up his duffel bag. He'd charged his cell last night at the firehouse, so he had it with him now. Once he got into the hallway outside her room, he would call Trent and make sure that he would protect Brittney better than he had and that he would make sure she didn't slip away again and put herself in danger.

And he'd even wait in the hall until Trent got there, to make sure that she was never unprotected. He didn't want Brittney getting hurt. Not like Amelia had…

As he neared the door, he turned back to the bed to look at her one more time. Her hair had tangled across her face and across the pillow where his head had lain next to hers. He wanted to go back there, wanted to close his arms around her warm body and hold her close.

But it was that desire, that need burning inside him that scared him more than anything else right now. He needed some distance, some time to clear his head, so he could figure out exactly how to finally take care of what he should have five years ago.

He forced himself to resist the temptation of Brittney and turn back toward the door. When he closed his hand around the knob and just started to rotate it, she murmured in her sleep. He glanced back over his shoulder, watching as she settled back against his pillow. Once her body relaxed, as she slipped back into deep sleep, he pulled open the door and quietly stepped out into the hall.

He'd just closed it behind him when someone grabbed him roughly, jerking his arms behind his back, preventing him from fighting.

And if he called out…

Brittney might try coming to his rescue. But she had no gun, nothing that would protect her and save him. He had to figure out some way to do that, but he had a feeling that he was outnumbered this time. It wasn't just one shadow looming over him in that hall but two.

But he'd never given up before. Not when Amelia had betrayed him or when that plane crashed.

He wasn't giving up now. Just like before, he wasn't giving up without a fight. And now he wasn't just fighting for his life but for hers, too.

Brittney jerked awake, her arms outstretched, reaching…

Reaching for Rory, but he was gone. The bed was cold. How long had he been gone?

Snippets of a dream came back to her. Men's deep voices. Sounds of a scuffle…

Had that been a dream?

Or had something happened to Rory?

She jumped up and hurriedly dressed. Then she searched

her room and the adjoining bathroom. Rory was gone, and so was his duffel bag. How long had he been gone?

The light was already dimming outside. How long had she slept?

Had the entire day slipped away from her? Just like Rory had?

A twinge of regret struck her heart. Not over what they'd done. She would never regret that. He was amazing in bed. Had brought her so much pleasure...

She had needed that. She'd needed him. Her regret was that he was gone now. And she didn't think she would find him as easily as she had earlier that day. He probably wasn't going back to the firehouse.

Where would he go?

That island where he was a forest ranger?

Or somewhere else? Wherever he was from?

Did he have a home? Family? He'd never said much about anyone but his hotshot team.

And yet, he didn't seem as close as the rest of them were to each other, either. Rory VanDam was a loner now, but had he always been alone?

Despite having dressed in a sweater and wool pants, she shivered. She wasn't cold so much as she felt alone. And despite the closed door, she had that uneasy feeling, that sensation that someone was watching her even though there wasn't even a peephole in the door.

Then the knob rattled, as someone tried to turn it. "Who's there?" she called out. "Rory? Trent?"

The knob rattled more and so did the door as someone tried to force it open. It definitely wasn't Rory or Trent. They would have answered her. They wouldn't want to scare her like this person obviously did.

But if this was the one who'd fired shots at her and

tried to run her down, this person didn't want to just scare her anymore. They wanted to kill her.

Trent had never felt like killing anyone more than he had Rory. When he and Ethan had caught the man sneaking out of his sister's hotel room, fury had coursed through him. And if not for Ethan stopping him, he wouldn't have killed Rory, but he certainly would have messed him up.

If he could...

His jaw still ached a bit from where Rory had nailed him the night before. Even with a serious head injury, the guy was strong.

And stubborn.

He'd resisted Ethan's efforts to encourage them to go somewhere and talk it out while Ethan stayed behind to protect Brittney. Rory had insisted there was nothing to talk about it.

And even though Rory had finally agreed to go to the Filling Station with Trent, he had yet to say much of anything. Trent wasn't sure what to say, either. He was almost too damn mad to talk.

From the way Rory had looked, sneaking out of his sister's hotel room, he could pretty much guess what had happened between them. That was bad enough, made Trent's empty stomach churn with disgust.

But then to sneak out like the man had...

Like he'd been trying to get away from her without waking her up...

A growl bubbled up the back of his throat, but he didn't want to think about why she would have been sleeping. Why she would have been with Rory at all...

Sure, the guy had saved her life. Twice. That Trent knew of. But what if he was the one who'd put it in danger?

He growled again.

"I don't speak Annie," Rory said. "So if you've got something to say to me, just say it." He squared his shoulders and leaned forward a bit, as if bracing himself.

After how Trent had pounced on him in the hall, he was smart to be wary. But Rory was always wary no matter what.

The first time Brittney had come to town, he'd worked damn hard to stay away from her. Why hadn't he done it this time?

But if he had…

She would be hurt or worse: dead.

He released the growl in a groan of frustration. Then he said, "Thank you."

Rory's forehead furrowed, and he leaned farther across the booth and peered at Trent's face. "What did you say?" he asked as if he hadn't heard it or, if it had, he didn't believe that Trent had said it.

"Thank you," he said. "You saved my sister's life. Twice. I can't thank you enough for that…"

Rory's mouth curved into a slight grin. "But?"

"I know she acts tough and all that," Trent said. "But she's got a really soft heart. She's hurt a lot more easily than you'd think. And she's been through a lot."

Concern filled Rory's eyes. "What do you mean? When?"

"We lost our dad when she was really young," Trent said. "Sometimes I think she doesn't remember him, and then sometimes I think she remembers him too much, that she remembers how hard it was for us to lose him."

"On *all* of you, I'm sure," Rory said with sympathy. "Especially your mom."

He shook his head. "My parents were already divorced when he died. He was married to Brittney's mom then."

A muscle twitched along Rory's cheek, and he cleared his throat and asked, "What happened to him?"

"He was deployed, roadside bomb," Trent murmured, and he felt that hollow ache in his heart.

"I'm sorry…"

The sympathy was genuine. Not for the first time, Trent suspected that Rory knew how it felt to lose someone and maybe not just because of that plane crash.

Trent nodded. "A few years later my mom died," he said. "Moe, Brittney's mom, had remarried by then, and Brittney convinced them to take me in, to foster me. She'll fight fiercely for those she loves, and she loves fiercely."

"Why are you telling me all of this?" Rory asked. "Why are we even here?" He gestured at the food untouched on the booth in front of them. "You should be back at the hotel with her."

"And what about you?" Trent asked. "Where are you going?"

Rory's gaze dropped down to the table then. That was clearly a question he didn't want to answer.

"Does this have anything to do with you?" Trent asked.

Rory shrugged. "I don't know."

"I think you know more than I do."

"You haven't had your detective girlfriend looking into this?" Rory asked.

Trent grinned at just the thought of Heather. Talking about fierce women, there was no one fiercer than her. Not even Brittney or Moe.

"What did Detective Bolton find out?" Rory asked.

"That a certain producer has been creeping on my sister."

That muscle twitched in Rory's cheek again when he clenched his jaw. "The one that calls her cute…" he murmured.

Trent bristled with anger over the thought of someone harassing his sister. "He's not been at work, either. Brittney's coworkers told Heather about him."

Rory didn't look as convinced of the man's guilt as Trent was.

"What?" he asked. "What do you know that I don't?"

"She got a couple of notes," Rory said. "One was shoved under her windshield wiper. Told her to drop a story or she'd regret it."

Trent groaned. "That would just make her more determined."

"The next was a text that told her she was going to die for not dropping it, or something to that effect, and after she got that somebody shot at her windshield. That's why she went off the road."

Trent cursed and jumped up from the table. "Why the hell didn't she tell me this? Why didn't you?" Then his fury turned back on Rory as he realized why. "The story she's supposed to drop... It's about that damn plane crash!"

"Or about the sabotage," Rory said. "She's still looking into both of those."

Trent cursed again. "Probably the sabotage even more now after what happened after the holiday party. Who the hell is doing this?" And he glanced around the bar all the hotshots frequented. Usually they would have been jammed into the big corner booth, but none of them were there now. They'd been at the firehouse earlier, though, so most of them were still in town.

Because Rory had been hurt? Or because Rory had recovered? Was whoever hit him worried that he was able to identify him?

"You really didn't see who hit you?" Trent asked him.

He shook his head. "Brittney wanted a list of all the hotshot team members. She intends to look into everyone."

"And I intend to stop her," Trent said. "Are you coming with me?"

Rory shoved his hands in his pockets, and his face got a little pale. "Damn. I must've left my keys…"

"You didn't have them," Trent reminded him. "Brittney drove you back from the firehouse." He wasn't happy that his friend had probably crossed a line with his sister, but it was clear that Brittney had been the instigator. Like she usually was.

But as she was learning from those threats, some people really resented the instigator and would do anything to stop them from meddling.

Even murder them…

Chapter 17

Rory didn't know why his pulse quickened as he and Trent neared the hotel. Was it just because, in order to get his keys, he was going to have to see her again?

After…what had happened between them?

But the feeling churning his stomach was more than anticipation, more even than nerves. It was fear. Not of her but for her.

But Ethan was watching her room from the adjoining one that Trent had booked the night before. She'd locked the door on the other side, though, so all Ethan could really see was the hall through the open door of his room. And if he was focused on the hall, he wouldn't be able to see the fire escape…

The one Rory had gone out the night before when he'd sneaked up on Trent. He glanced up at it now and saw that the window to Brittney's room was open, the curtains and blinds hanging out as if someone had exited it in a hurry.

Or dragged someone out of it?

"Trent!" He grabbed his friend's arm and pointed up. "That's her room!"

Trent cursed and started running toward the hotel. While he went through the lobby, Rory jumped on the ladder dangling down from the fire escape and climbed up it. As he ran up the landings, he looked for blood or for any other sign of a struggle. Because he doubted that Brittney had just opened that window for some air...

Not with as chilly as the wind was now that the sun had dropped. It was cold. Too cold to leave a window open.

The escape swayed beneath his pounding feet as he hurried up the last landing to that open window. He leaned over, peering inside, before sliding his leg over the jamb. "Brittney?" he called out.

The door to the hall stood open, spilling light into her room. Into the empty room...

The door and the window were open? What the hell?

He climbed through the window and checked the bathroom. It was empty, too. And he noticed that the door to the hall hadn't just been opened, it had been kicked in, the wood cracked and the jamb splintered.

Hearing footfalls on the stairs, he stepped out into the hall and nearly fell over a body.

"Ethan!" He dropped to his knees and felt his friend's neck, checking for a pulse. It was there. Strong and steady.

But Ethan didn't move. And Rory was almost scared to move him. Had he been shot? Or stabbed? There was blood on the carpet near him.

"What the hell!" Trent shouted, standing over them in the hall. "Is he—"

"He's alive, but we need to call for a rig."

"And Brittney?" Trent asked, his voice cracking.

Rory shook his head. "She's not in there."

Trent stepped around him and looked inside, too, as if he didn't believe Rory. He unlocked the adjoining door from her side and looked in his room, too.

Maybe she'd gone in there. Maybe she was safe. But Trent walked out of it into the hall. He was shaking his head, and tears shone in his eyes.

He was scared for Brittney, as scared as Rory was. He never should have left her.

But Ethan…

He was so damn big. So indestructible…

Then Rory saw where the blood was coming from, a wound on the side of Ethan's head. Someone had struck him just like Rory had been struck those weeks ago.

He hoped that Ethan recovered faster than he did. The man had already been through too much. The Canterbury curse couldn't claim him now, not when he was so happy.

"Owen, get a rig here to the Lakeside Inn," Trent spoke into his cell. "Ethan's unconscious—"

"He was hit over the head!" Rory said, speaking loud enough that Owen could hear him.

"And Brittney is missing," Trent added. "So we need to get Braden and Trick and whoever else we can find to help look for her."

Rory shook his head.

Trent clicked off his cell and asked, "What? Why are you shaking your head?"

"We don't know who we can trust," Rory said. "Besides you and me and Ethan—"

Trent pointed at Ethan's prone body. "He's hurt, man. And I trust Braden and Trick."

But Rory noted that he didn't add any other names. Not even Rory's…

Rory shook his head with disgust. How could Trent doubt Rory now?

Because of the damn story.

Because of the plane crash.

Was that what this was all about? If it was, Brittney was right about getting the truth out. Keeping secrets certainly wasn't keeping her safe.

He needed to get back to the island. He rushed back into Brittney's room.

"She's not there," Trent said.

But Rory wasn't looking for her now, he was looking for his keys. They weren't on any of the tables or the desk. Not lying on any of the furniture...

He didn't have the keys, so Brittney must have taken them with her. Had she used them to get away? He rushed back to that open window and climbed through it. The fire escape shuddered beneath his weight.

"Rory!" Trent called to him. "You can't leave Ethan alone!"

Sirens were already wailing in the distance. Help was on its way. And there wasn't much Rory could do about Ethan's head injury when he was still recovering from his own.

Ignoring Trent, he continued clamoring down the escape and dropped off the end of the dangling ladder onto the sidewalk. Where had Brittney parked his truck?

Hadn't it been here, close to the hotel? He peered up and down the street and didn't see it.

Whoever had broken into Brittney's room must have taken her and the keys and his truck...

Taken her where, though?

And why? Why wouldn't he or she have just left Brittney in the hotel room like they'd left Ethan lying in the hall? Maybe Trent was right, maybe the person who'd been after her was her obsessed producer.

But then why shoot at her and try to run her down if he'd wanted to abduct her?

"Brittney, where are you?" he wondered aloud as he looked around the street again.

Lights flashed on and off. On and off.

And he noted they were coming from the alley where he and Trent had been standing the night she'd nearly gotten run down. But now there was a vehicle in it instead of two men.

He started down the street toward that alley, stepping in front of it just as the lights flashed on again and the motor revved up. He could see the US Forest Service insignia on the side door.

He'd found his truck.

But was it about to run him over?

Brittney lowered the driver's window and gestured for Rory to hurry around the front. To jump into the passenger's door. But he stepped up to her door instead and pulled on the handle. "Let me drive," he said with a quick glance around.

Brittney had already stayed longer than she should have. "He's probably out here somewhere—"

Rory reached through the window and unlocked the door and opened it. "Slide over, quick," he said.

She scrambled over the console. "I can drive—"

"You don't know where we're going, or you would have left already," he said, and he pulled out of the alley onto the street.

Obviously he knew where he was going.

"I couldn't leave," she said. She'd been so disoriented when she'd awakened *alone*. Had he snuck out after they'd made love? But she hadn't known if she was really alone or if Rory was somewhere else, if he'd heard whoever was at that door before she had. But that person hadn't been him or Trent or they would have answered when she'd called out to them. "I didn't know who was supposed to be *protecting* me and what had happened to them."

She'd been so scared that he or Trent had been hurt. Because how else would someone have gotten past them?

"What happened?" Rory asked.

She shivered as she relived those terrifying moments. "I heard some arguing earlier, but that didn't wake me up fully. I'm not really sure what did, but then I heard someone trying to get in the door. I grabbed your keys and my purse and went out the window onto the fire escape," she said.

"That must have been right before someone broke through that door. Did they follow you?" Rory asked, and he was glancing into the rearview mirror as he drove. As if looking for that SUV…

The person trying to get into her room must have been whoever drove that SUV straight at her the night before and who'd shot at her and Rory at the firehouse.

She shivered again.

So the lock and the door hadn't held, hadn't kept her would-be killer out. She'd been smart to run. But what happened…?

Lights flashed and sirens whined as an ambulance passed them. She knew where it was headed: the hotel.

"Who's hurt?" she asked, her heart pounding.

After going out the window, she'd pulled the truck into the alley, shut off the lights and hunkered down inside. But she'd seen Trent and Rory coming back from wherever they'd been, and relief had surged through her. Now she felt a twinge of guilt.

"Who is it?" She reached across the console and clutched Rory's arm.

It was already tense, like his tightly clenched jaw.

"Who's hurt?"

"Ethan," he said. "He must've gotten hit over the head. He was unconscious."

"Shouldn't we go back?" she asked. "Make sure he's all right?"

He drew in a shaky breath. "I want to," he said, his voice gruff with emotion. "But I don't think it's a good idea."

"Why not?" she asked.

"Because someone is trying very hard to kill you," he said. "And I don't think either of us want anyone else to get caught in the crossfire."

She sucked in a shaky breath.

"I assume that's why you didn't tell your brother about the threats you—"

"You told him?"

"Yeah, why didn't you?"

"Because I knew he would get crazy overprotective," she said.

"Like he's been since your van crashed?" Rory asked. "You think holding back that piece of information worried him any less than he's been worrying?"

She sighed.

"Holding back that information misled him," Rory said.

"What do you mean?"

"He had Heather checking out your coworkers and—"

"What?" she asked. "Not that I care…" After nearly getting killed and knowing that she was still in danger and putting others in danger, Brittney had a different perspective on her career. She still wanted the story, but it wasn't so she would be taken seriously as a reporter. She just wanted to make sure nobody else got hurt.

"She heard a lot of things about your producer, and he's been conspicuously off work since you left," Rory said with a glance across the console at her.

She shivered again.

And Rory reached for the heat, turning it up.

Despite the warm air blasting out of the vents, she was still chilled. "As big a creep as he is, I don't think he would go to all this trouble to hurt me. My career, maybe. But my life…" She shook her head. "And he has no reason to want to stop me from pursuing any stories. He doesn't even know that I've been trying to get enough information to do a follow-up to the plane crash and with the hotshots."

"Who does know?" Rory asked.

"I've tried talking to Mack McRooney," she said. "And I've called the FAA with questions about the flight path and the black box…"

"And?"

She shrugged. "Ethan. I'm always bugging Ethan for a follow-up," she admitted.

"Well, Ethan didn't hit himself over the head."

"He was hit like you? Do you think the same person hit you both?"

He shrugged. "I don't know what to think anymore, but I know this needs to stop."

"How are we going to stop it?" she asked.

He glanced across at her again, his pale eyes glowing in the dim light from the dashboard. Clearly he had some idea, but he said nothing, just kept driving. Rory had saved her over and over again, so he had to be heading someplace safe. But with how tightly his jaw was clenched, how grim he looked, he had obviously realized the same thing she had. No place was safe.

Somebody was pounding. Hammering away at something…

Was it an axe chopping through a door? Or a wall? Or a tree?

Ethan breathed deeply, waiting for the burn of smoke, for the tickle that would make him cough. But it didn't come. There was no burn. Did he have his helmet and oxygen on?

He raised his hand to his face and found a mask over his nose. But not the kind that came with his helmet.

What was the pounding? Where the hell was he?

Ethan opened up his eyes to two guys leaning over him. Owen, with a pinched and serious look on his face, and Trent, who looked even more anxious.

But maybe not for him…

Ethan pulled the oxygen mask aside. "Where's Brittney? Is she safe?"

Trent grimaced, and Ethan reached up and grabbed his friend's shoulder. "What happened to her?" he asked, his voice gruff with concern. Despite her pestering him, Ethan had grown fond of Brittney, and he would always be grateful for her help in saving Tammy's life.

If he'd lost her…

That pounding intensified again, and he realized it was inside his head. He grimaced at the pain.

"We need to get you to the ER for a CT scan," Owen said.

He shook his head and grimaced again. "Where is she?" he asked. Then he glanced around the hotel corridor. "Where's Rory?"

"He went to find her," Trent said, "out the fire escape. The window was open."

The tension eased from Ethan, and he relaxed a bit against the hotel carpeting. "She got away."

Of course she would have. She was smart and resilient, like Tammy, which was probably why the two of them had become fast friends. He emitted a little wistful sigh for their missed cruise. He would have to reschedule once he knew everyone was safe.

"How do you know she got away?" Trent asked, his topaz eyes bright with either unshed tears or hope.

"The guy stepped over me again after he broke the door down."

"You saw him?" Trent asked. "Who was it?"

"I didn't see him when he hit me over the back of the head. I went down, but I didn't lose consciousness right away." But he hadn't had the strength to get back up after that first blow. "I just saw his legs when he stepped over me and headed back down the interior stairs."

"Why didn't he go out the fire escape after her?" Owen asked.

"He probably didn't want anyone to see him, in case someone was walking by, or Rory and I were walking back up," Trent said. "Rory saw that open window right away."

"Rory probably found her," Owen said. "I'm sure they're safe. So we need to get you to the hospital, Ethan."

While Owen was certain they were safe, Trent didn't look as convinced.

"Rory's smart and resourceful," Ethan reminded him. "He'll figure out how to keep her safe."

"What if she's in danger because of him?" Trent asked. "She got threats telling her to stop pursuing the story."

"What story?" Owen asked.

Ethan didn't have to ask. "The plane crash."

"Is there more to that story?" Trent asked. "Something someone else might not want made public?"

The pounding resumed inside Ethan's skull. But he didn't know now if it was because of the blow or because of the pendulum of the past swinging back toward him. He'd made a promise five years ago.

He and Rory both had. Rory had kept his promise all these years. And Ethan had, too.

But now…

He'd kept Rory's promise to keep him safe, but Rory was

obviously not safe any longer. And Brittney wasn't safe, either, because she wouldn't give up the damn story. And Ethan was afraid that it might cost her more than her career.

It might cost her everything.

Chapter 18

Rory kept glancing into the rearview mirror, looking for lights on the road behind him. Then he would know for certain that he'd been followed. Right now, he just had that uneasy feeling, that twisting of his stomach muscles that made him suspect that he had been.

But maybe he was just paranoid.

But his paranoia was for good reason after everything that had happened to him and had happened to some people who'd been unfortunate to be around him.

He glanced across the console at Brittney. Was he protecting her by taking her with him or was he putting her in more danger than she already was? Because she had something going on with her, too, and was it really related to him? Or was it her producer?

Or that damn saboteur…?

Brittney was digging inside her purse and cursing.

"What's wrong?"

"I must've left my phone on the charger," she said. "Can I use yours to call and check on Ethan?"

He wanted to know how his friend was, too, but he hesitated for a moment.

"What?" she asked. "Did you forget yours, too? I still don't understand what all happened at the hotel, how Ethan was hurt and where you and Trent were coming back from…"

"The Filling Station," he said.

"The Filling Station?" she asked. "Why were you…?"

He was trying to focus on the road, on finding the turn-off to what he was looking for, but that wasn't why he wasn't filling in the blanks for her. Recognizing the bend in the road, he turned onto the two-track road in the middle of the national forest. This was what he'd been looking for…

While she was looking for answers.

And with her life in danger now, she deserved those answers. "I snuck out when you fell asleep," he admitted. "Trent and Ethan caught me in the hall. Trent was probably going to kill me, but Ethan stopped him." And then might have lost his life, as well.

No. His pulse had been strong and steady, just like Ethan. The man was a survivor, like Rory, so he had to make it. He had to be okay.

"And so you two went to get a beer together?" she asked.

"We needed to talk."

"That was when you told him about those threats."

"You shouldn't have kept it secret from him," he said.

"Like you're *not* keeping any secrets, Rory?" she asked.

Damn. She was smart. Too smart.

"I'm sorry," he said. If this was all his fault, if people were getting hurt again because of him…

"Don't be," she said. "I made the moves on you. I wanted what happened to happen. You didn't need to sneak out, though, so fast that you left your keys behind."

"I don't regret what happened," he assured her, his heart pounding fast as he thought of how amazing it had been, how they'd fit so perfectly, moved so much in sync and had had such a mind-blowing release. "That's not why I took off like that. It's just…"

"What?" she asked. "What is it, Rory?"

"The last woman I got close to wound up dead."

She sucked in a breath then released it in a shaky sigh. "Well, someone was trying to kill me before we ever hooked up, so I can't blame you for that."

Even though there were other possibilities, he was not so sure.

"So did you leave your phone behind with your keys when you made your fast getaway?" she asked again.

"No, no, I have it," he said. "I just… I don't want anyone to know where we're going."

"Why not?" she asked.

"I'm not sure who we can trust," he admitted. He knew all too well how easily some people could be bought, people he'd believed had cared about him. People he had cared about.

The truck bumped along the rutted path between tall trees, but the lights shone up ahead on a clearing in the forest, then glinted off the metal of a big building.

"Don't worry about me telling anybody where we are," she said. "Because I have no freaking idea…" She leaned forward, peering around, but the sun had slipped away a while ago, leaving the area pretty much in darkness but for the lights of his truck.

He braked the truck next to the service door to the hangar. The overhead doors were on the other side of the building by the airstrip. One of his team would realize where he'd gone soon enough, but maybe by that time, he would have gotten what he wanted off the island and made it back already.

He reached into his pocket and drew out his phone. "I have to get something ready," he said. "You can make the call…"

He would leave it up to her who to trust. He'd learned long ago that his judgment sucked when it came to that, or he wouldn't have been betrayed like he'd been.

So was he making another mistake trusting her?

Because that last woman he'd cared about had nearly gotten him killed.

Brittney watched through the windshield as Rory unlocked the door to the massive metal building in the middle of the forest. But there weren't as many trees around here, like they had been cleared away for this...

Whatever it was.

No, like she'd told him, she had no idea where he'd taken her. Then the headlights of the truck went out, leaving her totally in the dark. He'd shut off the engine, and he must have taken the keys with him.

To prevent her from leaving?

But then she couldn't blame him if he didn't want to be left stranded out here in the woods. She wouldn't, either.

Sitting like she was in the dark, she was very aware of the silence. There weren't even birds or animals making noises now. Then an engine started up, and light shone around the corner of the building and from beneath that door.

There was something in the metal structure that had an engine. So Rory wouldn't have been stranded.

She might be, though.

Something vibrated in her hand, and she jumped, realizing that she'd been holding his phone. She glanced at the screen that was lit up with Trent's name.

She accepted the call. "Hi."

"Brittney!" Trent exclaimed. Then he released a shaky sigh that rattled the phone. "Are you all right?"

"Yes, is Ethan?" she asked with concern. The guy wasn't just her brother's best friend, he was also the love of Tammy's life and a really good man.

"He regained consciousness right away, even before we got him out of the hotel hallway," Trent said.

Not like Rory, who'd spent those two weeks in a coma.

"That's good," she said. Hopefully that meant it wasn't a bad concussion.

"We're at the ER now, so he can get a CT and make sure he's as all right as he keeps claiming he is."

"Is Tammy all right?" Brittney asked. "Is she there?"

"She's here, with him," Trent said. "Where the hell are you?"

"I don't know," she answered honestly.

"You're with Rory, right? You have to be since you answered his phone."

"Yes, he's here," she said. She just had no idea where here was.

"You need to get away from him," Trent said with such urgency in his voice that Brittney shivered.

"What do you mean?" The man had saved her life. He wasn't going to hurt her. At least not physically...

Emotionally. She shut that down, refusing to think about that, about what they'd done and how he'd snuck out when she'd been sleeping.

"You were right," Trent said. "You've been right all along that there was more to that plane crash..."

"What?" she asked, her pulse quickening. "What did you find out about it?"

"Ethan didn't know a whole lot, just that when it first happened Rory was blaming himself..."

"Why would he do that?"

"He was the pilot," Trent said. "He went through hotshot training with Ethan, but he was also able to pilot the planes they were jumping out of. He already knew how to fly. And Ethan doesn't think his name is really Rory Van-

Dam. Somebody else on that flight, somebody who didn't make it off the mountain, called him something else."

"What?"

"Mario."

Even though Trent couldn't see her, she shook her head. But she had no idea why she would deny it. She'd known there was more to the plane crash story and more to Rory VanDam.

"Mario what?" she asked.

"That was all Ethan heard, and when he asked him about it later, when they were stranded, Rory denied it, said he had to be mistaken."

"Maybe he was," Brittney said.

"You got those threats about dropping a story—"

"And Rory was the one who told you about those threats, and he wouldn't have done that if he'd been the one sending them," she reminded him.

"You should have told me."

"Why? So you could overreact?"

"Someone's trying to kill you, Brittney," he said. "So I'm not overreacting. You're underreacting."

She was scared to death, but she wasn't about to admit that aloud or she might fall apart. And she had to keep it together. The side mirror on the truck caught her attention through the passenger's window. She saw something…a flicker of light. But it appeared to be some distance back down that narrow driveway. But what was the message on the mirror? Objects are closer than they appear.

Someone had been following them.

"Trent, I have to go—"

"Where?"

The door through which Rory had disappeared opened again, and he gestured toward her.

Had he seen that light, too?

"Brittney!" Trent yelled. "You have to get away from him. You can't trust him."

"He keeps saving my life, not putting it in danger," she reminded her brother and herself.

"But your life might be in danger *because* of him, Brittney. You have to get away from him and stay away from him," Trent demanded.

The last woman I got close to wound up dead...

Rory stood there, gesturing toward her again, but he wasn't looking at her now. He was looking behind her.

Objects might be closer than they appear.

She pushed open the passenger door and jumped out. Trent might be right, but she didn't have a choice right now. Somebody else was out there, and it wasn't Trent.

It sounded like anyone else she could trust was at the hospital with Ethan.

So the only person left was Rory.

Or Mario...

"Brittney!" Trent called out again.

But she clicked off the cell and dropped it into her purse. And as she headed toward the door to the building, something pinged off the metal.

Someone was out there, and he or she was shooting at them. "Hurry up!" Rory said, and he reached out the door and grabbed her arm, pulling her inside with him. He slammed that door and locked it.

But she didn't know why he bothered—wide and tall doors were open on the other side. And outside, a helicopter sat.

"Come on," he said, and he wrapped his arm around her, nearly carrying her toward that machine. "We have to get out of here." He cursed. "We were followed."

She'd been aware of how often he'd checked in his mir-
rors because she'd been checking, too. There was no way
they would have missed someone tailing them unless...

Someone had guessed where they were going. Like a
member of his team. Maybe they weren't all at the hospital with Ethan and Trent and Tammy.

"We have to go now!" Rory said. And he swept her
around the helicopter, opened the door and lifted her up
into it. Then he jumped into the cockpit or whatever it was
called on the other side.

He touched buttons and switches, and the blades began
to swish above them. Then he reached for some levers and
the helicopter lifted. He pointed toward her belt and a set
of headphones.

Her hands shaking, she buckled up and put the headphones over her ears. The sounds were muffled, but the
noise was still there.

Even the pings as bullets struck the metal of the small
helicopter. But it continued to rise above the metal hangar,
above the woods.

The gun must have had a long range because it kept firing at them. And on the ground below, Brittney could see
little flashes of light as the bullets left the gun. But she
couldn't see the shooter.

As fear overwhelmed her, she closed her eyes entirely
and hung on tight, terrified that they were going to crash.

Maybe to reassure her, Rory spoke to her, his voice coming through her headphones. "We're going to be all right,"
he said.

But she didn't know if he was lying to her or telling the
truth...about anything.

Then he muttered, "I am not going to crash again."

* * *

The shooter wasn't really worried about the reporter. Not anymore. Not now.

Because the shooter had finally realized the truth of what had happened five years ago and who Rory VanDam really was. They'd been worried about that damn woman, about the reporter, pushing others to look for that wreckage, to find out why it had crashed.

That helicopter needed to go down, or the shooter was the one who was going to suffer. So the gun kept firing; hopefully a bullet would hit the gas tank and that helicopter would blow up like they did in the movies when bullets hit them.

One of the bullets had to hit the target, if not the pilot then the gas tank. This helicopter had to go down like the plane had five years ago. But unlike that crash, there could not be any survivors this time.

Chapter 19

The helicopter was going down...

Right where Rory intended to land it, on the section of rock that stood atop the hill on the island. No trees could grow out of the rock, and none of the ones near it were tall enough to stand above it. So this was the clearest place to land. Nothing to catch at the blades, and a solid place for the landing skids to rest.

Once Rory sat it down and shut off the engine, he waited for the blades to stop rotating. Then he turned toward Brittney. Her eyes were closed. He could see her face in the moonlight that streamed through the windows of the helicopter. Her eyes weren't just closed but squeezed tightly shut as if she was bracing herself.

Maybe for a crash.

He reached out and pulled off her headphones, and she jumped and flinched. "You're okay," he assured her. "We're okay." For now. "We're on the ground."

And none of the bullets that had struck the helicopter had caused any damage.

Brittney opened her eyes and peered around them then. "Where the hell are we?"

"Bear Isle," he said, and he opened his door and jumped down to the ground. Then he rushed around to help her out.

When she stepped onto the snow-covered rock, she slipped, and he caught her, closing his arms around her trembling body. Maybe she hadn't slipped. Maybe her legs had been shaking too badly to hold her. "We're safe here," he said.

She swung her head around, staring into the shadows of the trees and rocks. "How do you know that?"

"The only thing we have to worry about here might be a bear or a coyote," he promised her. "Whoever was shooting at us back there isn't going to be able to make it out here."

At least not for a while.

Rory's was the only helicopter within a couple hours' drive of Northern Lakes. And if the shooter tried to come by boat, there were still enough chunks of ice around the island to make it hard to get ashore.

As if on cue, a coyote howled somewhere close. Close enough to make Brittney jump again and to make Rory uneasy. "Let's go," he said, and he helped her down from the rock ledge onto the path that wound through the woods to a cabin. His cabin. His sanctuary, really.

"Your hideout," she presumed.

And she wasn't wrong. It probably was more his hideout than anything else. He'd been hiding for a long time. But he had a feeling that he'd been discovered. That the people he'd never wanted to learn the truth knew now that he wasn't dead. He hadn't died in that crash.

Rory opened the door to the cabin and stepped inside, looking around to make sure that it was as he'd left it. Empty. Not just of people but of animals, too. He lit a match to the kindling he had laid in the fieldstone fireplace, and flames flickered to life, illuminating the wood floor and log walls. He turned back toward Brittney, who stood on the outside of the door, hesitating like she had back at the hangar.

"What's going on?" he asked. Then his stomach pitched. "You called Trent. Isn't Ethan…?" He swallowed hard on the emotion suddenly choking him. He and Ethan had been through hell together. He couldn't have lost him, especially now when Ethan was so damn happy. He cleared his throat and asked, "Isn't he okay?"

"He's conscious," she said. "And he's *talking*…"

Rory tensed, waiting for it, because from her tone, there was clearly more to come.

"Mario…"

He could have denied that it was his name, like he had to Ethan all those years ago. And with Ethan assuming another name, he'd had no room to judge him.

Or so he'd thought.

After all, they'd both been afraid for their lives…just for different reasons. Ethan had been convinced that damn Canterbury curse was trying to claim him. And Rory had a curse of his own.

"I'm glad he's okay," he said, then released a heavy sigh of relief.

But she stood there looking all tense yet.

"He is okay, right?"

"They were waiting for a CT scan to confirm it, but he is conscious."

Which was better than Rory had been after the blow to his head. Maybe it hadn't been the same person who'd struck Ethan.

He shuddered, and not just from the cold, but from the thought that there could be two people that cold-blooded in Northern Lakes. But he knew, all too well, that anyone could be cold-blooded, especially when it came to money or their own well-being.

He'd even once been that way himself, when he hadn't

come forward with everything he'd known about the plane crash. When he'd let the people responsible for it escape justice.

But he'd done that for his sake, so that the people who'd wanted him dead had believed they'd succeeded. Playing dead was the only way he'd been able to stay alive.

The door slammed, and he whirled away from the fire toward Brittney. Had the wind slammed the door? Or…

She was bristling, her body tense. "I'm tired of this," she said. "Tired of being in danger. I want to know the truth, *Mario*."

"It's Rory," he said.

"Now. But it wasn't always, was it?" she asked.

He shook his head. "No. But it wasn't always Mario, either."

"So who and what are you really?" she asked. "A hotshot? A pilot?"

"Yes and yes," he said.

"And?" she prodded. Then she sucked in a breath and seemed to be holding it, waiting for his answer.

It had been so long since he'd told anyone the truth. So damn long…

His legs shook a bit, like hers must have from the helicopter trip, and he dropped into one of the big plaid easy chairs that sat in front of the fire. "I was… DEA," he said. "An undercover agent."

In a ragged sigh, she released the breath she'd been holding. She must have been convinced he'd been the criminal, not the cop.

Sometimes, with as deeply undercover as he'd gone, he had felt more criminal than cop. Which had reminded him of how he'd grown up.

"Mario was my undercover identity, my way into the organization," he said. "But I grew up with people like that, so it was easy for me to be Mario. Probably easier than it is for me to be Rory."

"Where did you grow up?" she asked.

"Baltimore."

"And where was Mario?"

"LA."

"And what is your real name?"

He leaned back in the chair and sighed. "When I woke up from that coma, with that concussion, I didn't even know…" He shook his head. "I couldn't remember who I really was. Mario was not my only undercover assignment, my only fake identity. And then there was the Special Forces ops and so many other things that I wanted to forget…"

"The woman?" she asked. "Who was she?"

"Someone who fell for Mario," he said.

"And did Mario fall for her?"

"She seemed sweet. Special. She was also the sister of the guy I took down."

"For drugs?"

"For murder," he said. "My undercover assignment, Mario, was a pilot for a drug cartel. While I was flying their private jet, I witnessed a murder." Remembering that murder, how he'd been unable to stop it, how the whole damn plane could have crashed if he hadn't stayed in control then even as everything had spun out of control around him. "It happened while I was flying, so I didn't have any time to react. I had no idea what was coming. This guy was so cold-blooded, so vicious. He shot this man right between the eyes." He shuddered as he remembered the scene, the blood, the…

But that wasn't even the worst he'd seen.

"Why?" she asked. "Why did he shoot him?"

"Because he thought he was a DEA agent," he said. "He knew someone had infiltrated their organization. He just suspected the wrong man." So that man had died because of him.

She dropped into the chair next to him then as if her legs had given out. "So you're talking about very dangerous people."

"Yes. People who don't forget," he said. "And damn well don't forgive that I arrested the killer and testified against him."

"You were just doing your job," she said. "And why would they go after a DEA agent, especially after you'd already testified and put him in jail?"

"Because the guy I arrested got shanked in jail before his sentencing."

"Then who's after you?" she asked.

"His father."

"I don't understand… You said the woman who got killed was related to them, too. Would the father have killed his own daughter?"

"She set me up," he said. "Got me to meet with her, swore she wanted to leave town with me, start a new life with me, when all she really wanted was to end my life." He rubbed his shoulder, but that wound was nothing in comparison.

"She tried to shoot you?"

He nodded. "She did. And it wasn't just for revenge. Her father had promised her a huge amount of money if she killed me. But a US Marshal killed her before she was able to finish the job."

"The scar on your shoulder?"

He nodded again. "Yeah, she wasn't a very good shot. The Marshal was."

She leaned back in her chair now and closed her eyes, probably overwhelmed with everything he had told her. "I… I don't know what to say…"

"Or what to believe?" he asked.

"It's a pretty wild story," she said. "If I wanted to sell this, I would need proof. Corroboration of the facts."

"So you still want to sell a story?" he asked, his stomach churning with disappointment. "Even though it might cost you your life?" And him his.

He'd started to think there was more to her than ambition, that she genuinely cared about people. At least about her brother. And Ethan and Tammy.

But she apparently didn't care about him.

"I want some proof," she persisted. "Some way to know what the truth really is."

He sucked in a breath now and nodded. "You don't believe me."

"I don't know what to believe," she admitted. "That's why I need corroboration."

He had proof. But for some reason he wanted her to believe him without it. He wanted her to see him for the man that he was, instead of all the different men he'd pretended to be. But how could he expect her to see what he struggled to?

"The person trying to kill us isn't corroboration enough?" he asked.

"Why is that person trying to kill you now?" she asked. "Why didn't that person go after you right after the plane crash?"

"Because the pilot, at least the man who'd been listed as the pilot, didn't survive," he said. "That's what all the reports said. That man was really the US Marshal who had helped set up my new identity."

"People didn't realize he was missing?" she asked.

"He went through the hotshot training with me as my protection. That's why he was on the plane, too, because everybody knew about the hit out on my life," he said. "And after the crash, his presence on the plane was kept quiet. Most people probably believed he'd taken money for killing me and that he'd retired on some Caribbean island."

"But there was coverage of the survivors," she said. "I dug up old articles and news coverage, although you and Ethan both looked pretty worse for wear…" She narrowed her eyes as she studied his face. "And you both did a pretty damn good job of not looking directly at the cameras."

He shrugged. "It wouldn't have mattered. Mario was the disguise. Dark wig, dark contacts, dark beard… I didn't have to wear a disguise for Rory."

"So this is how you really look?"

He shrugged. "Pretty much. I used to wear my hair longer except when I was in the Marines." He rubbed his hand over his short, spiky hair and felt that ridge of a scar beneath it in the back. Where he'd taken that blow.

Had that been the hotshot saboteur or someone who'd started digging a little deeper into the plane crash after Brittney had brought it all back up again? Could someone have realized what he would have looked like without the Mario disguise? Could someone have figured out who Rory VanDam really was? A wanted man?

She stood up and walked around the cabin then, pacing like she was nervous. Or searching? She glanced at the desk in the corner, at the filing cabinet next to it.

"You want to look for that collection of passports you searched my duffel bag for earlier?" he asked.

"Was that today…?" she murmured. "It seems like so long ago."

So long since he'd kissed and held her and made love with her. It seemed like a lifetime ago now. Like a dream that would probably never be repeated because she didn't believe him.

"I don't have any proof, any identification, anything to show I was ever anyone but Rory VanDam," he said. And no one, not even other US Marshals, had known about that identity. He'd created it himself after Amelia had tried to kill him because he'd known there was no one he could trust.

"But you must have something."

"Why do you want it, Brittney?" he asked. And he stood up then because she wasn't going to find what she was looking for without his help. He'd hidden it too well. But then he'd thought he'd hidden well, too, and someone had figured it out.

Or maybe they hadn't.

Maybe they were just trying to hide their involvement in the plane crash. Because that crash hadn't happened due to pilot error. Rory and the US Marshal had discovered a bomb in the cockpit. If they'd tried to dismantle it, it would have exploded. Not wanting to freak the others out too much, Rory had claimed that the engines were failing and urged everyone to parachute off. The timer had given them long enough for everyone to get clear before the plane exploded. But in the chaos, the US Marshal had urged Rory to go before him.

He wasn't sure even now if the plane had exploded. He hadn't seen it go down, and they hadn't found the wreckage. But maybe that was because the bomb had destroyed everything, leaving nothing left for anyone to find.

Except, if Brittney was being threatened to drop her story about the crash, someone must have been worried that the wreckage and the bomb would be discovered. Maybe that bomb could be traced back to the killer.

Rory had something else that could be traced back to him, too. But that crash had proved to Rory that he couldn't trust anyone. Could he really trust Brittney? Because if he or Brittney put his insurance into the wrong hands, Rory had no hope of ever finding a safe place to hide where he wouldn't be found.

He had no hope of staying alive.

Brittney hadn't answered his question. And it wasn't because she was being petty over how many of her questions he left unanswered. It was because she didn't have an answer herself. Why did she want proof?

Because she wanted to sell the story? Could she do that if it would put him in danger?

But then he was already in danger.

He wasn't acting like it now, though. He was moving around the cabin, working in the small kitchenette area, opening soup cans, thawing bread that had been in the freezer. "There's electricity out here?" she asked.

He shook his head. "Power is solar and wind only, but it's enough to run some small appliances and lights."

"Any way to communicate?" she asked as she pulled his cell from her purse and held it up. There was no signal and the battery was draining fast.

He pointed toward a radio on the desk in the corner of the small log cabin. Besides the door to the outside, there was another that opened into a small bathroom. Then the cabin itself had the big stone fireplace with two plaid easy chairs pulled close to it. That fireplace and a king-size bed dominated the space. But there was also a kitchen table and chairs next to the short row of cabinets.

"Are you hungry?" he asked as he carried the food from a small gas stove to the table.

She nodded and joined him, pulling out the chair across from him. He held out a bottle of wine he'd uncorked. And she nodded again, more heartily. But it didn't matter how much she drank, there wasn't enough alcohol to calm her fears or wash away the nightmares she was bound to have.

The only reason she was still alive was because of Rory. He'd saved her twice now. A third time on the helicopter. If they hadn't gotten away, they would have been shot for certain at that hangar in the woods.

No matter what he called himself, he was a good man. Only a good man would have jumped in front of a speeding SUV to rescue her and into the line of fire to save not just her but the firehouse dog, too.

She took a sip of the red wine, which was just a little sweet and a little dry. Kind of like the man sitting across from her, ladling stew into bowls.

"I trust you," she said.

He pushed the bowl across to her. "I didn't poison the soup or the wine," he assured her, his mouth curving into a slight grin.

"Not just about the food," she said. "I trust you about your story."

"It's so wild that it does sound like something made up," Rory acknowledged. "But I don't have a big enough imagination to make it up."

"You lived it," she said. She'd seen the scars on his body. But the real scars, she suspected, were deeper than his skin. They were on his heart. In his mind…

"And you trusted me with this information," she said, awed that he could trust anyone after what he'd been through. "You trusted me with the truth."

He shuddered a bit as if he was cold. The fire was dying down in the hearth. But then he said, "I didn't think I would ever trust anyone again."

"You didn't even trust your team with the truth or Ethan." And he'd been there with him. "Why me?"

"If it's because of me, because of this story, that you're in danger, you deserve to know the truth," he said.

She realized what he meant, that if she died because of this, she should know why.

Braden hated how often he and his team had had to wait out here, outside the ER room, worrying and wondering about one of their own. Dirk was the only one who hadn't survived. But their luck was bound to run out again.

The more times they had to come here, the greater the odds that another life was going to be lost. Was this time because of that damn saboteur again?

"I'm not going to die," Ethan said as he stepped through the doors from the ER. Tammy was under one of his arms, her arms wrapped around him as if she was, with her slight weight, holding up the giant of a man. Ethan lifted one hand to his head and knocked his fist against his forehead. "Hard as a rock."

"More like full of rocks," Trent Miles said. His teasing him seemed like just a reflex. He was preoccupied, worried about his sister and Rory.

Braden was worried about them, too.

Ethan made his way through the crowd of concerned hotshots to where Braden and Trick stood near Trent. Owen had had to leave for another call. Dawson Hess, the other paramedic-firefighter-hotshot, was with his wife in New York City, so Owen was pulling extra shifts.

"Have you heard from Brittney?" Tammy asked Trent,

Lisa Childs

her voice full of concern for her new friend. Tammy befriended everyone, she had such a big heart. But she also owed Brittney for helping save her life. She had been the one who'd put it in danger, though.

Trent nodded. "She called. She's with Rory."

"Where?" Ethan asked.

Trent shrugged. "She didn't say."

"The island," Trick said. "I checked the hangar. The helicopter is gone." A muscle twitched beneath the reddish stubble on his jaw.

There was more to the story. Braden knew it. Trick had already told him. But he must have been leaving it up to him to share or keep it from the others. Seeing the concern on Trent's and Tammy's and Ethan's faces, he was tempted not to share. But they deserved to know the truth, and they all damn well knew how much danger they were in.

"He found bullet holes in the metal walls of the hangar and spent shells."

Trent sucked in a breath. "So someone was shooting at them."

Trick nodded now. "Looks like it."

Trent cursed.

Tammy reached out and touched his arm. "But you talked to her," she reminded him. "She's safe. She's with Rory."

Trent shook his head. "She's not safe with Rory. Rory isn't Rory." He pointed at Ethan. "Tell them what you told me and Owen."

Ethan touched his head again, but he was holding it instead of knocking on it. While he was going to be all right, he had a concussion. Fortunately, it wasn't as bad as the one Rory had.

Rory hadn't just had that concussion, though. He'd had other scars. He was a man who'd been through a lot.

That plane crash. Ethan shared that Rory blamed himself for it, that he had been the pilot.

Trick nodded. "I knew he was a pilot from how he flies the helicopter."

"And he stepped in on previous wildfires, flying the plane when nobody else was available," Braden added.

"But he was here, in the hospital, when Brittney had her accident with her van," Tammy said. "He didn't hurt her, and I don't think he would."

"He wouldn't hurt any of us," Ethan said.

But one of them had. The saboteur. "We don't know that any of this has to do with that plane crash," Braden said. "Brittney was also investigating the things happening with our team. And someone hit Rory that night. Maybe Rory saw who it was and doesn't realize it. He's been so out of it since he regained consciousness."

But now Braden understood why the man hadn't even recognized his name at first. Because it probably wasn't his real name.

"Brittney was trying to talk to my dad," Trick said. "Maybe he knows what's going on, too. I tried calling him, but he didn't pick up."

Mack was a busy man, but he usually answered for Braden. "I'll try."

Trick chuckled. "You'll probably get more out of him than I could. I think you're his favorite son now."

"Son-in-law," Braden corrected him. "And it's easy to be his favorite since he only has one daughter."

One amazingly strong woman.

"I only have one sister, too," Trent said to Trick. "And I need to do everything that I can to make sure she stays safe. How can we get out to that island tonight?"

"Rory took the helicopter," Trick said. "So next best

would be a boat, but it's dark and the water's rough with some ice chunks in it. It wouldn't be safe to go out until morning."

But from the look on Trent's face, he was afraid that his sister might not make it until morning. With how the attacks on her and Rory had escalated, Braden was worried about the same thing.

That the next hotshot he lost would be Rory...or whatever his name really was.

Chapter 20

The wind howled around the cabin, louder than the coyotes had been howling earlier. It would be too dangerous to try to fly back tonight.

Too dangerous for someone to try to fly out here tonight or even to take a boat. Knowing how protective Trent was of his sister and how worried he was about her, Rory pointed to the radio. "You need to talk to your brother," he said. "Make sure he doesn't try to get out here."

Brittney wrapped her arms around herself and nodded. "It sounds like a storm's coming."

"The storm's been here," Rory said. Ever since she'd done that story about Ethan and the plane crash, the storm had been brewing. Then it had just been a far-off rumble of thunder, a warning of what was to come.

The past.

It had come back to get Rory.

He had to make sure that it wasn't out there now. "I need to make sure the chopper is secure." And that nobody had made their way onto the island already. "But first I'll connect you with the firehouse radio where someone should be able to get patched through to Trent's cell," he said. "And I'll give you some privacy."

Brittney narrowed those pretty topaz eyes and studied his face. "Can I tell Trent what you told me?"

He nodded. "It's fine." It was all going to come out, any-way. Because probably the only way to protect her…was to put himself in even more danger…

Once the truth got out, nobody would have any reason to try to stop Brittney anymore. But him…

He still had that hit out on him. So he'd have to go back into hiding, have to leave this life as Rory VanDam and the people in it behind him because he didn't want any more lives lost because of him. "And tell Trent to sit tight on the mainland," he said. "He can't try to get out here tonight. It's too dangerous."

So was staying here with her…

Staring at her across the table as they'd eaten and drunk wine had had Rory hoping that it wasn't just one night, like the aberration making love with her had been.

A one-off.

A dream.

Something he wouldn't be able to repeat…even if he didn't get killed. If his old enemies didn't come for him, Rory was making new enemies among his team. They wouldn't like that he'd kept the truth from them.

And Trent probably wouldn't accept it as easily as his sister had. Hopefully he wouldn't risk his life trying to get out here, though, trying to get to her.

Now if the killer had…

Maybe it would all be over tonight.

Rory turned on the radio and connected it to the fire-house, then he handed the speaker and headphones to Brittney and walked to the door. When he opened it, cold air and icy rain rushed in, soaking him.

"Rory!" Brittney called to him.

But he ducked his head down and headed out into the storm. It was the lesser threat of all the ones he'd recently faced, like his feelings for Brittney. He didn't just trust her, he was beginning to fall for her.

And he couldn't do that…not when they both had so much to lose: their lives.

The door closed behind Rory, but the cold stayed inside the cabin, chilling Brittney deeply. What if that person who'd been shooting at them had managed to catch up to them somehow?

What if he or she was out there, waiting for Rory? He wasn't armed.

As a former lawman, wouldn't he have a weapon somewhere around? Some kind of gun or taser? Something to protect himself, especially when there was a hit out on his life…

No. On Mario's life.

"Brittney!" Trent's voice crackled through the headphones she'd slipped on.

She pressed the button on the microphone and leaned forward. "Trent."

"Stanley said he patched the call through the radio. Are you on the island with Rory?"

"Yes."

"Sit tight. We're trying to figure out how to get there tonight—"

"No!" she shouted, and her voice echoed in her headphones, making her flinch at the volume. "It's too dangerous."

"Why? What's happened? What has he done?"

"Rory hasn't done anything." But save her, protect her, feed her and make love to her.

She sucked in a breath as she realized she was falling

for him. And she had only his word that he was who and what he said he was.

What if she was wrong to trust him?

What if he was lying to her?

But why?

Unless he had been the one responsible for the crash.

"Rory's not even his real name," Trent reminded her.

"No, it's not," she agreed.

"He admitted that to you?"

"Yes, he told me all about his past, and the plane crash," she said.

The headphones crackled. Brittney didn't know if that was just static on the line or her brother trying to talk to her. "What?" she asked. "Are you there?"

"Yeah, I'm waiting for you to tell me what he told you," Trent said.

And Brittney hesitated. Dare she share Rory's secrets?

"Maybe it's better that you don't know," she admitted. For Trent's sake, but mostly for Rory's.

Trent groaned. "If it's that bad, you shouldn't know, either."

"Rory is not the bad guy," Brittney insisted. "But there are some dangerous people after him." She didn't want her brother to be one of them.

"You need to get away from him," Trent said. "Now."

The wind howled so loudly that the windows rattled. Then sleet slashed across the glass. Rory shouldn't have gone out in this, not even to secure the helicopter.

Was that all he was doing?

Or had he taken off and left her here?

"Rory won't hurt me," she said, but she felt a pang in her heart even as she made the claim. He wouldn't hurt her physically, but if he'd taken off, even with the intent of keeping her safe, she was going to be hurt.

He'd already left her once, at the hotel.

And this time they hadn't even made love first.

"The weather's bad, Trent. Don't do anything stupid," she said.

Instead of being offended, he chuckled. "I'm not used to you talking to me like this…"

"Like I'm the calm sensible one and you're…"

"You," he teased.

She wasn't calm and sensible, either. She was scared to death. Not of what she'd learned or even of that killer.

She was scared that something had happened to Rory. He'd been gone for a while. Maybe she needed to go and look for him…

Make sure he hadn't fallen on the rock when he'd gone back up to the helicopter. Or that the killer wasn't out there, that he or she hadn't hurt Rory or worse…

"I need to go, Trent," she said.

"Brittney! You can't go anywhere, either."

"I meant off the radio." But she intended to go somewhere, wherever she had to in order to find Rory.

"Brittney, you need to be careful," Trent said in his best big brotherly voice of concern.

"I'm always careful," she said. But even she couldn't say it without smiling.

Trent snorted. "I mean it. I don't like this, any of it."

"Rory's a good guy," she said. But she wondered now if she was trying to convince her brother or herself.

"Even if that's true, that doesn't mean he's good for you," Trent pointed out.

And it was a valid point.

One Brittney chose to ignore as she'd begun to ignore

most of the unsolicited advice she received. "Stay where you are," she told him. "Don't worry about me."

She wasn't sure how to sign off the radio. But she pushed buttons until the headphones stopped crackling and whatever lights had been lit up went dark.

Just like the cabin had begun to do as the fire died down. She needed to find Rory, make sure he was all right. But she didn't even make it across the room to the door before it opened.

The wind swept into the room along with the hard pellets of sleet and rain. Had the door blown open? Because she didn't see anyone.

Then a dark shadow stumbled across the threshold, his arms laden down with wood. Rory's hair and jacket were soaked, some of the ice clinging to his hair and his chafed skin.

Brittney rushed forward and closed the door behind him, shutting out the wind and rain.

"It's getting cold," Rory said. "We're going to need more wood than this…" He dropped his armload near the hearth and headed back toward the door, as if he intended to go back out into the storm.

But Brittney stood in front of the door, her heart hammering. She'd been so scared that something had happened to him. That he wasn't coming back…

"What's wrong?" he asked with concern, and he slid his cold fingertips along her jaw. "Did Trent upset you? Is he coming out here anyway, despite the storm?"

She shrugged. "I don't know. I tried to talk him out of it."

"Did you tell him about me?"

"I told him you're a good man," she said.

He closed his eyes then and leaned forward, pressing

his forehead against hers. "If I was, I wouldn't want you again like I do…" he murmured, his voice gruff with desire.

Her heart hammered even faster and harder. And she reached up to wrap her arms around his neck, to pull his head the rest of the way down to hers.

He kissed her deeply, and she tasted the beef stew and the wine and her desire. It rushed up, overwhelming her with its intensity.

"I was so worried about you out there," she admitted. "Worried that something would happen to you."

He stared down into her face, his pale blue eyes so intense. "You were worried that I wasn't going to come back?"

She nodded.

"Did you think I'd take off and leave you here?"

"If you thought it would keep me safe, you might," she said.

He nodded, and rain droplets sprayed from his hair to her face. He wiped them away like he was wiping away tears. "I might," he agreed. "But I'm not sure either of us will be safe anywhere until…"

"Until what?" she asked. Then she stared up at him. "You have a plan?"

"Yeah."

She should want to hear it, want all the details, but at the moment, she just wanted him. "Tell me later," she said. Then she rose up on tiptoe and kissed him. She reached for his wet flannel jacket. After unbuttoning it, she pushed it from his shoulders. Then she reached for the bottom of his sweatshirt, tugging it up over his washboard stomach.

He was undoing her buttons and zippers, too, pushing down her jeans, pulling off her sweater…until she stood before him in only her bra and panties.

And even that was too much. She wanted nothing between them. So she unclasped her bra and let it drop onto the clothes that littered the hardwood floor around them. And she slid her panties down her hips.

Rory shoved down his jeans and boxers and stepped out of them and his boots, so that he was as naked as she was.

She shivered, a delicious shiver of anticipation for the pleasure she knew he could give her. But he must have mistaken it as cold because he picked her up and carried her to that big bed.

"Get under the covers," he said. "And I'll add more wood to the fire…" As he threw in a couple of logs, sparks hissed and sprayed back at him.

"Don't get burned!" she said with concern.

"I'm a hotshot," he reminded her as he walked to the bed wearing only a slight grin. The firelight played across his skin, turning it gold, making him look like the painting of some mythical god. "I'm used to playing with fire."

"You jumped out of the frying pan of your old career literally into the fire when you chose your new one, your new identity…" When he neared the bed, she reached for his hand, tugging him toward her. "Why?"

"Fires are more predictable than people," he said with a heavy sigh.

"Trent says that they're anything but, that they can shift and turn at a moment's notice."

"But you know they're always capable of great destruction, of harm," he said. "You can't always tell how badly a person might hurt you, but a fire leaves no illusions." He stared down at her intently, as if he suspected that she would hurt him.

She didn't want to. That was why she hadn't told Trent any of the details yet. Maybe not ever…

This would have been the story to make her career, to

take her permanently off the fluff pieces, but if it cost Rory his life, it wasn't worth it. Nothing was worth that...

But everything was worth this...

Making love with him again. Even though she was putting not just her life but her heart in danger, too.

She tugged on his hand again, pulling him down with her, onto her. His body covered hers, naked skin sliding over naked skin.

"I told you to get under the covers," he reminded her.

"I don't need them," she said. "I need you."

He groaned then kissed her, his mouth making love to hers. And as he kissed her, he touched her, sliding his fingertips in light caresses along her side, over the curve of her hip. He pulled back, panting for breath, and said, "You are so beautiful. So sexy..."

He was the sexy one. She touched him like he'd touched her, just gliding her fingertips along his skin. First it was cold, damp, from the sleet and the wind, but it heated as she touched him.

Then she lowered her hand and wrapped it around his erection, and he began to sweat, beads forming on his upper lip.

"You're dangerous, Brittney Townsend," he said. "You can hurt me more than anyone else."

Before she could ask what he meant, he kissed her again. And his hands continued to move over her, caressing her breasts, cupping them.

He brushed his thumbs over her nipples, and she moaned. The tension was winding up inside her, twisting her muscles into knots. Making her desperate for release...

Then he was inside her, filling her, and they moved together like they'd choreographed a dance. She arched and he thrust. Then finally the tension broke, and the orgasm moved through her with such force and pleasure that she had to cling to him.

Then he called out her name as he came, too. And she knew that he was just as dangerous to her as she was to him because she was definitely starting to fall for him.

And she hadn't ever wanted to fall for anyone, let alone someone in a dangerous career, someone she could lose like she'd lost her dad.

Way too soon…

Way before their time and way before she was ready to let them go…

The killer waited inside the SUV, which rocked and shuddered as the wind battered it. Rain and sleet swept across it so thick and fast that the wipers couldn't keep the windshield clear.

And the driver had to peer through the rain and the darkness to see the dock by which they'd parked, waiting for the boat that was supposed to be coming, that would take them to where the reporter and the hotshot must have gone.

That island, which was part of a national forest, was where the hotshot firefighter also worked as a forest ranger. They'd asked around the bar in Northern Lakes about the helicopter and the man who flew it.

Rory VanDam.

The tall, lean blond guy didn't look anything like dark-haired burly Mario Mandretti. But Mario had been a disguise, a cover for the DEA agent. For the former special ops Marine. With the expert flying and that ability to escape death over and over, Rory VanDam had to be Mario.

The killer had been worried about the wrong thing this whole time, that the reporter's quest to delve deeper into the plane crash would have the FAA and the US Forest Service resuming a search for the wreckage. And DNA had been left behind when the bomb had been planted in the plane they'd known Mario would be flying. They just hadn't realized why he'd been flying it, that he'd gone through hotshot training. That he was a hotshot now.

How the hell hadn't *anyone* known that the DEA agent hadn't died? Why the hell had the DEA agent been hiding out here all this time, posing as some hotshot firefighter?

Why hadn't he gone to anyone? Let the authorities know he was alive?

Was it because he'd realized there was no one he could trust? That the people who wanted him dead were just too rich and too powerful to be stopped?

Chapter 21

Rory wanted to stay on the secluded island, in the cozy cabin, in that warm bed with Brittney forever. But he'd realized long ago, with the careers he'd chosen and the enemies he'd made, that forever wasn't possible for him.

Especially now.

The sun was shining. The storm had ended with the break of dawn. While the water was calmer now, there was still ice in it that could make it hard to get a boat to the island. But there had been time for someone to get another helicopter.

So they couldn't stay. They had to leave as quickly as they could before the shooter found them. But Brittney seemed as reluctant to go as he was.

She was making the bed that they'd messed up so many times last night, kicking off the blankets, tangling the sheets…as they made love. His pulse quickened just looking at it, at her, and his body hardened.

He grunted and shook his head. "We have to go, Brittney. Now."

She must have heard the urgency in his voice because she stepped back from the bed and pulled on her jacket and hooked her purse over her shoulder. "Okay…"

But instead of heading toward the door, Rory walked over to the desk in the corner. He didn't open any drawers, though.

What he wanted wasn't inside it. He pulled it back from the wall to reveal a small safe between joists in that wall. His hand shook a bit when he twisted the lock and opened it.

There was a gun inside, his old Glock. It had come in handy while he and Ethan had been stranded those months in the mountains. But he hadn't used it since.

And the other thing. The small USB drive beside it, he hadn't used it at all. And he probably should have.

But in order to use it, he would have had to come out of hiding. He would have had to blow up the life he'd made for himself here in Northern Lakes with his hotshot team.

"You do have a gun," she said.

He nodded. "This will do more damage, though," he said as he handed the USB drive to her.

"What is this?" she asked.

"This is the proof," he replied.

"What?"

"This is a recording of the US Marshal who was with me on the plane. He gave it to me when he gave me a parachute to get off the plane before the bomb we found on it went off. He said it was my *insurance*. This will prove what I told you is true. It's the corroboration you need for that big story you've been chasing," he said. "Even bigger than Jonathan Canterbury IV."

She shook her head. "I don't want it."

"What?"

"The big story," she said. "I don't want to put you in danger because of it. If that family is still paying people to try to kill you, you will be in terrible danger."

"If someone is after you because of that damn plane crash, because of me," he said, "the only way to make you safe is for you to tell the story, the whole story. Then there is no reason for anyone to try to stop you anymore."

"But those people, that family, want revenge on you," she said.

"They don't want revenge on you," he assured her. "You won't have to worry about losing Trent, like you lost your dad."

Tears suddenly filled her eyes, either over the loss of her dad or maybe the thought of losing her brother.

"Nobody will die because of you," he assured her.

"You might," she said, her voice cracking. "If I do this story, those people will know you're alive."

He sighed. "Yeah, they won't like that…" But who were they anymore?

He didn't even know what had become of the Falcone family. Amelia's dad had sworn out the hit on him, the vendetta, but he'd already been pretty old five years ago. That was why he'd had his son take over his business interests.

The drugs. Then after Felix Jr. had died, Felix Sr. had promised the empire to his daughter if she killed Mario. He'd thought she was different than her family, like Rory was different from his.

And just as he'd left his family for the service and never looked back, he hadn't wanted to look back at the Falcone family. He also hadn't wanted to draw any attention to his past, to himself. Until now…

"I think it's already too late for that, Brittney. You need to go with your story." He pointed to the flash drive she held. "With that."

Her brow furrowed as she stared up at him. "I don't understand you…" She shook her head. "You wanted nothing to do with me, with the press…and I understand why that was. But why did it change?"

Because he'd fallen for her.

He couldn't tell her that now, though, not when he was

probably going to have to go into hiding again soon. And she wouldn't be able to hide, not with as famous as she was becoming. She was on the verge of the career she wanted, that she deserved. He couldn't take any of that away from her.

"Somebody's trying to kill us," he reminded her. "That's why everything changed, and it's why we have to get the hell out of here."

This time, he didn't wait for her to move. After tucking the gun into the waistband of his jeans, he grabbed her hand and urged her toward the door. As they headed up the path to the rock and the helicopter, he heard another motor.

Someone was coming.

"We have to hurry," he said. If they didn't get away with that tape, Brittney would never get her story. Nobody would probably ever learn the truth about what had happened.

But he wasn't sure that he knew the whole truth now. Maybe there was more going on than he'd even realized. Because was it really some minions for the Falcone family that were after them both?

The threats to Brittney and the blow to his head. Or had the saboteur been responsible for some of the things?

Brittney had been on edge ever since they'd left Bear Isle. He had proof. And he'd given it to her.

The responsibility of it weighed on her, making her bag heavier as she'd carried it from the helicopter to his truck. The entire flight, the entire drive…they'd both been so on edge, so certain that another attack was about to come.

Someone shooting at them.

Who?

Would she find out from playing that flash drive?

"You can play it," Rory said. Somehow, he'd known exactly what she was thinking. But they'd already pulled up to the firehouse.

Other trucks and vehicles were parked in the lot. A lot of the team must have been there. The side door opened and Trent walked out, Trick close beside him. Trick hit his shoulder and looked up, meeting her gaze through the windshield.

"Play it," Rory said.

But Trent was opening her door, pulling her from the passenger's seat into his arms. "Oh, my God, thank God you're all right," he said, his voice gruff with emotion. "I was so afraid I was going to lose you."

"I'm right here," she assured him as she pulled back. His weren't the arms she wanted around her, comforting her, holding her.

But Trent didn't give her a chance to reach for Rory again. Nor did Trick. He was standing by the driver's side. "Braden talked to my dad."

Rory's breath had a catch in it. "Your dad is a good man."

"Mack knew you were more than you were saying you were," Trick said. "He knew because you know my brother Mack. My brother vouched for you with my dad."

Rory's lips curved into a slight grin. "Mack…"

And Brittney didn't know which one had brought out that affectionate smile, the father or the son who were both apparently named Mack.

Trick continued, "My dad said that he kept quiet because Mack told him you had your reasons, whatever they were, for laying low."

Rory turned toward her again. "Play them that recording. That's what's on the drive."

"Recording?" Trent asked.

Brittney pulled the flash drive from her purse with a

shaking hand. "This. His proof… But I need something to put it in."

"Let's use the computer in Braden's office," Trick said. "Let's play it there."

Brittney got swept up between the big red-haired hot-shot and her big dark-haired brother. They hurried her toward the firehouse, as if worried that someone might shoot at her again, and once inside, they rushed her to Braden's windowless office. He glanced up from his desk then widened his eyes and released a ragged sigh of relief.

"Thank God you're all right."

She smiled. "I never expected you to be happy to see me."

Braden chuckled. "Well, I am, very happy that you're all right."

Trent, with his arm wound around her, tugged her closer. "Me, too."

"You're not too embarrassed to claim me now," she murmured.

He hugged her now with both arms. "I'm really sorry, Brittney. Very sorry that I've given you a hard time."

"Not just me," she said. But she couldn't see around her brother to Rory. All she could do was grant his wish. She pulled back from Trent and held out the flash drive to Braden. "We need to play the recording on this."

Braden took it from her hand and pushed it into the side of his desktop. Then he pressed his fingers on the keyboard. "There's just one file on this. An audio file."

Her stomach flipped and dropped. Did she want to hear this? Did she want to know everything about Rory?

"Why do you want to play this?" he asked.

"It's proof." Trick was the one who said it now, not Rory.

She glanced back over her shoulder. But he must have been standing behind Trick. She couldn't see him.

"Proof of what?" Braden asked, but instead of waiting for an answer, he pressed a key and a voice emanated from the speaker on his computer.

"Your DEA agent crossed the wrong family," a male voice was saying. "Felix Falcone is not going to forgive or forget that this Mario whatever cost him his son and his daughter."

"She tried to kill him," another male voice remarked. "She would have if I hadn't been there."

"It wasn't supposed to be you there."

The man gasped. "Who was it supposed to be?"

"Me. I've been paid for this job. To make sure that Mario dies."

"You're a federal agent…"

Brittney held her breath, waiting for a name. But neither of them used each other's.

The federal agent continued, "You can't help him start over with some new identity."

"Why not?"

"Because you're on Falcone's hit list, too, for killing his daughter. The only way for you to stay alive and keep your family alive is to give him up."

"I don't have any family," the man replied.

"What about your life? Don't you care about that?"

"Sounds like I'm a dead man anyway."

"Be a dead rich man. Start over yourself, someplace warm and far away."

The US Marshal sighed. "Sounds tempting…"

Sounded sickening to Brittney, that the people who were supposed to protect Rory had given him up instead. But the woman who was supposed to have loved him had given him up, too. No. She'd tried to kill him herself.

"He's flying you somewhere, isn't he?" the agent asked.

"Make sure that plane goes down and the pilot with it." He chuckled. "Like the captain going down with his ship."

"Do you recognize those voices?" Brittney asked, and she tried peering around Trent and Trick again. "Rory? Do you recognize those voices?"

Trick and Trent both turned around, but Rory wasn't there. He'd slipped away. To go where?

Then she remembered what she'd heard as they'd headed up to the helicopter. The other motor.

But that hadn't been Trent heading toward the island. He was here. So who was there?

"We have to stop him," she said, and she tried to get around Trent to head out the door, too. But her brother held on to her arms, keeping her between him and his boss's desk. "He's going back."

"Back where?" Trent asked. "To his old life?"

She shook her head. "Back to the island. Someone was heading there when we were leaving. It was probably that person who's been shooting at us, trying to stop us."

"The US Marshal or the agent?" Trick asked from behind her brother.

"I think the Marshal died in the plane crash. There was a bomb in the cockpit, and he made Rory and the others parachute out. Before he did, he gave that recording to Rory, maybe so he would know not to trust anyone."

"What do we do with it?" Braden asked. "If we hand it over to the authorities, we risk this agent getting it or destroying it."

Brittney turned around and reached for the USB drive, pulling it out of Braden's computer. "I know what to do."

"This isn't just some story," Trent said. "This is Rory's life."

"Yes, it is, so go after him!" she said. "Don't let him face that killer alone!" She wanted to go, too, but she knew that since her brother wouldn't even let her out the door there was no way he would let her go back to that island, back to danger.

To the danger that Rory was facing alone.

He had a gun. But did it even work anymore? Would he be able to save himself like he had her so many times? Or was he determined to go back and confront the person in order to protect her once and for all?

FBI agent Barry Shelton had a trace on Felix Falcone's landline. But he'd had to get far enough away from the damn island before he got enough reception on his phone to play the call that had come in.

"Falcone? Felix?" a familiar voice said.

"Uh, yeah, this is Felix," the old man replied, his voice weak.

He was weak now. But he still paid. He had no power anymore, but he had money. And nobody to give it to…

"Felix, this is Mario," the former DEA agent told him.

"Mario?"

"Yes, Mario Mandretti," he said. "Do you remember me?"

"Uh, I… I don't know…"

"I was a friend of your son Felix's, and I was close to Amelia, too," he said.

"Felix?" Felix asked, and his voice was muffled, as if he was calling out for him. He chuckled. "I don't know where that boy is off to. Probably down at the basketball courts. And Amelia… She'll be playing with her dolls…"

"Yes," the man replied. "Yes, she will be."

"What's your name again?" Felix asked.

"Mario."

"I don't remember you," he said.

"What about any federal agents?" the man asked. "Do you remember them? Paying them?"

"Paid a lot of them…paid a lot of them…but I don't remember why…"

"I know," the man calling himself Mario again assured him. "I know why, and I know who. I have a recording of his voice. You don't have to pay him any more money, Felix. He didn't earn it."

Barry cursed. A recording.

He'd figured the Marshal might have recorded him. Barry hadn't trusted him. That was why he'd followed him and figured out he was getting on that plane with Mario. So, while they were at that training center in Washington, Barry had planted the bomb in the cockpit of the plane. He'd watched Mario inspect it, and then when he'd gone back inside the building, Barry had acted fast, planting the bomb he'd brought along.

But he'd had to move so fast, he wasn't sure it was going to work. Or what evidence he might have left behind. But when he'd heard about the crash, he'd figured his plan had played out how he'd intended. But the pilot hadn't gone down with the plane.

He was alive.

He was Rory VanDam.

And he had evidence.

It should be gone now, though. If it had been on the island, it would be gone soon.

Unless…

Unless Rory VanDam had already done something with it…

Had already given it to someone?

That reporter. She hadn't dropped the damn story. After she'd run the first story about Jonathan Canterbury, Barry had tapped her phone line. He knew what calls she'd been making, who she'd been trying to contact and question. And she hadn't stopped reaching out, trying to follow up and find out more about the crash.

If she'd gotten that damn recording…

Barry had to do whatever he could to get that recording back. He'd made too much money, but he'd also advanced too far in his career to give it all up for somebody who should have died five years ago.

Chapter 22

Rory figured the FBI probably still had a tap on Falcone's line. When he'd gone undercover with the DEA, they'd coordinated with the FBI on the investigation.

After talking to the man, who obviously had dementia or Alzheimer's disease, Rory wasn't sure if his calls were still being monitored. But just in case, he'd made certain to mention the recording. But would his plan work how he wanted it to?

Would it flush out the killer toward him or toward…?

Rory sucked in a breath as he realized what he might have done. And his hand slipped a bit on the control of the helicopter, making it dip toward the lake below. Through the windows, he could see the smoke.

The son of a bitch had set the island on fire.

And that had been even before he would have heard that wiretap, if there was even still a tap on the line. The son of a bitch had set Rory's sanctuary on fire.

His heart ached for the animals and the cabin and all the trees and nature. Then he noticed through the window that a boat was heading toward the island.

A US Forest Service boat. His team members were heading out there. They would save what they could.

And Rory had a feeling, since that other boat was already gone, that he had someone he needed to save, too. If he wasn't already too late.

If he hadn't just made a horrible mistake by baiting a murderer...

Brittney was supposed to lock herself into Braden's office and open the door to nobody until Heather got there or the hotshots got back from the island. That was the order that Trent had given her before he left with his crew.

But she'd had things to do.

A promise to keep to Rory.

She should have made him make her a promise, as well. A promise to stay alive.

Where the hell had he gone?

Straight to danger? Or maybe he'd taken off entirely, knowing that his secret was soon to be revealed. It was what he wanted, she reminded herself, as she wrapped up and sent off not just the audio file of the recording but also a video of her coverage of it.

She wasn't sure if her station would play it. But she knew somebody who would. And she didn't even care if she took all the credit for it. Avery Kincaid had done the first story about the hotshots back when the Northern Lakes arsonist had been terrorizing them and the town. Avery had once worked out of the news station in Detroit where Brittney worked. But after that story, Avery had been offered a job in New York City and had moved there. She was Brittney's idol, who Brittney wanted to be. Career-wise.

Maybe even personal-wise.

Avery had married one of the hotshots. Dawson Hess. Not that Brittney intended to marry a hotshot. She just wanted to make sure that a certain endangered one of them stayed alive. And because Avery knew the hotshots well,

Brittney trusted her to do the right thing with the recording and the video she'd sent her. The video she'd taken outside Braden's office but still inside the firehouse, in the conference room on the third floor in front of the podium the superintendent used for hotshot meetings.

While waiting for the large file to finish sending, Brittney walked over to the windows and peered down at the street below. A black vehicle pulled up outside the firehouse. A long black SUV.

A chill rushed over her.

Then a man stepped out of the driver's door. His hair was salt-and-pepper, and he wore dark shades. He just had that look…that federal agent look to him.

Her pulse quickened. Was this the guy who'd tried running her down? Who had shot at her?

She rushed to the door of the conference room, intent on locking it to keep out the federal agent. But then she heard Annie's bark echo up the stairwell from below.

Annie and Stanley were down there, in the garage area. Stanley was polishing the trucks. Maybe the guy wouldn't hurt him. It wasn't as if Stanley understood anything that was going on, he just knew that people he cared about were frequently in danger.

But then he worked in a firehouse, so everyone he worked with put themselves in danger. Stanley hadn't signed up for that job, though. He was just a sweet kid.

A kid that Brittney needed to protect. But how…?

Maybe she was overreacting, maybe this person driving that black SUV wasn't the same one who'd tried running her down, who'd shot at her and Rory.

She slipped out of the conference room and started down the stairs to the ground floor.

Annie's bark got more frantic, and then she growled.

This person was a stranger to her, unlike the person who'd attacked Rory the night of the holiday party. So maybe there had always been two different threats to them.

"I'm sorry," Stanley said, and his voice sounded strained, as if he was wrestling with Annie. "She usually likes everybody."

"I'm not really a dog person," a man replied. And his voice sent a chill running down Brittney's spine. She recognized it all too well from that recording.

She hadn't been paranoid to think he might be that FBI agent—she'd been right. And now she had no idea what to do...

"If you're here to talk to Braden or any of the hotshots, they're not here," Stanley said. "They probably won't be back for a couple of hours."

And Brittney nearly groaned. The teenager had inadvertently let the man know exactly how much time he had before he might be caught. Because she was absolutely certain that he intended to commit a crime...

Especially when he asked, "What about Brittney Townsend, the reporter. Is she here?"

"Uh..."

Annie barked louder, as if the dog knew Stanley shouldn't answer this man's questions.

"She's supposed to be locked inside Braden's office," Stanley said.

The kid was sweet, too sweet to realize that he shouldn't always tell the truth, especially to strangers.

"Why would she be locked up like that?" the man asked with amusement in his voice.

"She's in danger," Stanley replied. "Somebody's been trying to hurt her."

"Why?" the man asked. "Has she been putting her nose where it doesn't belong?"

Had he seen her shadow on the stairs? Did he realize that she was standing there, listening?

Stanley chuckled. "That's what some of the guys say. Rory used to say it the most…"

"I bet he did," the man remarked.

"But now he seems to like her…" Stanley muttered as if he was confused about Rory's turnaround.

Brittney was, too. Had Rory developed feelings for her? Feelings like she had for him?

Where was he?

Had he gone back to the island?

Or was he around here somewhere? Ready to rush to her rescue again?

She couldn't count on that, though. She had to figure out how to save herself and Stanley and Annie, too.

"If he liked her, he wouldn't have let her keep pursuing her story, and he certainly wouldn't have given her what I think he gave her…"

"I… I don't know what he gave her," Stanley stammered. "I… I don't know anything…"

But from the fearful crack in his voice, Brittney knew that he'd figured out that the man he was talking to was not a good man. Annie had already figured it out because she kept barking and growling.

"Shut up that dog!" the man yelled. "Or I will!"

"Annie," Stanley whined at the dog.

And Brittney could hear the struggle between the kid and the animal. He was trying to hold on to her leash. He was getting out of breath, and Annie's nails were clawing against the concrete as she tried to drag him closer to the man.

They needed to get farther away. Out of the line of fire…

Out of the damn firehouse…

Brittney edged down a few more steps until she could peek into the garage area. The big doors were closed, and the man stood between Stanley and the side door he'd entered. It was closed now.

They were all shut inside with this man unless Brittney could figure out how the overhead doors opened. If it was possible there would be witnesses, the agent wouldn't try to hurt Stanley or Annie.

But as she peered around, she saw that the controls were on the other side of the garage. Not far from where Stanley stood. If only she could catch his attention…

But he was focused on his dog, on trying to pull her back from the man. Brittney had caught someone's attention, though, as the man stared up at her. Then he drew his weapon and pointed it, not at her, but at the kid. "You know why I'm here," he said. "So hand it over."

"How…" Her voice cracked. "How do you know about that?"

He smirked. "How do you think?"

Her pulse quickened even more, and she hurried down the last of the steps to join them in the garage area. "Rory told you? What did you do to him?" She wanted to hit him, to shove him back, to shout at him for hurting Rory. Because surely he would have had to hurt him to get him to say so much…

The man chuckled and nodded. "Uh-huh, I was right."

Brittney swore. He'd tricked her into confirming his suspicion. He hadn't known for certain that she had the recording until she'd just admitted it. This was a trick that, as a reporter, she knew and shouldn't have fallen for herself.

"Hand it over," the man said.

She lifted her empty hands. "I don't have it."

He pointed the gun barrel at Stanley, and she edged between it and the kid. Annie jumped on the back of her legs, nearly knocking her down. She turned and pushed the dog back along with Stanley, trying to steer them behind one of the engines, out of the line of fire. And as she shoved, she looked at those controls for the overhead doors, hoping that Stanley would notice what she was looking at...

That he would understand what she needed him to do.

"Get that dog under control or I will shoot it right now!" the man shouted.

And Stanley pulled harder on Annie's leash, pulling her behind the engine.

Some of the tension eased from Brittney. She didn't want them getting hurt. She didn't want anyone getting hurt but this man.

"You damn well have that recording!" he yelled at her. "And you need to hand it over or I will shoot you right in the head. And I'll kill that kid and the dog, too."

"Then you won't find the recording," Brittney said. "I hid it." In plain sight on the third floor, but hopefully he wouldn't make it that far.

At least not before the recording and the video file finished sending to Avery Kincaid.

"You're going to get it now," he said. "And bring it back down here or I'll shoot the kid and the dog."

"You're going to shoot us all anyway," Brittney said. "We've all seen your face. I know you have no intention of letting us live."

Stanley let out a little cry of fear, and Brittney glanced at him to see tears in his eyes. She tried to make eye contact with him before she looked at the controls again. *Please, Stanley, open those damn doors...*

If only he could read her damn mind...

The agent laughed. "You're not wrong, Ms. Townsend. I am going to kill you all. I guess it just matters how you want to die. Slowly and painfully or quick and relatively painless."

She snorted. "I don't want to die at all." And she certainly didn't want Stanley's young life cut short. If only he would move toward those damn doors...

"Get that recording," the guy threatened.

She shook her head. "It's too late anyway."

"What do you mean?" he asked, his body tensing.

"You don't think I would share that kind of bombshell recording the minute I received it? You don't think I got that out to as many news sources as possible to pick it up and run with it?" she asked. "Your voice is going to be played on every news program at every station in the country. It's over for you, Agent. It's all over."

He lowered his brow a bit. "You don't know my name. It's not mentioned on that recording?"

"You don't think someone will recognize that voice as yours?" she asked. "I recognized it the minute I heard you talking to Stanley. You don't think it can be voice matched to yours? That your coworkers and the US Marshals won't start pulling your financials and figure out that you took money to carry out a hit on a DEA agent?" She laughed and shook her head. "Then you're not as smart as you think you are."

"Neither are you, Ms. Townsend," he said. "Because you just pointed out to me that I have nothing to lose. I might as well just kill you and the kid right now." And he raised the gun and moved his finger toward the trigger.

Brittney moved, shoving Stanley and Annie farther back behind the engine as the first shot rang out.

Chapter 23

He was too late. Rory had known it the minute he'd seen the black SUV parked outside the firehouse. And he'd made a horrible mistake on that phone call.

He'd thought mentioning the recording would get the agent to come out in the open, to come after him, or at least get him to leave Northern Lakes, to leave the whole damn country for one with no extradition. Then Brittney would be safe.

But he should have known that the guy was smart. Or he wouldn't have gotten away with his crimes for as long as he had. So the guy had figured out to whom Rory would have given that recording.

The reporter.

Brittney.

And somehow he'd figured out she was here, at the firehouse. Or maybe he'd just wound up here after checking the hotel and other places in town.

Rory had snuck up to the firehouse, to that side door, since none of the big ones were open. But when he touched the knob, it didn't turn. It was locked. He doubted Stanley had remembered to do that since he rarely did.

And the kid was here. His car was in the parking lot.

And Annie was here. Rory could hear her barking.

She sounded ferocious for once. But underneath that

ferociousness was an element of fear, too. Fear probably more for her people than for herself.

Annie was a protector.

And for years, Rory had been, too. But he hadn't done everything he could have the past five years to protect people. He should have tried to figure out who the hell this agent was earlier. He should have made sure he would never hurt anyone else again.

Rory pulled his keys from his back pocket. Thank God he had one to the firehouse. All the hotshots did. He slid it into the lock now and slowly and softly pushed open the door a bit.

Annie barked louder, but she didn't give him up. Maybe she hadn't even noticed him. She was focused on the man with the gun.

But Brittney stood between that man and the teenager and the dog. She had made certain that barrel was pointed at her, not the kid.

And Rory's heart swelled with more love for her. She was so damn brave. So strong. So smart.

He listened as she tried to talk to the agent, as she tried to buy more time for her and Stanley and Annie. Had she really done with the recording what she'd claimed?

Was it really all over for the agent?

He must have thought so because he flicked off the safety and began to squeeze the trigger. And Rory squeezed his, firing off a shot.

He got the guy in the arm, spinning him around...toward Rory. But when Rory fired again, there was just a click, as either the gun jammed or it was out of ammo.

He hadn't checked it when he'd grabbed it out of the safe. He hadn't checked it once during the nearly five years it had been locked inside the safe because he hadn't wanted anything more to do with guns. He'd wanted to leave that life and that violence behind him and just be Rory Van-Dam, a hotshot firefighter.

But he'd always known that it would catch up to him someday. He'd just hoped that nobody else would get hurt because of him.

"It really is you," the agent murmured as he stared at him. "These past five years, I thought for sure you were dead, just like Mitchell."

"I'm not dead," Rory said. "You didn't kill me the first time you tried, but you killed some other people, some innocent people."

"You think Marshall Mitchell was innocent?" The FBI agent snorted. "He was willing to take bribes. He was willing to kill."

"He only said that because he was setting you up, getting you on that recording," Rory said. "He was going to deal with you once he got me safely established in my new life."

The agent snorted again, then grimaced as he moved his shoulder. But he grasped his gun tightly in his other hand, the barrel pointed at Rory now.

Not Stanley and Brittney…

But had they been hit?

Rory couldn't even see them now. They were behind one of the engines. And all he could hear was Annie whining…

Had the dog been hurt?

Or was she whining because one of the humans with her had been hit?

"He recorded me to get more money out of me," the agent replied. "He probably wanted a bigger cut."

Rory shook his head. "Not everyone is as greedy as you are…"

The agent laughed. "God, you're an idiot. Everybody

has a price. Money. Or fame. With this reporter here…"
He gestured behind him with the gun, but at least he wasn't
pointing at her any longer. But maybe that was because she
wasn't moving…

His heart hammered with fear that she'd already been
hit. That she was lying there bleeding…

Needing help.

Rory had to help her.

"She couldn't wait to send that recording out everywhere," the agent continued. "She used it, used you, just
for her career."

A little jab of pain and doubt struck Rory's heart. Was
the agent right? Had Brittney been using him for her career just like Amelia?

While Brittney's job meant a lot to her, people meant a
lot to her, as well. Her brother…

And even though she didn't know him, she'd put herself
between Stanley and that gun. She'd been doing her best
to protect him and his dog.

The dog continued to whine.

"You're wrong about Mitchell," he said, just trying
to stall for time now. While he couldn't fire his weapon,
maybe he could find one close enough in the garage that
he could use. Like a wrench or an axe. "Why do you think
he didn't tell you my new identity?"

"It doesn't matter," the agent said. "He died. He's gone.
And soon you will be, too."

"Why?" Rory asked. "Felix Falcone doesn't even know
who I am let alone want me dead anymore. He's senile. He
doesn't even know his kids are dead let alone want to
avenge their deaths. You don't need to do this. To do any
of this…"

The agent glanced at his bleeding shoulder and shook

his head. "It's too late now. Too late. She already sent the recording. It's all over, and I'm not going down alone. I'm taking everyone with me that I can."

And he pointed that gun directly at Rory's heart.

Brittney was hurt. But it was more her heart than her body. She would probably have bruises from how hard she'd hit the concrete when she'd pushed Stanley and Annie back and flung herself behind that truck.

The bullet the agent had fired had struck the rear bumper of the rig and bounced back. But another gun had fired, too, the shot echoing so loudly in the garage that it had scared Annie. And Stanley...

While the dog whined, the teenager cried. With his eyes closed, he couldn't see the gestures Brittney was making at him. So she crawled closer, while the two men talked, and she whispered in Stanley's ear.

And finally he opened his eyes and met her gaze. There was fear in his brown eyes but also resolve. He knew what he had to do.

She listened to the men's conversation, waiting for that moment, that distraction that would give Stanley time to get to the controls and get him and Annie out of the garage. And she heard what the agent said about her using Rory just for fame, for her career.

Would he believe that?

Would he think that was all she'd wanted from him, to further her career?

Or would he know that she'd fallen for him?

She didn't dare speak out now. It was better to be as quiet as they could be, so that the agent would forget about them for now. But he hadn't because he said even more, that because she'd sent that recording out nothing mattered anymore.

And she knew in that moment that he was going to kill Rory.

She nodded at Stanley, who moved surprisingly fast toward those controls. He smacked all the buttons, sending the doors up, the motors grinding.

But over that noise, she could hear the gunshots. The bullets pinging off the metal. She hoped that Stanley had followed through with the rest of her plan, that he and Annie had gotten out through one of those big doors.

That they were safe at least. Because she could hear shoes scraping on concrete, could see feet moving toward her. And she knew that she wasn't safe.

And Rory…

She was so damn scared that he'd been hit or worse. That he was dead…

For real this time.

Trent was exhausted from sleepless nights and worrying and that damn futile trip out to the island. He'd seen the helicopter. Rory hadn't even landed. Maybe he hadn't been able to because of the smoke and the flames.

Or maybe he'd realized what Trent had…that Rory's would-be killer wasn't there any longer. He must have set the fire and taken off.

For where?

Northern Lakes.

Brittney was there. Heather on her way. Two of the people he loved most in the world. Two of the smartest, most resourceful people he knew. Surely, they would be all right.

And yet he had this sick feeling, this chill that he couldn't get rid of. He made his team leave early and head back.

And nobody had argued with him, as if they'd all realized what he had.

That something wasn't right.

That people they cared about were still in danger, and it wasn't just Brittney and Heather, but Rory, too. He was the one the killer wanted dead the most, the one he thought he'd killed years ago.

Until Brittney had started digging up the past, pursuing a story that the agent hadn't wanted anyone to pursue.

The closer they got to Northern Lakes, the more anxious everyone got. Braden and Trick kept checking their phones.

Trent checked his, too.

He had no messages from Brittney. But then he wasn't even sure she had her phone or if she'd left it in that hotel room when the killer had been coming for her.

When he'd hurt Ethan…

Ethan was back in Northern Lakes, too, but he was supposed to be resting. Tammy had promised that she'd take care of him, that she would make sure nobody hurt him, including himself.

He smiled a bit at how his friend had met his match in the salon owner. And Trent had met his match, as well, with Detective Heather Bolton.

A text came in from her:

I'm here, heading to the firehouse

She'd sent it several minutes ago, but it probably hadn't come through until the boat had gotten closer to land and cell reception.

He wasn't the only one who'd gotten a message. Trick was staring at his phone and murmured, "I'll be damned…"

"What?" Braden asked.

Hopefully it wasn't something from Trick's significant other. Henrietta "Hank" Rowlins was a hotshot, too, but she and Michaela had been busy at their firehouse up in St. Paul, nearly an hour north of Northern Lakes. Hopefully they were safe.

"I think Mack's in town," Trick remarked.

"Your dad?" Braden asked.

Trick shook his head. "My brother…" There was awe and surprise in his voice, like he couldn't believe it, like he hadn't expected to see him.

Maybe his relationship with that sibling was strained or strange. Trent's relationship with his only sibling had been strained, too. He'd been so angry with her for investigating his team, for running that article about them and Ethan and that damn plane crash.

He'd barely spoken to her lately. And when his life had been threatened, he'd pushed her away instead of pulling her closer. He'd thought he was doing the right thing, protecting her.

Just like she'd tried protecting him when she hadn't told him about those threats. She hadn't even told him about that creepy producer of hers.

That was his fault, that she hadn't trusted him to respect her, to protect her without trying to smother or control her. Not that she'd ever listened to him…

So no doubt she hadn't locked herself in Braden's office like he'd ordered her to do.

As the boat pulled up to the dock, Trent jumped off before even tying it off. He needed to get back to the firehouse, to make sure Brittney was okay.

To find out where the hell Rory was…

And Heather…

Braden and Trick caught up to him, running alongside

him as they rushed toward Braden's truck. They'd ridden with the hotshot superintendent to the dock.

Braden clicked the locks, and they all jumped into the vehicle. The boss must have felt his urgency because he drove fast, making the trip to town and to the firehouse in record speed.

But the lights that flashed weren't behind them. No officer followed him. They were already at the firehouse. Lights flashed on police cars and an ambulance. And parked alongside one of the curbs was that black SUV that had nearly run down his sister that night, that would have if not for Rory rescuing her.

Trent had been right to be worried. Something bad had definitely happened here. Had he lost anyone he loved? Everyone he loved?

Chapter 24

Rory felt like he was in that coma again. He was caught somewhere between consciousness and sleep. And Ethan was right. He could hear voices around him.

"I'm so sorry, Trent," a female voice was saying. It wasn't Brittney's, though. It was huskier. Heather. The detective. "I got here too late."

Too late?

Too late for what? Was Brittney okay? Had she been shot like he'd feared? Then he'd been too late, too. He hadn't saved her at all.

Where was she?

He dragged his eyes open and peered around. He could see concrete and people's shoes. He was on the ground. He reached out, trying to shove himself up. "Brittney…" he murmured.

Big hands caught his shoulders, holding him down. "Take it easy," Owen said. "You've been hurt."

"Me?" He shook his head. "Brittney…"

Where was she?

He had to find her. She had to be here somewhere.

He turned his head and noticed what he'd missed before. The sheet. There was a sheet lying over someone. Blood stained it. He couldn't see who was under it.

The sheet covered the face of the person. Whoever it was hadn't survived.

"Brittney…" He coughed and gasped for breath as fear and grief overwhelmed him.

"You're aspirating, man. You've got to stop fighting me. Let me treat you."

"Help her…" he murmured, but he could see that it was already too late. Brittney was gone.

Fury coursed through Brittney. She'd never wanted to assault an officer before, not until Trooper Wells insisted on interrogating her instead of letting her go back inside the firehouse to check on Rory.

Was he going to make it?

How badly had he been hurt?

Those were the only questions she cared about, not the ones Trooper Wells was asking her. "Did you see the shooter?"

"What shooter? I saw that agent. He shot at me and Stanley and—" her voice cracked with fear and dread "—and he shot Rory. I need to check on Rory." She tried to step around the woman, but she'd trapped her between her body and the side of her state police SUV. She'd acted like she was going to put Brittney in the back seat and arrest her.

For what?

For trying to see the man she loved? The man who might be dying on that firehouse floor.

The blood had been spreading across his shirt when she'd scrambled over to him. And she'd tried stopping it with her hands, tried helping him. But then other people had rushed in. The police. Owen and another paramedic.

And she'd been pushed and pulled aside, taken away from him. And now he was being taken away from her.

Over the trooper's shoulder, she saw Owen and that other paramedic carrying him toward the open doors of the ambulance.

"They're taking him away," she said. "I have to go!"

"I need to get your statement while everything's fresh in your mind," the trooper insisted.

Was this how people felt about her when she kept firing questions at them that they had no time or inclination to answer?

"I need Rory!" she cried.

But the ambulance didn't wait for her. It sped off, lights flashing and siren wailing. Rory was alive, but they obviously needed to get him to the hospital fast.

And that was how Brittney needed to get there, too.

"Please," she said, her voice cracking with a sob now. "I need to see how he is."

"You can't do anything for him," Wells said. "He's getting the help he needs."

Was she implying that he didn't need Brittney?

Maybe he didn't. All she'd done was turn his world upside down. But it didn't matter if she couldn't help him medically, she still needed to be there for him emotionally.

"I need to be with him," Brittney insisted.

And the woman just stared at her.

And Brittney's fury turned to pity. She understood now why Wynona Wells didn't understand her. "You've obviously never been in love."

Brittney could have said the same for herself until recently. But even before that, she'd known what love was like from watching the people she loved. Her mother and her father had loved each other so much. And her mom and her stepdad…

And Trent and Heather.

They walked up to her now. "You've asked enough questions already, Wells," Heather told the other law officer. "Brittney needs to be checked out, too."

"She hasn't been shot."

Trent pointed toward the torn sleeve of her shirt and her jeans. "She's been roughed up." And his voice was rough with emotion when he said it. "She needs to be checked out at the hospital."

She shook her head. "I need to make sure that Rory is all right."

"I have questions about him, too," Wells persisted. "I don't understand what's been going on here."

Heather snorted. "You're not alone in that, Trooper, but we'll figure it out. Right now, we need to get Brittney to the hospital."

Heather was smart. She knew Brittney wasn't hurt badly, but she must have figured she needed to be at the hospital for another reason. For Rory.

But was Heather's urgency an indication that his condition wasn't good? That he might not make it…?

Tears sprang to her eyes, blinding her. But Trent wrapped his arm around her, guiding her toward Heather's vehicle. And Heather, ever the law officer, put her hand on the top of her head as she helped her into the back seat. Brittney could have felt like a perp again, like Wells had made her feel, but there was affection and understanding in Heather.

She knew how upset Brittney was because she was in love. She understood. Brittney needed to be with Rory for however long he had left.

Braden's firehouse was a crime scene. Again.

Blood spattered the concrete and the side of one of the rigs. Lives had been lost.

At least one...

He wasn't sure about Rory. He'd regained consciousness for a minute, but then he'd lost it and his ability to breathe on his own.

Owen had done something with a long needle and rushed him to the hospital. The man had already spent three weeks there. Had already cheated death recently and then again five years earlier.

Braden stared down at the dead body. A sheet covered him, but his black pants and shoes stuck out from under one end of it. The gun that had been clutched in his hand had already been bagged and taken into evidence along with his badge.

FBI special agent Barry Shelton. His was the voice on that recording. Brittney had verified it to Trooper Wells, but according to the trooper that was pretty much the only question that the reporter had answered.

Braden couldn't blame her. She wanted to be with Rory. Just like Braden wanted to be with Sam.

But she was gone. On a case out west.

He needed her here.

But he had her brothers. Not just Trick.

Mack was here. He'd sent the text to his younger brother, and he'd made his presence known even though he hadn't shown himself yet. Braden gazed around the area. Where was he?

Why hadn't he come forward yet?

He had to be the gunman. The one who'd shot the FBI agent and saved Brittney and Stanley and hopefully Rory, as well. Heather had said she'd gotten here too late.

So why hadn't Mack stuck around?

What was the deal with Braden's mysterious brother-in-law?

Mack knew Rory. No. He'd called him something else when he'd told his dad to talk to no one about that plane crash. But at the time he'd thought the man he knew had died. Mack hadn't been in the country then.

He very rarely was. What the hell was Mack? Not that it mattered much right now. He'd taken out the bad guy. Unfortunately, Braden suspected Agent Shelton wasn't the only bad guy who was messing with his team.

There was still the saboteur among them. Too many things had happened to them, too many things that hadn't been accidents. And Braden doubted the FBI agent had had anything to do with those incidents. He probably wasn't even the one who'd started up the trucks and hit Rory over the head, because he would have made damn certain he'd killed him then.

Stanley rushed up, away from the officer who'd been talking to him. And Braden closed his arms around him. "You're okay," he assured the kid. "You did good."

Annie jumped up, as if wrapping her long legs around them both, as if she thought this was a group hug.

"Brittney told me what to do," he said. "To open the big doors. She thought it would stop the man from shooting us if there were witnesses. But he shot Rory anyway." He started shaking. "He shot him anyway…"

Rory had to make it.

He had to. He'd already been through too much.

Chapter 25

Rory could hear her voice in his head. She was talking about how a man who'd risked his life for others had had others give up his life for money. How people he should have been able to trust in law enforcement and even in his personal life had betrayed him…

How a hero had had nobody to turn to, and yet he'd continued being a hero, working as a hotshot firefighter. And his name was Rory VanDam.

"Cory…" he murmured. No. Not anymore. Cory was from a long time ago. A few lifetimes ago. Cory didn't matter. Even Rory didn't matter.

Only Brittney did.

That was her voice. She had to be here. But when he opened his eyes, he found himself alone but for the TV. It sat across from the bed where he lay with tubes and machines hooked to him.

"Déjà damn vu…" he murmured, but this time he didn't have a tube down his throat. He was breathing on his own. But his throat was dry as if he'd been asleep for a long time again. How long had he been out this time?

And why?

He felt his head, but he had only that ridge of a scar on the back of it. The stitches were gone now. So his head hadn't been injured again. Then he patted his chest and felt the bandage between his heart and shoulder.

"Damn…"

He must have gotten shot. He remembered the agent raising that gun, pointing it at his chest.

And he remembered the body with the sheet over it.

"Brittney…"

He'd heard her voice earlier. Or had he just imagined that? Then he focused on the TV again and saw her on the screen. She looked to be standing at Braden's podium, talking about Rory, playing that recording…

She had gotten it out just like she'd told the agent she had. Agent Barry Shelton. The reporter covering her, Avery Kincaid, showed his picture and reported about his life and his death.

Rory didn't recognize him, wasn't sure he'd ever met the man until that moment in the firehouse. The moment he'd been afraid the man had killed Brittney.

Was she alive?

That video from the firehouse, of her standing at Braden's podium, had probably been shot before the agent had showed up. Before Rory had.

He fumbled around, looking for a remote, a way to turn up the TV. What about Brittney?

He waited for more coverage but the program switched to a commercial. And he cursed.

"You're awake," a woman said, her voice cracking with emotion.

And he turned to find Brittney standing in the doorway. Was she dead? She looked like an angel with her brown curls and pale brown eyes. She was so beautiful.

Or maybe he was dead and he was just imagining her.

But the machine beside the bed recorded his blood pressure, which seemed to have gone up at just the sight of her.

"Are you all right?" he asked.

"I am now," she said.

He glanced at the TV. "Yeah," he agreed. "You're famous. You're on the national news now."

She had everything she'd wanted. The respect. The career. So what was she doing here? With him…

His heart seemed to shake in his chest, trying to swell, to warm, with hope. But Rory had never had much luck with love or anything else, really. Everybody who'd ever claimed to care about him had betrayed him.

Even a member of his hotshot team was willing to hurt the rest of them, kept sabotaging the damn equipment. So if he couldn't trust them, how could he trust her?

Maybe Agent Shelton had been right. All she'd wanted was the story.

"Are you here for a follow-up interview?" he asked. He gestured toward his door. "Got a camera crew out there?"

Her topaz eyes widened and she sucked in a breath. "Wow. Screw you. I can't believe you listened to what that creep was saying. That all I care about is my career."

He pointed toward the TV. "You got your big story."

"I gave that story to Avery Kincaid. I just did the video to let her know what was going on. I wasn't counting on her to use my part of it."

He sucked in a breath now. "You gave it up? It nearly got you killed. Why would you give it to someone else?"

"Because it didn't matter anymore who covered the story, it just needed to get out there," she said. "The truth needed to get out there."

"And you should be the one getting the credit for it," he insisted. She'd worked so hard that she deserved it.

She shook her head. "I thought you got shot in the shoulder, not the head. But you're not making any sense. First you act like you're mad I did the story, and now you're insisting that I should be the only one getting the credit for it. What's wrong with you? What do you want?"

You. Just you.

He wanted to say those words, but he couldn't bring himself to utter them now. He had no damn idea what was going on, how badly he was hurt. And how much danger he might be in now that the truth was out.

But Felix Falcone had dementia. "Is that FBI agent dead?" Was that who'd been covered with that sheet?

She nodded.

"Who killed him?" he asked. His gun had jammed. He hadn't been able to protect her and Stanley or even himself.

She shrugged. "I don't know."

"You haven't been investigating?" he asked.

She cursed again. "I told you that I'm not here for that damn story," she said. "I'm here for you. To make sure that the man I love wakes up."

"You love me?" he asked, and his heart swelled now with that hope as warmth flooded it. Was it safe for him to tell her how he felt about her? Would she be safe if he told her?

She'd been so happy to open that door and see him sitting up in bed, awake. It had been a long week since he'd been shot. And of course, he woke up when she was gone. When she'd finally given in to Tammy and Trent's nagging for her to get a shower and some sleep.

But the way he'd been acting since she'd walked in…

"You really believe what that agent said about me, how all I care about is my career?" she asked, her heart aching. But did she have a right to be upset about that? For so long that was what she believed, too, what she'd wanted to be true. She'd wanted to only care about her career so that she wouldn't love someone and lose them.

Like she'd nearly lost Rory.

Maybe she had.

Not to death but to his own doubts about her. Did he even believe that she loved him?

And if he couldn't believe that, he probably didn't return her feelings. Tears rushed to her eyes, and she turned toward the door but was too blinded to find the handle. She fumbled around, searching for it.

Then strong hands gripped her shoulders, turning her around. She blinked her tears away to stare up at Rory. "You shouldn't be out of bed." He'd dragged some of the machines with him. Hell, he'd dragged the bed behind him in his haste to stop her from leaving.

"I love you," he said. "I love you so much that I don't want to be around you if that will put you in danger." His hands moved from her shoulders to her face now, cupping it. She could feel a tremor in him, moving through him. "I love you so much."

"I love you," she said. "And the only danger I am in is getting my heart broken if you try to push me away."

He pulled her close to him now, wrapping his arms around her. "I'm not going to push you away," he said. "I'm tempted to never let you go. But I know you have your job—"

"I don't care about—"

"I do," he said. "It's your career. And you've worked too damn hard to walk away from it now. Take the credit and the opportunities that come up with that story and know that I will always be here for you."

"What about you?" she asked. "What are you going to do now that the truth is out?"

He shrugged. "The truth was always out that I'm a hotshot and a pilot. That's what I intend to keep being once I'm medically cleared to return to duty."

"You don't want to go back into law enforcement?"

"I think I lost my touch for that," he said. "I haven't figured out who the saboteur is, and I've probably been working right alongside whoever it is."

She shivered as she realized that he and her brother were still in danger. "I don't want you getting hurt again," she said.

"I wish I could promise that I won't, but we both know how unpredictable life is," he said. "It's not just officers and firefighters who get hurt. Anybody anywhere can have an accident or become a victim of a crime, even children. So loving anyone is a risk that you might lose them."

She closed her eyes on a fresh wave of tears. "I know you're right."

"You survived losing your dad," he said. "And you were a kid then. You're strong, Brittney, so much stronger than you give yourself credit for being. You can handle anything."

"Even loving you?" she asked, opening her eyes to stare up at his handsome face.

"Am I worth the risk?" he asked.

She nodded. "You're worth every risk. I love you so very much."

"I love you," he said, and he pulled her even closer to his madly pounding heart.

Hers was pounding hard, too, but with love, not fear this time. She wasn't afraid of falling for him like she'd once been. She knew that he was a survivor, too. He'd already survived so much and was still here. She wasn't worried about loving and losing him. She wasn't worried about anything anymore. Not even the saboteur, because so many people were determined to figure out who he was and stop him, that he wouldn't escape justice much longer.

A while ago the saboteur might have felt guilty over how hard they'd struck Rory over the head. But Rory might have seen them leave the bunk room before the trucks started. VanDam had been the only one not snoring or breathing hard like everyone else.

But the saboteur didn't even feel guilty anymore, didn't feel anything at all anymore except for anger and resentment. And the only time they felt less angry and resentful was when something went wrong or somebody got hurt.

Somebody was going to have to get hurt again.

Soon.

* * * * *

LOVE HARLEQUIN ROMANCE?

• DISCOVER

SCAN ME

Find which books are coming next month
from your favorite series at

Harlequin.com/Shop/Pages/Coming-Soon.html

• EXPLORE

SCAN ME

Sign up for the Harlequin e-newsletter and
download a free book from any series at

TryHarlequin.com

• CONNECT

SCAN ME

Join our Harlequin community to share your thoughts
and connect with other romance readers at

Facebook.com/groups/HarlequinConnection

**Be the first to find out about promotions, news and exclusive
content by following our socials @HarlequinBooks.**

SERIESIBC2024

A KILLER'S AFTER THE MAN
...HE USED TO BE

Who's more dangerous: The saboteur targeting Rory VanDam's hotshot team or Brittney Townsend, the hot reporter asking too many questions? Maybe the secrets Rory has had to keep since he survived a plane crash are more dangerous than both of them. When a killer pursues the guarded firefighter and relentless journalist, it's Rory's past that could cost them their lives. And his reluctant attraction to the newswoman could make him expose the shocking truth.

A HOTSHOT HEROES NOVEL

CATEGORY: **SUSPENSE**

$7.99 U.S./$8.99 CAN.

ISBN-13: 978-1-335-59400-6

50799

9 781335 594006

EAN

S

Danger. Passion.
Drama.

H HARLEQUIN
ROMANTIC
SUSPENSE
harlequin.com